THE SWARM OF HEAVEN

The First Renaissance Mystery –
set in the rumbustious Italy of the 15th century.

In pursuit of a private vendetta, the young Niccolo Machiavelli leaves his beloved Florence in the grip of the fanatical friar, Savonarola, and travels to Rome only to be lured into the service of the appalling Borgia pope Alexander VI and his power-crazed son Cesare. Niccolo's employment on confidential missions involves probing the death of the Sultan of Turkey's brother, an investigation that puts his own life in danger. The only way to save himself? – to outscheme the schemers.

THE SWARM OF HEAVEN

THE SWARM OF HEAVEN

by

Derek Wilson

Magna Large Print Books
Long Preston, North Yorkshire,
BD23 4ND, England.

British Library Cataloguing in Publication Data.

Wilson, Derek
    The swarm of heaven.

    A catalogue record of this book is
    available from the British Library

    ISBN   0-7505-1652-6

First published in Great Britain, 1999
by Constable & Company Limited

Copyright © 1999 Derek Wilson

Cover illustration by arrangement with
Constable & Company Ltd.

Published in Large Print 2001 by arrangement with
Constable & Robinson Ltd.

Magna Large Print is an imprint of Library Magna Books Ltd.

Printed and bound in Great Britain by
T.J. (International) Ltd., Cornwall, PL28 8RW

I see Ambition, with that swarm which Heaven at the world's beginning allotted her, flying over the Tuscan mountains.

Niccolo Machiavelli, *Tercets on Ambition*

PROLOGUE AND EXPLANATION

15 March 1518
Sant'Andrea in Percussina

To Francesco Vettori,
Most Worthy Florentine Ambassador to the
Supreme Pontiff in Rome.

Magnificent Ambassador,
I am bored.
Let me prove it to you. Yesterday the god of love served me a dish of young maidenhood, fresh, sweet and ripe for the tasting. How do you suppose I received it, savoured it, devoured it? I'll tell you – but I warn you in advance you won't believe me.

I had repaired to my olive grove, as is my habit towards noon – the habit of a neglected man who fools himself that he enjoys solitude – and settled with my *Plutarch* in the shade of a sprawling oleander. After a while I drowsed, only to be awakened by the sound of voices. Peering through a gap in the shiny leaves I

9

recognised Giovanni, the young son of one of my woodcutters, in the company of a girl from the village, a pretty black-haired creature of some fifteen summers. As I watched, they stopped and reclined together on the other side of my bush, so that I could see and hear all. You may imagine with what amusement I listened to the fumbling seductions of this *cavaliere servente* and how I had to bite my tongue to prevent my laughter betraying me. The poor Leander, not knowing whether to trim his arrow with ardour or persuasion, missed the target altogether so that, when his Hero made the obligatory protest of violated modesty, he took her at surface value, jumping up shouting that she did not love him and stumbled angrily away down the path.

After a while the girl arose and walked slowly in the opposite direction, muttering to herself – the very embodiment of frustrated desire. You of all men will know that the opportunity was too good to miss. Slipping from my place of concealment, I took a circuitous route through the trees and met up with the maiden as though by chance. She curtsied prettily and said 'Good-day, Messer Machiavelli', very respectfully. I greeted her and asked her why she was so sad. She hid her face and said she didn't know what I meant. I told her that I had seen enough of the world throughout my long years to know an unhappy young woman when I saw one. She looked at me, then, with wide, forest-pool eyes. Was it true what folk in the village said, she wanted to know, that I had been to Rome? 'Yes,' I replied, 'and to Venice where they have rivers instead of streets and to Paris far away over the mountains. Would you like to hear about them?'

We sat on the bank and I told her stories that made her by turns laugh and gasp with amazement. Of course, it was easy to turn her thoughts in the direction I wanted. When I told her about the lovely ladies at the court of Louis XII she sighed and asked whether I thought she would ever be beautiful. I considered the matter with philosophical detachment: hair? Yes, possibilities there. Eyes? Good. Complexion? Well, the application of powdered chalk would cover the glow that cultured gentlemen found vulgar. And so on and so on – until we reached her breasts. I shook my head. Ah no, I regretted, too small. My little dryad pouted. 'Not so, Messer. My mother and my sisters tell me they are of good size for my age.' 'Ah,' I said, 'but they cannot judge by the standards of Paris and Rome.' Well, of course, she had to prove her point and I promised her a disinterested adjudication and so we progressed from observation to those finer points of evaluation which can only be arrived at by manipulation. In short, it was but minutes before I had her skirts about her ears. And then?

Nothing! I remembered some important engagement, bade the girl run along home and commend me to her family. She thanked me for my advice and curtsied, and I returned to my villa. There. Did I not say that you would be astonished? I hear you laughing and telling me that I have old man's droop. Not so; my affliction is far worse than that. I am losing my taste for all life's pleasures.

I only live to serve Florence but Florence does not wish to be served – not by a man who has already given her fourteen years as diplomat, military strategist and administrator. All the members of the Signoria know I'm here, rotting on my little farm a mere ten miles away from their council chamber. How could they fail to know it? I've written enough entreaties to cover their frescoed walls. Not one of them is ignorant of all I have done for my beloved Florence or of the ideas that teem in my brain concerning her future welfare. How often have I told them that I would gladly take any office that would contribute something to the good of the state? Yet scarcely a week passes without some vacant post being filled by a talentless boy from one of the families in favour, or a place-seeker with more in his purse than his head while I, like blind Belisarius, am forced to beg for favours from the ungrateful and the forgetful...

3 April 1518
Sant'Andrea in Percussina

To Francesco Vettori,
Florentine Ambassador at the Papal Court in Rome

...Yes, I was in an ill humour when I wrote and remained so until Tafano came with your letter. Your stories of affairs there made me laugh out loud. How I should love to have seen Cardinal Ferino's face. And as for that pompous fool, Secretary Benini, I hope you told him you were writing to me about his dowsing in the cesspool. After the way he used me at our last encounter I relish his discomfort now. Vengeance is a wine all the better for the maturing.

I have given much thought to your advice, old friend. You say that the best fruit is always the least accessible and you apply that to my career. Well, it is certainly true that the Signoria are sated with my more obvious accomplishments and unaware of those confidential services I performed for Alexander VI, Cesare Borgia, Louis XII, Pope Julius and Doge Leonardo. You suggest that my talents at pursuing truth through labyrinths of deception, of un--masking secret enemies and bringing evil men to justice might be of greater value to the new rulers of Florence than my diplomatic skills. You may well be right but, as you know, those clandestine missions on which I was engaged were always *in petto*, not to be bruited abroad. Is it time to bring some of them into the open, in order to rescue Niccolo Machiavelli from the pit of obscurity? I don't know. What I do know is that this inactivity will suffocate me if it continues much longer...

Little has been heard about the remarkable Escobaldi Papers since their discovery four years ago caused a ferment of excitement in the world of Renaissance scholarship. Then, three volumes of papers, loosely bound together in eighteenth-century calf, in the Umbrian library of a ducal family were found to contain hitherto unknown documents by Niccolo Machiavelli, the Renaissance author and diplomat whose amoral advocacy of *realpolitik* in *The Prince* has added a new word to the vocabulary of most European languages. At the time experts were vigorously – sometimes violently – divided over whether to regard these writings as the find or the fraud of the century. So extreme were the reactions that the owners of the papers withdrew them from scrutiny and resolutely refused very substantial offers for their purchase.

It seemed to the present editor that it would be tragic for this remarkable collection to be returned to the obscurity from which it had so recently emerged. Negotiations were therefore opened with the owners with a view to translating and publishing at least some of the Escobaldi

Papers. This volume is the first result of the arrangement that emerged from those discussions. It is offered to the public without any claims as to its authenticity, upon which subject every reader must form his own judgement.

The Swarm of Heaven has been compiled from that substantial part of the collection which is autobiographical in nature. The extracts already quoted from two letters to Machiavelli's friend Francesco Vettori seem to provide the *raison d'être* for the remarkable narratives which follow and to date their composition to the period 1518–19. In the latter year Machiavelli celebrated his fiftieth birthday. Most of his adult life had been spent serving his beloved Florence in a variety of roles but when a sudden change of government in 1512 restored the ducal house of Medici and put an end to the eighteen-year-old republic, officials who had served the old regime were sacked. Machiavelli was one of those who suffered in this purge and he retired to his family farm outside the city where he wrote most of the treatises by which his name is now remembered, most notably *Il Principe*. But he never gave up his ambition to return to office. 'I hope and hoping increases my torment,' he told Vettori, 'I weep and weeping feeds my tired heart; I burn and my burning is hidden beneath the surface.'

If the following pages are, indeed, from the pen of Niccolo Machiavelli they provide a remarkable narrative covering those early years of the author's life about which we have, until now, known tantalisingly little. They give us valuable glimpses of a man travelling the road from arrogant young scholar to cynical *politique*. Reading between the lines of a frustrated exile reflecting upon more exciting times we can detect his passionate patriotism and his desire to be at the centre of affairs. We see that Machiavelli, no less than the princes and prelates he served, was motivated by ambition and that he, too, knew what it was to be visited by the swarm of heaven.

I

1494, then – since one must begin some-where.

1494, the second choice for the world's death-year.

1494.

The gullible had prepared themselves for the Apocalypse twenty-four months earlier, anno 7000 in the eastern calendar, a date hallowed by ancient prophecy and flame-tongued, soul-grasping preachers. There were, I confess it, a few days in the spring of 1492 when I joined the muttering old women and perfervid priests prostrating themselves upon the chilling marble of Santa Maria del Fiore. Had not the very heart of Florence, the Magnificent Lorenzo, ceased its beating amidst dreadful portents? Caged lions tore themselves to death in the Via di Leone; lightning shattered the highest pinnacle of Santa Reparata; ghostly giants fought in the public gardens; and a mad – or divinely possessed – woman interrupted the mass at Santa Maria Novella screeching lurid prophecies. Surely these portents presaged some catastrophe.

All that was 1492. But the world survived. Italy survived. And so did Niccolo Machiavelli. The doom-mongers adjusted their almanacs and bade us watch for the four horsemen in 1494. For my part, I determined they should not snare a second time the well-read young philosopher-poet-historian who was already regarded with favour by members of the Signoria. Stupid, blind arrogance! I should have read the signs – not in the heavens but in the schemes of pope and princes. 1494 *was* the end not, manifestly, for the world, but certainly for Italy, for Florence and for poor Niccolo.

It was the year the shambling, broken-backed, beak-nosed King of France crossed the Alps to grab the crown of Naples and, in the act, cast down the precarious political edifice composed of all our little dukedoms and republics. After Charles VIII's invasion, the self-adjusting balance of Italian rivalries passed into history. Our lands, our armies, our peoples were martialled by the clash of Habsburg and Valois ambitions. Colonna, Vitelli, Orsini – the pope's barons – sold their swords to whichever power would guarantee their independence from Rome.

The Milanese usurper, Ludovico Moro, played a dangerous double game between the Emperor and the King of France. Venice watched like a hawk, ready to swoop upon any victim weakened by warfare or shifting alliances. And Florence? She fell under the sway of that mad friar, Girolamo Savonarola, who inflamed the citizenry against the Medici and welcomed King Charles as though he had been the returning Son of God. To recall it now, across the years of misery inaugurated by those events, turns my stomach.

Now I can only repine, like Alcibiades in Phrygia, condemned to watch my native land sucked into the cesspit that is Italy. How different things were then... Ah, then I was at the very centre of affairs – and understood nothing!

The twenty-five-year-old scant-bearded young man bearing the name Niccolo di Bernardo of the *familia Maclavellorum* is a stranger to me. I look at him now, across the years that separate us, and see an innocent, masking his ignorance and uncertainty behind swaggering braggadocio, ready wit and the gregariousness that surrounded him with companions he eagerly mistook for friends. In the spring of 1494, while the

Frenchman and his allies mustered their invasion force of mercenary soldiers, while courtiers on lathered horses sped between Rome, Milan, Venice, Ferrara, Florence, Naples and every town whose rulers had cause to welcome or fear the coming conflict, while diplomats bargained frantically for peace and stone masons and cannon founders put defences in readiness for war, Niccolo Machiavelli thought only of one thing – marriage to Baccia Vernacci, which offered a delicious combination of profit and gratified lust.

The courtyard of Bernardo and Bartolommea Machiavelli's modest house in the Borgo Santo Spirito was seething with good humour on that April afternoon when the younger son of the house was joined in matrimony to the fur trader's beautiful daughter. From a wide-thrown upper casement jaunty music from shawms, lutes, viola da gambas and viola de braccios cascaded down upon a crowd enthusiastically devouring their host's food and drinking his wine. Bernardo sat at a long trestle table beneath the window with the elderly Guido Vernacci and their more exalted neighbours and kin. The space before them was filled with a milling throng of young people, children, servants, foraging dogs and the regulation quota of local paupers. The couple whose union was the occasion for all the festivity were situated, in obedience to their custom, at either end of the table, each surrounded by their chosen friends and same-sex relatives. They were able to exchange occasional smiles and glances but, for the most part, were involved in conversation – largely ribald – with their companions.

'Well, Nicco, there's not a man in Florence who doesn't envy you today.' Totto, Bernardo's firstborn, a pallid, long-faced serious man, who smiled patronisingly at the groom, was older by six years and still unwed.

'We'll envy him much more tonight!' Niccolo's close friend, Francesco Bardi, already well flushed with Vernaccia di San Gimignano, tugged his red cap from his perspiring brow and hee-hawed from his ample stomach.

Niccolo edged away to avoid wine from Francesco's goblet splashing over his new doublet of plum-coloured silk. 'Francey, you have a wonderful well-developed talent for stating the obvious.'

His friend was not abashed by the jibe or

the laughter it evoked. 'Well, we're not all blessed with Niccolo's wit,' he muttered into his wine.

'Nicco,' a voice called from further down the table, 'what was that verse you made up the other day about our beloved Piero de'Medici?'

Niccolo waved a hand dismissively. 'Oh, I really can't remember.'

'Nonsense,' the voice insisted. 'No man has a better memory either for his own compositions or the writings of the ancients.'

'Perhaps he's frightened of his satires floating across the Arno, right into the Palazzo Medici.'

The taunt drove Niccolo to his feet. 'I don't care if the tyrant himself hears it. It goes like this:

'Balls are my mark, O Florence note.
Note, Florentines, you are by balls.
A spade my standard, digging gold.
Dig Florentines, my naught-but-spades.
A race I run, it is my fate.
Fate, Florence, marks you for my mount.
My stake is fixed in Florence soil,
And Florence fast bound to my stake.'*

*Footnote on next page

23

There was general applause and laughter, but Totto did not join in. 'For God's sake be careful, Nicco. Men have ended up in the bowels of the Palazzo Medici for less. Piero isn't like his father: ready to applaud wit and literary skill even when they are turned against him.'

Niccolo laughed and clapped an arm across his brother's shoulder. 'See how Totto still looks after me,' he called out. 'He doesn't realise that I have a wife to take on that responsibility now.'

'See to it that she's not soon a widow. That naked, headless corpse found last week in an alley off the Via Tornabuoni – you remember?' Totto gazed round at his companions, pausing till he had their full attention. 'Well, I have it on good authority that it was Brother Jacopo who prophesied from the pulpit in the Duomo that Piero de'Medici's reign would be measured in months rather than years.'

Nicco shook his head. 'If our leader is so

---

*Translator's note: These lines represented an extended play on words: the Medici's heraldic device being six red balls – *palle* – on a gold ground; a spade *pala*; a horse race *palio*; and a stake *palo*.

vengeful, why has he not struck down the mad friar?'

'Savonarola?'

'How many fanatical Dominicans do we have in Florence?' Niccolo scoffed. 'Of course, Savonarola. Day after day he preaches against the House of Medici. I hear he speaks of an armed saviour, a second Cyrus, who will march into Italy, ridding the land of unjust rulers and purifying all our morals.'

'You haven't heard him yourself, Nicco?' someone asked.

'Not I.' The young bridegroom waved his goblet for a servant to refill with the lush white wine. 'I've better things to do than listen to madmen – and I certainly don't want my morals purified.'

Several round the table laughed but others reacted without their usual whole-hearted approbation of Niccolo's ribaldry.

'You should go along to the Duomo and hear him,' Francesco suggested. 'Most of Florence is turning out for his sermons. If nothing else, you'd find plenty of material for your wicked pen.'

'My dear Francey, you should know by now that I don't do things just because other people do them. I grant that this

Savonarola is, by all accounts, a fine preacher and very popular...'

'Aye, and that's why Piero is afraid to touch him,' Totto said. 'People say he tries to laugh off the friar's criticisms, affecting his father's sang-froid, but underneath he's furious.'

'I've heard he just shrugs the fellow off,' a slightly older man in a blue satin doublet observed. 'The same as he ignores everyone who doesn't tell him what he wants to hear. Like the ostrich, he buries his head against unpleasantries.'

Totto nodded enthusiastically. 'While all Florence looks anxiously beyond the Alps he has eyes only for balls – tennis balls, footballs. Why...'

'Stop!' Niccolo shouted the word and silence clamped itself on the entire company. He glared round at his friends in mock anger. 'The next person to talk politics at my wedding feast will be taken straight from here to the Ponte Vecchio and dropped in the Arno. Come, let's have dancing.'

With applause and cries of delight the crowd pressed back against the walls to leave a space in the centre of the courtyard. The musicians struck up a lively *gagliardo* and Niccolo led Baccia out to start the *danza*.

Throughout the rest of the day the groom set the pace for all the merry-making, as ubiquitous as he was tireless. Not a man failed to be back-slapped and pressed to more wine; not a woman escaped being kissed, fondled and danced with. If Niccolo was assiduous in attending to his guests it was less out of concern for them than out of determination that *his* day should be a success.

Well, he was young and there is something about a first marriage that cannot be repeated – a sense of having taken hold of destiny, of having laid a vital emotional cornerstone, established an undisputed place in polite society. I suppose the bumptious young fool had some cause for celebration. Anyway, it was certainly true that everyone caught the jubilant mood – or, if they did not, it was no fault of Niccolo Machiavelli's.

Of course, the libations of Bacchus are not all pressed from the grapes of mirth. Some there are whom drink makes into raging bulls, some are possessed of Herculean strength. During the Olympian nine-day feast Doge Jacomo organised in Florence to distract the populace from the corruption of his regime I saw a man ... God damn me, I rambled. How tedious old men's anecdotes are.

As I was observing, wine takes men in a variety of ways. It may overwhelm them with hilarity, amorousness, aggressiveness or lethargy. Totto – dear, earnest, well-meaning Totto – invariably became maudlin. Nicco observed him several times sitting, usually alone, and watching the laughing throng with rheumy eyes. He was aware that his brother was following his movements particularly closely. Niccolo knew exactly what that meant – and he kept well away. The last thing he wanted on this special day was a slurred sermon from his tediously censorious and over-protective sibling.

He escaped until late in the spring night, by which time the lamps had been lit and the ebb of departing revellers had begun. It was then that Niccolo was caught off guard. He had staggered to a corner of the court-yard to relieve himself when he felt a heavy hand on his shoulder.

'A word, brother – a brief word.'

Nicco groaned. 'Not now, Totto, I have to bid farewell to our guests.'

'Won't take a moment.' The taller man leaned heavily against him. 'Just want to remind you of your promise.'

'Yes, yes, of course. I hadn't forgotten.' Nicco, whose head seemed to be full of viscid honey and droning bees, squinted at Totto. He took him by the arm to steer him back into the crowd. 'Come along; you haven't done nearly enough dancing.'

But the older man stood his ground. 'You will look after her, then, as I would have done?'

Nicco shook his head – and wished he had not. 'This ... no time for riddles, Totto. Look after whom?'

'There, just as I thought.' Totto took on the old, familiar, scolding look. 'You're not rel ... relubble ... relia... You can't be trusted. You've already forgotten your solemn promise – before Father Bernardino. I waived my elder brother's right to Baccia and you vowed to care for her – always.' The tall man hiccuped noisily and he almost fell as his gangling legs got in each other's way.

Patiently Niccolo led his brother to a bench set against the wall and lowered him onto it. 'Totto, for God's sake stop wet-nursing me. Of course I haven't forgotten my pledge but I only made it to humour you. There was no need for it. I *love* Baccia

– passionately. I'd never let anything or any-one harm her.'

Totto belched. 'Hm! Until the next pretty woman comes along, that is.' He waggled a finger and went cross-eyed staring at it. 'I know you too well, little brother. Just you remember, if you mistreat beautiful Baccia or desert her I'll kill you.'

He slumped against the wall and Nicco turned to make his escape.

That was the moment that Francesco Bardi waddled up. 'Ah, there you are,' he gurgled, 'and Totto, too. That's good. The time has come to take the groom to his bridal bed. Baccia retired with her maidens a full half-hour ago. She'll be growing impatient. Come on, Totto, we must carry your good-for-nothing brother up to paradise. I've found three or four others but we need you, too. Stefano, Michele and Paolo are all dead to the world. Truth to tell I'm not much better.' He belched loudly. 'So, up you get.' He tugged at Totto's sleeve.

The elder Machiavelli gazed up im-ploringly into Francesco's eyes. 'You tell him, Francey. You tell this wastrel... Must look after Baccia. Just as I would have done ... poor old Totto, steady, 'dustrious, 'sponsible Totto... Tell me.' He jabbed a finger into Francesco's chest. 'How big is Baccia's dowry? Do you know that?'

'Four hundred florins – everyone knows.'

'Aye, four hundred florins. Enough for a nice house. Enough to start a business ... *and* have plenty over to invest... But what do you think dear Nicco will do with four hundred florins...? We mustn't let him squander it on horses and whores and embroidered clothes and backgammon and dicing...'

Francesco winked at Niccolo as he dragged Totto to his feet. 'That's right, we must keep an eye on this young rake. Though I'll wager Baccia will do a better job. You'll see, she'll have him trained soon enough. But now we must see him bedded as well as wedded.'

The three friends weaved their way across the courtyard and Francesco rounded up four other young men who still had the use of their legs. They gathered round the groom, lifting him shoulder high, lurched a few paces in raucous triumph, then fell to the ground in a laughing heap. Hastily Francesco organised a less ambitious procession. The bearers picked Niccolo up by arms and legs. Accompanied by the remaining revellers, they bore him into the house, with some difficulty up the narrow staircase, to the door of the main bedchamber, given up, on this one night, by Bernardo and Bartolommea, for the pleasures of a younger generation. Someone knocked, then pushed open the heavy oak door.

The room, dimly lit by candles in two wall sconces, revealed a cassone, two wooden armed chairs with cushions on the seats, a low table bearing a statue of the Virgin and the curtained bed. With whoops, whistles and many bawdy and salacious comments they carried Niccolo across the open space. Someone pulled back the light drapes.

Everyone fell, momentarily, silent. Bartolommea's best coverlet – blue diaper patterned in gold thread – overspread the bed. The slight movement of Baccia's breathing beneath it variegated its contours sufficiently to catch the candle-light. The seventeen-year-old, girl-woman lay very still with the counterpane up to her chin. Her eyes were wide and sparkling, her long hair arranged over the pillows like a halo of radiating silver-gilt strands.

For long seconds the men gazed, raucous ribaldry frozen on their lips. Then someone cried 'Have at her, Nicco' and they heaved him onto the bed. With more shouted advice and laughter, the escort fell back towards the door. At last it closed behind them and Niccolo and Baccia were alone.

With a slight groan he let his head fall back on the soft pillows.

She propped herself on one elbow and looked down at him. 'I thought you were never coming,' she said with a slight pout.

'I'm sorry. It was Totto; he couldn't let me get married without the benefit of a fraternal lecture.'

Baccia smiled. 'Dear Totto. He cares very much for his little brother. I expect the habits of a lifetime are hard to break. Well, now you are here – husband – what now? Don't you want me?'

He reached up and pulled her face down to his. 'I always want you; you know that,' he said between kisses.

She giggled. 'Shh! Everyone's supposed to think this is our first time.'

He laughed a light laugh that immediately faded into another groan.

'What's the matter?' She pulled back, real concern in her eyes now.

'My head feels like molten lead.'

'I'm not surprised after the amount you've drunk. It's not the best preparation for our wedding night, is it?'

'What do you mean?' He blinked and tried to focus on the pale face a few centimetres from his own.

'Well, Cousin Bianca told me that when a man has had too much wine he can't … do it.'

'Oh did she!' He sat up suddenly – regretting it. 'Well let's put that theory to the test.'

He rolled into a sitting position on the edge of the bed and began tugging at the fastenings of his doublet. He made some fumbling progress until he bent to loosen his shoes. Then all sense of balance deserted him. He fell to the floorboards and began to vomit uncontrollably.

Baccia leaped lightly from the bed. She helped Niccolo to his feet and led him to a chair. Then, soaking a cloth in a bowl of water standing on the table, she wiped his face. The convulsions stopped. 'Better now?'

'Yes, I think so. Baccia, I'm so sorry. I…'

'Shh. Let me help you out of these clothes.' Deftly she undid the bows tying Niccolo's sleeves and doublet. She rolled down the hose and unbuttoned his shirt. 'Now, into bed with you.'

When he was lying, naked, between the sheets she cleared up the mess, folded his clothes and laid them on the chair. By the time she had done that Niccolo was fast asleep. With a sigh, she extinguished the candles and slipped gently into bed.

She woke with a start. The first thing she was aware of was the faint light through the chinks in the shutters. The second was her husband's hands wrenching the bedclothes away then grasping the edge of her night-gown. 'Now, about that absurd hypothesis of Cousin Bianca,' he breathed. She felt his warmth against her as she turned towards him, arching her back to help him remove the obstructing garment. Four times they made love before the chamber door was thrown open by a smiling Bernardo and Bartolommea and, once again, they had to share each other with the world.

Niccolo believed, as all idiot lovers do, that no one else since Adam and Eve in the perfection of Eden had experienced such intensity of passion – a conviction shared by his adoring bride. The couple leased a small house on the Via del Proconsolo, near the cathedral, which belonged to Signore

Vernacci's brother. There they received friends almost every day, for all the world like a ducal couple holding court. Thither came not just Niccolo's drinking companions, but young artists, men of letters, those who shared their host's love of the ancient authors. The pretentious, posturing philomath really considered himself the doyen of the younger Florentine intelligentsia, patron of a new Platonic academy like the one that had assembled at the court of the great Lorenzo. For one all-too-brief summer a medley of talented friends resorted to the happy little house on the Via del Proconsolo and basked in their own wisdom. To Niccolo and Baccia it seemed that the sun shone exclusively on their small garden with its lemon trees and vine-shaded arbour.

But the deluge was about to break and it should have taken no great acumen to read the significance of the massing political clouds. As I contemplate across three decades the wilful innocence of that other Niccolo Machiavelli I can scarce credit his blind self-absorption. All Italy was vibrating with fears and rumours. Charles VIII had moved to Lyon and was there gathering his invasion force. He had made costly peace treaties with enemies and rivals in the North in order to concentrate all his energies on the reconquest of Naples. This was to be only the first step in the realisation of his megalomaniac ambitions – after Naples, Constantinople, after Constantinople, Jerusalem and ultimately sole sovereignty over a reunited Christendom. Madman! By August news came that the massive French war machine was on the move – 50,000 infantry and cavalry some said; others 100,000. Soon came intelligence of the first engagements – a force of thirty Neapolitan galleys repulsed off Portovenere, less than 150 kilometres from Florence across the lower Apennines. Charles's rage at being opposed was vented on Rapallo. We heard with horrified disbelief how the town had been sacked by the king's terrifying Swiss mercenaries and every one of its inhabitants slaughtered. Even the sick and infirm had been dragged from their hospital beds to be butchered in the streets.

Italians were shocked by the stories of repeated atrocities. Yet few allowed themselves to contemplate the collapse of order in the city states. For decades the great Houses – Medici, Sforza, Aragon, d'Este – had maintained their own regal splendour but also internal control and external power balance. Any other political reality was unthinkable. Thus, in Florence, our masters pursued a policy of consummate inactivity. Piero de'Medici did nothing because he lacked the character to face facts. The Signoria did nothing because it had long since lost the faculty of independent thought. Only the demented prior of St Mark's Convent advocated a clear course of action – and claimed divine sanction for it. That was why Florentines crowded to hear him in ever growing numbers. Savonarola's tongue flayed them for their sins and menaced them with the imminent fiery judgement to be visited on them by the Lord's anointed, but he did offer them hope, a positive route to salvation and safety via repentance and accommodation with the invader. Of course, he was right – and profoundly wrong.

As the summer heat intensified the city divided into two clearly defined factions. Some held firm to their Medici allegiance. Others put their faith in Savonarola. Only, it seems, did that superior student of human frailty, that expert in the writings of the Latin poets and philosophers, Niccolo Machiavelli remain aloof from the conflict.

He had friends in both camps and it amused him to argue with them in the taverns, always taking a contrary line to the company he was with. Thus, to Savonarolans he represented the shameful indignity of allowing French troops transit through Tuscany while to the supporters of Piero, who eventually decided to resist Charles's demands, he protested the folly of opposing a hugely superior military force. Niccolo's pen was for hire to all. For a few scudos he would write a lampoon of Savonarola or Piero or one of their prominent supporters which, within hours, would be circulating in handmade copies or run off the presses and selling in the print shops.

All young Machiavelli's burlesques were published anonymously but few of those he held up to ridicule were ignorant of their authorship. As many Florentines as hailed him cheerfully in the piazzas or toasted his wit in the taverns spat or tugged their hoods at him as they passed. But that other Niccolo cared not a fig for man's enmity or their attempts to still his pen. Oh, but he was above petty party squabbling, that one, and about to be taught a lesson for his Olympian pride.

On a morning in July he was roused by his

manservant. The room was still dark and the features illuminated by the uncertain light of the tallow candle Timeo held aloft were unwashed and anxious.

'Sir, there are men here who demand to see you.'

Niccolo struggled into consciousness. 'What men?'

'I don't know, Sir. They're wearing cloaks over their livery. I told them you were not…'

'Nicco, what is it?' Baccia sat up in the bed, peering into the candle-lit gloom.

'It's nothing, Darling.' Niccolo subsided again beneath the covers. To Timeo he said, 'Tell them to call at a more convenient hour.'

The next instant the chamber door crashed open. Framed in the rectangular space was a tall figure whose face was a featureless smudge within the blackness of his hood. 'Messer Machiavelli, you are to come *now*. Our master is not to be kept waiting.' The tone of the man's voice made it clear that he was not accustomed to being defied.

Naked beneath the sheets, Niccolo felt vulnerable but tried not to show it. 'And I am not to be dragged from my bed in the middle of the night. Tell your master to send his lackeys at a more sociable time.' He turned on his side and closed his eyes.

He heard the heavy tread of boots upon the floor and felt something cold against his neck. At the same moment Baccia uttered a frightened scream. Rolling over, Niccolo saw the point of a narrow sword hovering centimetres from his eyes. The stranger leaned forward and, with his free hand, pulled down the bedclothes. The candlelight fell aslant his face as he stood back, gazing at Baccia's exposed upper body with an appreciative leer.

Niccolo grabbed the moment. He slipped from the bed, at the same time clutching a pillow and swinging it at the intruder. As the man staggered back, Niccolo fastened both hands onto his sword arm and twisted it. The rapier clattered onto the boards and Niccolo stooped to pick it up.

That was when Timeo yelped with terror, dropped the candle, which immediately went out, blundered into his master in his rush for the door and sent them both sprawling. For several seconds there was a confusion of scuffling and shouting, embellished with Baccia's screams. Then more footsteps sounded on the stairs. A stronger light filled the room. When Niccolo

41

regained his feet there were three strangers in the chamber and one was holding a close lantern aloft.

The leader calmly bent to pick up his sword. Then, very deliberately, he swung round, smashing the hilt into the side of Niccolo's face and sending him reeling against the wall. 'Now get dressed – unless you want me to take you as you are.'

'Where are you going with him?' Baccia demanded, kneeling on the bed with sheets draped around her.

'Don't worry, pretty one. He'll be back.' The tall man laughed. 'Perhaps. If he isn't, I will be.'

When Niccolo had hurriedly dressed, his hands were tied behind his back and he was bundled out into the street. The first glimmers of dawn were visible above the hills towards Bagno a Ripoli but the city's streets were still in deep darkness. Niccolo's captors rushed him along narrow thoroughfares towards the Ponte Santa Trinità. There they turned abruptly, along the road following the Arno down-river. After a short distance they plunged back into the tortuous streets of the wool merchants' quarter. Niccolo had enough wit about him as he stumbled along past the shuttered shop fronts to realise that he was deliberately being led by a circuitous route to avoid being seen and in the hope of confusing him. His captors stopped at last before a gateway in a high wall and, passing through, entered the enclosed garden of an impressive *palazzo*. A side door led them into the building and they traversed several rooms and came to a halt in a marbled antechamber. There Niccolo was left with two men to guard him. He waited.

And waited. Slowly light slithered into the room through chinks in the shutters, showing up elegant furniture and elaborate frescoes. Niccolo peered through the gloom for clues but neither the interior décor nor the vague geographical location of the building helped him to identify it or its owner. Without that information he could not calculate why he had been brought here or what was likely to happen to him. He was more curious than afraid – until a servant came in to throw back the wooden coverings over the windows. As the man turned again into the room the red and gold emblem on his tunic was clearly visible. The device of the *famiglia Spini*. Now Niccolo was frightened.

He waited almost two hours in a sweat of

anticipation before the tall man returned and led him across a wide hall, knocked on a door and ushered him into a dining salon.

At a table of shining walnut, well spread with silver dishes of meat, bread and fruits sat a solitary young man. His black hair hung lank to his shoulders. His doublet was unlaced and he lolled in his chair. He was eating a peach speared on a poniard but looked up as Niccolo was placed opposite him. 'Signore Machiavelli, how good of you to come.'

'I couldn't bring myself to refuse your gracious invitation.'

The other man wiped juice from his chin with his sleeve. 'I suppose that kind of smart answer passes for wit among your set.'

Niccolo made no reply.

'Anyway, you are here. Tell me, do you know who I am?'

'All Florence knows Signore Doffo Spini.'

Yes, Niccolo's captor was none other than the city's most notorious ruffian, the leader of Piero de'Medici's cutthroats. You will remember them – the Compagnacci* they called themselves as they swaggered about the streets and piazzas overturning shop-

*Editor's note: 'Comrades in Evil'

44

keepers' stalls, breaking up church services for the devilment of it, terrorising any who voiced public opposition to the government and, though no one had yet proved it, removing several of Savonarola's supporters.

Spini smiled. 'Good. Since you recognise me I'm sure a self-professed scholar like yourself has calculated why I have had you brought here.'

Niccolo had no taste for this cat-and-mouse game but if it meant deferring whatever unpleasantness Spini had in mind for him he would go along with it. 'I cannot imagine, Signore. You surely do not consider me a political opponent. I am quite neutral in matters of state.'

This time the other man laughed. 'Humility? Well, well, that is not a trait I expected to find in Signore Machiavelli. Perhaps these will give you a clue.' He indicated a sheaf of papers before him. 'Do examine them.' He motioned to a servant to untie Niccolo's bonds.

Niccolo flipped through the pile. 'They appear to be some little verses of mine.'

'Indeed they are. What do you suppose they have in common?'

Niccolo shrugged.

'Come now, surely you are better acquainted with the children of your own genius? They are all about me and my friends, are they not?'

'Possibly.'

'Certainly.' Spini finished his peach and dropped the stone in a silver dish. 'Tell me, have you eaten this morning?'

Niccolo shook his head.

'Then you must join me.' He pointed to the papers. 'You will find these meaty enough to break your fast. Eat.'

Rough hands pushed Niccolo up to the table. 'Look,' he pleaded, 'is this really…'

'Eat! Or by God I'll ram your stinking verses down your throat myself. I'm going to enjoy watching you choke on your own empty wit.'

With trembling hands Niccolo picked up the top sheet of paper. He tore it in pieces and stuffed the fragments between his lips. They had a bitter taste and his fear-dried mouth produced little saliva to soften them.

'Hard to stomach, aren't they? I certainly find them so. Did you really suppose that I would stand aside and let you make a laughing-stock of me? Little men like you are pathetic. You call yourself *neutral*? What you really mean is that you don't have the guts for politics. All you can do is stand on the edge of the crowd and poke fun at those of us who do have the courage to take a lead in the city's affairs. Come along, eat up! Aren't you enjoying your meal? That's a pity – because it's your last.'

Spini pushed his chair back from the table and stood up. 'Well, take as long as you like. It makes no difference. When you have eaten your fill my friends are going to kill you. Then, tonight, they will slip your pitiable carcase into the Arno. And Florence will be rid of a vulture who could do nothing but feed upon the corpses of other men's reputations.'

II

Spini turned to leave the room but at that moment a servant entered. He held a whispered conversation with his master.

Spini's face creased in fury. 'What? How could they possibly discover...? How many of them are there?'

'About a dozen, Sir,' the man answered nervously.

Spini paced the room like a prowling, angry lion. At last he turned to the tall man. 'Throw this rubbish out,' he ordered and strode to the door. There he paused and glared at Niccolo. 'There'll be another time – when you least expect.' So saying, he marched out.

Moments later Niccolo was standing in the street outside surrounded by a group of friends who shook his hand, clapped him on the back and demanded the details of his ordeal.

'All in good time,' Niccolo spluttered, spitting out gobbets of half-chewed paper. 'I need a drink ... several drinks.' He paused.

'No, first I must send word to Baccia.'

One of the company was despatched to the Via del Proconsolo with news of Niccolo's deliverance while everyone else went to a nearby market workers' tavern. There Niccolo, sufficiently recovered to embellish his adventure, gave a highly coloured account of the morning's events. For his part he was eager to know how on earth his rescuers had found him. It transpired that Timeo, his servant, had recognised one of the men who came to collect his master as a member of the Spini entourage. Baccia had sent him straight away to rouse Francesco and Francesco had rushed around gathering a posse. They had discussed tactics and decided that the best course was a frontal attack on the Palazzo Spini. If Doffo was holding their friend there and intended him some harm, they reasoned, he would want his designs kept secret. They had gambled on the fact that if they confronted Spini and charged him with abduction he would not dare proceed with his plan. Their gamble had come off.

Young Niccolo was saved. For all that he bragged in private about his brave defiance of the Spini, he did curtail his literary output, for a time – or rather he turned his wit from the government to its greatest critic.

When the sand is running through the hourglass no grain can resist its pull. Everyone Niccolo knew had heard Savonarola preach. Many went to the cathedral three times a week to listen to him. All were moved by the friar's eloquence and passion. Baccia was openly intrigued by the crowds which swept, eager and chattering, past her casements on sermon days and returned, muted or sobbing, hours later. Her husband shared her curiosity but was certainly not going to admit it. He feigned amused indifference and only allowed himself with an indulgent smile to be entreated by friends to sample the Dominican's oratory. It was a remarkable experience. I even remember the date – Tuesday, 22 September 1494.

Francesco and Totto arrived mid-morning at the house on the Via del Proconsolo to collect Niccolo and Baccia. After a beaker or two of Artimino they made the short walk along the street, jostling with the throng which streamed towards the Duomo's gleaming, intricate massiveness. They entered by the west doors, shuffling forward with the crowd. Inside, Baccia and her maid had to part company from the menfolk. The nave was divided lengthways by a curtain and women were directed to the left into their own enclosed space. Although the friar was not expected to make his appearance for another hour the cathedral was already more than half full. Niccolo and his friends elbowed their way as close as they could to the pulpit and waited, wedged every man against his sweating neighbours. They chattered and laughed, Niccolo more than usually ready with jokes to lighten the atmosphere, making clear to everyone – including himself – that he was not about to be reduced to tears or breast-beating by a rabid *dominus canis*[*].

Conversation ceased abruptly, as though cut with a knife. A gaunt figure had appeared in the wide stone pulpit, mounting unseen from steps at the rear. He held his arms wide in benediction over the throng and every head bowed – every head except Niccolo's, who stared fixedly at the white-

[*]Editor's note: Dog Latin for 'hound of God'. The Dominicans were unpopular in many quarters for their over-zealous sniffing out of supposed heretics and their savage methods of interrogation.

habited prior with the black cowl thrown back from his shaven head. His first thought was that Savonarola looked like an aged fist fighter. His features were emaciated yet, in places, puffed out, distorted, disproportionate. The nose was huge, the lips thick and protruding. The eyes, though set deep in their sockets, bulged as they rolled to and fro, taking in the whole congregation. For a long moment it seemed to Niccolo that that intense gaze was directed solely at him.

Then the preacher spoke: 'Behold!' He paused and the two syllables echoed around the painted cupola far above. 'Behold, I send a flood upon the earth to destroy every living thing!'

Niccolo felt the hairs rise at the nape of his neck. The prior's voice was high-pitched and raucous. His cadences lacked grace. Yet there was an undoubted power in his slightest utterance. Savonarola gave no appearance of forcefully projecting his voice but that voice, with the timbre of a cracked bell, carried to every corner of the vast building.

'Have I not prophesied these past months; has not the God of storms warned you, O Florence, of the deluge to come? And is not that word fulfilled? Now! This chosen day!

O, Florence.' The preacher turned his eyes heavenwards and shuddered. 'I have received a vision this very morning. The flood is pouring down from the mountains. He who was foretold is come! He comes as a scourge! He comes to overthrow every tyrant! He comes to vanquish all Italy! He comes to purify the stinking wen of Rome! He comes to purge the Church! His armies will pour through your gates, Florence! An incarnadine flood! There will be blood in the streets! There will be wailing behind every shuttered window! Deep mourning! Rachel weeping for her children because they are not!'

Niccolo forced himself to look away, determined to break the verbal chains the preacher was binding round his mind. All about him men were crying out, snivelling, crossing themselves. The words rolled on: never shouted, sometimes almost whispered, so that the congregation leaned forward as one eager ear desperate to scoop up every trope, every cesura. Savonarola carved ever more elaborate embellishments around the circumference of his argument; festooned his prose with heavy garlands of dread.

'Florence, is your eternal woe upon my

head, that I have not warned you?' The preacher paused as though pondering the question in the depths of his soul. Someone called out 'No!' and Savonarola looked up quickly. 'No, day after day, I have held open for you the door of the ark. I have begged, implored, entreated you to come inside. For, as in the days of Noah, so even now the only salvation is within the vessel that God has provided.'

He stood back from the pulpit's edge, sighing deeply and the sigh was taken up throughout the audience. 'I am weary of telling you. Must I tell you again? Do I need to explain yet one more time how you may find salvation? How you may enter God's ark?'

'Yes!'

'Tell us!'

'Good brother, tell us!'

The responses erupted all over the cathedral.

'Very well. And yet I feel my strength ebbing. O, brothers and sisters, pray for yourselves. Pray as you have never prayed before.' Savonarola sank back out of sight.

'Well, that's quite a performance.' Niccolo found some torn shreds of nonchalance to drape round his numbed self-assurance. He looked at his companions for support but Totto was fervently telling his beads and Francey was on his knees, his lips moving in urgent and silent supplication.

Everywhere Niccolo looked he could see nothing but men – young, old, poor, rich, simpletons and scholars – deeply affected by the preacher's words. He felt panic surge up within him. He cast around for a way of escape but there was none. He was drowning in a sea of alien beliefs, superstitions. With the consternation came anger. But was it outrage at the thought of all these people being duped or resentment that they were experiencing something deep within themselves that he could not share? He was still debating the question when the friar resumed his discourse.

'O Florence, the door of God's ark stands ajar but it is fast closing. If you do not pass through today the opportunity will come no more. God will not suffer me to call you again.'

By now the preacher was having to raise his voice above a pitiful stridulation of penitential ecstasy. Wails, shrieks, sobs and cries of anguish rose from every part of the congregation. Over this cacophony of lamentation Savonarola's raven croaking called out the threefold message of Florence's salvation: forsake the sins of self-indulgence, luxury and pride; cast off the yoke of Medici tyranny; welcome Charles VIII, the Lord's instrument of judgement.

No one could be unaffected by this extraordinary experience. Not even Niccolo Machiavelli. He did not prostrate himself, or crouch foetally in self-abnegation, as many around him were doing, but the blood throbbed in his temple, he gasped for breath as though the friar's words were powerful talons squeezing his entrails, his mind fought against the surrounding hysteria and the power of the preacher's personality. Eventually it went numb with the effort and he ceased to be conscious of any sensation.

He could never afterwards say how much longer the sermon lasted or recall leaving the cathedral with the slow-moving congregation. His next sensation was of the brilliant sunlight and the dusty heat of the Piazza del Duomo.

Niccolo returned home with Francesco and was joined there by two other friends, Paolo Valori, whose father was one of Savonarola's most ardent champions, and Michelangelo Buonarotti, famed then in Florence and now known to all the world.

They sat under the vine, served by Timeo with cakes and wine. It was part of their regular ritual to gather there and amuse themselves with witty conversation, songs, cards and dice. This day was different. Francesco had not brought his lute and was not inclined to lead ditties of love or war with his rich baritone. Michelangelo, who often amused the company with caricatures and quick sketches, had little to contribute beyond the latest gossip from Bologna whence he had recently returned. Every man was too absorbed with his own thoughts for more than desultory conversation.

Niccolo thought seriously about the political implications of the friar's words. Had he the power to unleash a popular uprising? Could the Medici, after all these years, be displaced? And if they could, what then? Mob rule masquerading as democracy? People need leaders – the stronger the better. To whom could the citizens of Florence turn for a powerful yet wise head of state? He looked at Paolo, stretching his long limbs upon the grass. 'Paolo, if Piero de'Medici were thrown out, who would replace him? Your father?'

His friend stifled a laugh. 'Oh no, *padre*

mio is too much the friar's man.'

'But surely he doesn't think that Savonarola will leave the cloister for the council chamber?'

'He believes what the friar's visions tell him: the government, the fate of Florence will be decided by another.'

'The French king? But it's not certain that he will come or that, if he does, he'll be interested in anything but plunder.'

Francesco, sitting astride the low wall around the cistern into which the household's water was pumped, looked across at Niccolo sharply. 'Savonarola says the king, the Lord's instrument, has already come.'

Machiavelli shook his head. 'A device to stir up the congregation.'

His friend sighed. 'You still don't believe, do you?'

'I certainly don't believe just because the prior of St Mark's says it is so. Michelangelo, what news was there of the French when you were in Bologna?'

The artist, leaning against one of the posts supporting the aged vine, ran a hand through his matted black hair. 'As I said, the Bentivogli are worried enough to throw in their lot with Il Moro and his French allies. They want to make sure that any invading force keeps well away from their territory. That means they would have to come through Tuscany. But no one seems to know how real the threat is.'

'Then what man does not know God has revealed to Fra Girolamo.' Francesco spoke with total conviction. 'Nicco, why do you have such a problem accepting that?'

Niccolo let the matter drop. He had learned, even at his tender age, the futility of pitting reason against faith. Anyway, he did not know to what conclusion his own reason was leading him.

It was no more than half an hour later that a stranger was led into the garden by Timeo. It was a colleague of Michelangelo's who had been told that he might find the artist at Signore Machiavelli's. The two men strolled away a few metres under the trees and were absorbed in urgent conversation for several minutes.

After the messenger had gone Michelangelo resumed his position under the vine. He looked around the company and announced in an expressionless voice: 'Word has just arrived from contacts of ours in the marble quarries at Carrara. Yesterday the French sacked Fivizzano and slaughtered the garrison. They're pressing on southwards and must, by now, be in Tuscany. Piero de'Medici has already left to meet Charles VIII and talk terms.'

After a stunned moment the friends jumped to their feet and rushed to the Piazza della Signoria. That would be the place where any news or rumours or gossip would be buzzing around. They discovered very little more about the military situation but they did pick up the mood in the city. It was one of disgust and anger. For months Piero had adopted a defiant stance towards the dangerous alliance forming in the North, without taking any steps for the defence of Florentine territory. He trusted in strategically placed but undermanned outlying garrisons to block the advance of an invader. Now, at the first news of the French advance, he had panicked and hurried northwards with pack animals laden with gold to buy off the French. At three points on the square self-appointed orators were holding forth to little crowds. Niccolo moved from one to the other and found the demagogues strong on denunciation and weak on suggested action.

It was late when he returned home and Baccia was already in bed. She lay facing the wall, breathing steadily but Niccolo knew that she was not asleep. He slipped between the sheets and pressed himself against her back. He felt her stiffen. 'Darling, what's the matter?' he asked.

'I ... I don't want to.' Her voice was faltering.

Niccolo sat up, tired and irritated. 'Well, I do and I'm your husband.'

Baccia rolled onto her back and looked up at him with eyes reddened with tears. 'No, you mustn't make me. Dearest Nicco, you mustn't. It's sinful.'

'Sinful! What on earth do you mean?'

'We have been guilty of the sin of lust. That is why God is punishing us – and all of Florence.'

Niccolo laughed. He was never able to be angry with his wife for more than a few minutes. 'Signore and Signora Machiavelli enjoy lying together and for this reason cohorts of angels are being sent to destroy the whole city?'

'You mustn't speak like that, Nicco. It's blasphemy.' Baccia's mouth and eyes were circles of shock and dismay.

'You're quite serious, aren't you?'

She nodded, frowning.

'Then someone must have put these crazy ideas into your head. Who was it?'

Baccia sighed deeply. 'Oh dear, I shan't tell it very well. It was all so clear when he explained it.'

'He?'

'It was after the sermon. Outside the Duomo I met up with Cousin Anna and Cousin Bianca and Aunt Caterina – you know, the one who was married to Signore Lepari, the goldsmith.'

'Yes, yes, what's this got to do...'

'Shh, I am coming to that. Don't put me off. We went to Aunt Caterina's house on the street where Filippo Strozzi began building his *palazzo* before he was sent into exile. We noticed that we were being followed by one of the Dominicans from St Mark's; one of Fra Savonarola's men. When we reached my aunt's house he caught us up and asked if he might speak with us. Of course, Aunt Caterina invited him in and offered him refreshment, and we talked. Or rather he talked – Fra Roberto Attavanti; that's his name. He asked us what we thought of the sermon. He told us about poor Prior Savonarola's anguish. He receives visions – by day as well as night – terrible visions of the things to come unless we all repent. That's why he knows he must go on preaching, even though it takes such a terrible toll on his health.'

'So.' Niccolo frowned impatiently. 'He persuaded you what a great prophet Fra Girolamo is. What else?'

'He urged us, implored us, to examine ourselves – really deeply – to see what sins lay like black mud – those were his words, "congealed black mud" – besmirching our eternal souls. He told us to confess our sins so that he could wash them clean with his prayers.'

'And?' Niccolo urged her on.

'And that's when I realised that my sin was lust. All these weeks I have been taking pleasure from your body. I haven't been thinking about having children for you and for God; just how nice it is.'

'And you told this Fra Roberto about your "sin of lust"?'

'Yes.'

'And what did he say?'

'That I must purify my soul by real repentance and abstinence.'

'Abstinence? For how long?'

'Fra Roberto said the only way to be sure of forgiveness was to keep myself completely pure and spotless for Christ.' She faltered and turned her face to the wall. Her next words were part muffled by the pillows and Niccolo had to make her repeat them. 'He said I should ask your permission to become a Dominican tertiary – join the Sisters of Annalena.'

Niccolo felt a surge of mixed emotions: tenderness and pity for Baccia's confusion and distress; fury that this Roberto Attavanti was pestering silly women; and a weariness of soul – after all the turmoil of the day this was one aggravation too many. He sank back against the pillows.

After a long silence Baccia turned towards him. 'Are you angry with me, Nicco?' she whispered.

'No, Darling, just tired – too tired to discuss these things now. Go to sleep and don't worry. Tomorrow I will talk of this with Fra Roberto and decide what must be done.'

He extinguished the bedside candle, closed his eyes and stretched his limbs. But if his body rested, his mind clambered arduously over the boulders and crags with which the day's events had littered his life. Whichever route his mental scrambling took it always arrived in the same place and in that place was Prior Girolamo. Tomorrow he would confront Savonarola. Would that provide an answer to his questions? Which questions?

Niccolo walked to where the convent of St Mark's stood alone in open ground near the city's northern wall and presented himself there in mid-morning. He was shown into the wide cloister where, with a dozen or so other visitors, he had to wait the prior's pleasure.

He perched on the low wall flanking the space devoted to paved walks between beds of herbs, resting his back against a pillar and reading, from time to time, a book of Horatian odes. It amused him, in this place devoted to Christian piety, to dip into one of the great pagan authors. Men came to St Mark's from all over Italy and farther afield to gaze on the frescoes by the one known as Fra Angelico, the Seraphic Brother, and to consult the extensive collection of ancient religious documents bestowed on the library by Cosimo de'Medici. And here, at the heart of this shrine to Christian learning, sat someone reading verses, specifically the twenty-fifth ode, whose profanity would shock any curious person looking over his shoulder who could comprehend the language of Classical Rome.

Sweet is my bold endeavour now,
To chant unuttered strains divine,
And seek the god, who on his brow
Wears the green blossom of the vine.

It was the secret defiance of a young man far
from sure of himself. All the events of the
previous day had so far unsettled him that
he struggled to reassert old certainties.

He closed the book and one more time
rehearsed the arguments and questions he
would raise with Savonarola. He knew the
prior would agree to see him because the
written note Niccolo had sent him by the
hand of the brother who had admitted him
detailed a charge against one of his friars
which was very serious. Fra Girolamo was a
strict disciplinarian, very jealous of the
reputation of St Mark's. He knew of
Roberto Attavanti's earlier lapses and the
scandal that one particular incident had
created. Attavanti was a young man,
scarcely into his twenties, who had been
forced to take the habit, according to common gossip, after getting his own sister with
child. The rigours of conventual life had not
purged him of carnal desire and there had
been incidents of his insinuating himself
into female company for purposes not

entirely of a spiritual nature. Fra Roberto was one of those religious whose exploits – real or imaginary – were the stock-in-trade of tavern gossip. Niccolo had no intention of allowing his own name to feature in such tales. Nor would Savonarola, in the midst of his campaign for Florentine repentance and purity, want Brother Roberto's struggle with chastity bruited abroad. On that issue the prior and his visitor would be at one. And that agreement might lead on to discussion of other matters.

At length, Niccolo was escorted from the cloister and along a passage to a door at the far end. His guide knocked and held it open for the visitor to enter. Niccolo found himself in a simple cell scarcely different from those that housed the other brothers. Savonarola was seated behind a desk on which books and papers were arranged in neat piles. In front of the prior, and thus between him and his guest, stood a large crucifix.

'Brother Niccolo, welcome.' Savonarola did not rise to greet him and there was only the suggestion of a smile about his full lips. Close to, he was no less ugly than when seen in the pulpit, nor were the eyes less intimidating. They fixed themselves now on

Niccolo. 'You have a complaint to make about one of our fellowship?'

Niccolo reported all that Baccia had told him.

The prior listened in silence, then commented, 'Woman's thought is notoriously shallow and unstable, Brother. Are you sure your wife has not exaggerated or misunderstood Fra Roberto's words?'

'Fra Roberto caused her much distress. I am sure that she took his meaning accurately.'

'Let us see.' Savonarola rang a little bell.

The door was opened almost immediately by a diminutive friar and the prior gave orders that Fra Roberto was to be fetched.

Niccolo grasped his opportunity. 'Brother Prior, what will happen when the French king reaches Florence? The people are terrified of what his soldiers will do.'

'Are you terrified, Brother Niccolo?'

'I fear the breakdown of public order.'

'Fear rather God and his judgement.'

'I leave the study of the next world to theologians. My concern is with what happens here and now.'

'Tell me, Brother Niccolo, when a man's soul and body are separated what happens to him?'

Throughout this exchange Savonarola's bulging, unblinking eyes had never deviated from Niccolo's face. Stubbornly, with great difficulty, the young man returned the gaze. Like a wrestler locked in his adversary's grasp he refused to slacken his mental grip. 'The man dies,' he replied evenly.

'Just so.' The prior's uncowled head nodded almost imperceptibly. 'And if we separate this world from the world of heaven?'

Almost physically Niccolo felt the pressure of the other man's mind. 'I ... I think that is not a true comparison.'

Savonarola allowed himself a faint smile. 'Where is the world of the Romans you so much admire, Brother Niccolo? Dead. Its ruined temples and triumphal pillars are merely the scattered bones of its corpse. If any Christian state ever forgets that it lives *sub specie aeternitatis,* it too will die. I pray that you will not be led astray by your pagan authors, Brother Niccolo.' His brows creased into a frown. 'And yet I fear it.'

Niccolo rummaged for an answer but was saved by a knock at the door.

Fra Roberto sidled into the cell and sank to one knee before his superior.

'Rise, Brother. I think you do not know

69

Signore Machiavelli.'

The friar, a handsome young man with well-balanced features and a fringe of thick blond hair, nodded nervously at Niccolo.

'And yet,' Savonarola continued, 'you are acquainted, I understand, with Signora Machiavelli and some of her kinswomen.'

Fra Roberto gazed down at his feet. 'I believe I met the ladies yesterday, Brother Prior.'

'Are you not under my ban to avoid all female company?'

'Brother Prior, my zeal was so kindled by your sermon that I had to help those poor creatures... It was the Spirit of God that led me...'

'Silence!' Savonarola hissed the word. 'Do you dare blame God for your disobedience?'

Fra Roberto shuffled his feet and looked sideways at the visitor. What Niccolo read in the man's eyes was smouldering resentment.

'Tell me – precisely – what you said to these ladies?' the prior ordered.

'I ... I besought them to recollect their sins.'

'What sins?'

'The sort of sins which so easily beset beautiful women whose husbands do not direct them in the ways of holiness.'

'Watch your tongue, Friar!' Niccolo protested.

Savonarola reacted quickly. 'I will watch his tongue and I urge you to have an eye to yours.' To the friar he said, 'Did you press Signora Machiavelli to forsake the wedded state and embrace the life of our sister order?'

'Brother Prior, she confessed the sin of lust...'

'And you presumed to have the authority to dispense her from her marriage vows?'

'I ... I only ... advised ... suggested...'

'You advised a foolish woman to cleanse her soul by adding one sin to another? Vows, it seems, mean nothing to you, since you regard so lightly your pledge of obedience to me. Leave us. I will set your penance later.'

Fra Roberto dropped another obeisance and scuttled quickly from the room, but not before glaring again at Niccolo from beneath lowered lids.

'You have my word that Signora Machiavelli will not be troubled by him again.'

'Thank you, Brother Prior.'

'You will be able to set your wife's mind at rest?'

'I think so.'

'Then I bid you good-day – and I hope you will heed my advice.'

Niccolo made his way home slowly, impressed despite himself with the prior's assured control of his subordinates. Might such a man also be able to rule Florence? That question very soon received an answer.

The restoration of harmony in the Machiavelli household was in stark contrast to the mounting conflict and disorder outside. Piero de'Medici met Charles VIII on the march and grovelled before him, offering free passage through Tuscany and an indemnity of 200,000 florins without any such concession being demanded of him. Piazza orators in Florence told their audiences that a show of force would have deflected the invader or even halted him. Charles's large army was struggling through a barren area. Any delay would have weakened it by depleting its resources. Now, the French could make maximum speed and Florence lay at their mercy.

Like beetles in a disturbed midden, Niccolo's fellow citizens scurried to and fro, panicking and leaderless. When Piero showed his face again Florence rose against him almost to a man. He fled and the mob sacked all the Medici *palazzi*. This orgy of destruction might have assuaged the people's feelings but was no foundation for a new order. The Signoria declared a republic and appointed new assemblies to represent the people. But neither the greybeards or the novices had the first idea of how to frame and carry through policy. And every day the French army drew closer. There was only one man in the city who had any coherent political ideas and certainly only one to whom all factions and rival demagogues would listen. Savonarola took over the direction of events. It was he who led a second embassy to Charles VIII, secured the French king's support for the new constitution and arranged for the reception of his army in Florence. Nothing could remove the humiliation of temporary occupation but at least Charles, who was profoundly influenced by the prior of St Mark's, came to regard himself as a protector and deliverer rather than a conquering hero.

In the midst of all the confusion Niccolo took Baccia to our family property at San Casciano in the village of Sant'Andrea, some sixteen kilometres to the south of Florence. Here they passed three idyllic

October weeks. By day they walked among the hills in the autumn sunshine, watched the grapes being harvested and helped to tread them in the lofty *cantina* with its barrels stacked from floor to ceiling. In the evening they sat beside the fire in the little house's wide hearth and Niccolo read to his wife from the books he had brought from Florence or the poems he wrote in the peace of San Casciano's garden.

Most days news arrived from the city and, at the end of the month, Niccolo learned of the settlement Savonarola had achieved and the prospect of the peaceful entry of the French. He decided to return in order to safeguard his property and to see for himself this formidable army whose approach had been heralded by so many colourful rumours.

Charles VIII's army entered Florence on 17 November. Niccolo and Baccia had a vantage point at a second-floor window of Signore Vernacci's house near the Palazzo della Signoria. He sat with his wife's family looking down on the wide Via Calzaiuoli. Despite their amicable arrangement with the French king, the city fathers were taking no chances. The streets were lined with Florence's own militia and the walls and towers were well manned. Behind the flanking pikemen a crowd four or five deep pressed forward to catch a first glimpse of the alien force. The atmosphere, Niccolo reflected, was very strange. Though everyone was excited and curious, they were also apprehensive. This asserted itself in a muted murmur of voices. There was no cheering, even when the first armed ranks came into view.

At last the vanguard appeared. Niccolo was fascinated to see Europe's most feared fighting men, the Swiss mercenaries of whom he had heard so much. They were tall, decked in close-fitting multicoloured uniforms, which added to the impression of fierceness given by their long, square-bladed halberds. They came on, rank after rank, stepping briskly to the beat of side drums. They were followed by the French infantry and arquebusiers. After them the very different Gascon arbalisters swaggered by – stocky, unkempt troops, carrying their crossbows over their shoulders. When the foot soldiers had made their way into the square, the horsemen skittered along the street: first the heavy cavalry in full armour with lowered lances, each knight accompanied by his squire leading spare mounts.

Then came the light cavalry, wearing part-armour of corselets and helms, and carrying wooden bows in the English fashion. The size and variety of this military force was such as had never been seen in Italy since the days of the legions. But the chivalric zenith had yet to be reached. A gap of a hundred metres was left behind the cavalry. Then, with a fine sense of theatre, the royal escort blazed into the street – two hundred of France's best knights, fully caparisoned, shields and crested helmets gleaming and, after them, King Charles in their midst, resplendent on a white horse, the mounted royal archers in their purple gold-embroidered surcoats. It was magnificent, the opening paragraph of a new chapter on warfare – a chapter, as we now know, that was to tell a dismal story for Italy.

When the spectacle was over the company went in to dinner. Baccia and her cousins were excited by the splendour of it all and chattered excitedly. They sat together at one end of the long table, giggling and occasionally glancing in Niccolo's direction. Watching his wife as she jumped up to whisper something to Totto, who had just arrived, Niccolo fell in love again with her effervescent, easy grace. Then he was drawn back into the conversation of his neighbours who were sombrely trying to assess what the next few days would bring forth. In mid-afternoon Niccolo and Baccia said their goodbyes. While his wife returned home, Niccolo sought out friends who were members of the Florentine assembly and others who had access to the council chamber where Charles was received.

He wandered from tavern to tavern and house to house, gathering information and gossip about the rapidly developing situation. As the evening chill settled over the city and a mist drifted up from the river, Niccolo, Francesco and Paolo Valori were making their way across the Palazzo della Signoria. Suddenly they saw Timeo running across the square, waving and calling out. He was obviously in great distress. His hair straggled in sweating strands and he was so out of breath that for some moments he could not speak.

Niccolo was alarmed to see that the man had been crying. 'What is it, man? What's the matter?' he demanded.

'Oh, Signore, Signore, I have been looking for you everywhere. It is terrible, terrible. You must come.'

He turned back across the square and the

others followed him, running.

Niccolo outstripped the rest, reached his own door and rushed inside. Several neighbours were gathered in the downstairs room. Their faces turned to him with expressions of pity.

'What?' he shouted.

No one replied but all directed their eyes towards the staircase. Niccolo leaped up the stairs in four bounds. There were three women in the bedchamber: Baccia's maid and two of her cousins. All of them were wailing. His eyes went to the pale figure on the bed. Baccia lay naked, her golden hair fanned out around her head. The head lay at a strange angle and as Niccolo approached he saw purple marks round his wife's throat.

III

Grief is the fee the gods exact in return for love and Niccolo paid to the very bottom of his purse. For hours he howled and raged and wept. Now hugging Baccia's limp body, now prostrating himself on her disordered bed, now fiercely tearing at his clothes as though he would rip the very flesh from his arms and chest. The house rapidly filled with friends and neighbours but no one dared approach the stricken man. When faithful Timeo tried to draw him away from his wife's side Niccolo flung him across the room. It was Totto, with tears cascading down his own face, who eventually persuaded his brother to come into the cool night air of the courtyard and take a beaker of wine.

They sat in silence on the low wall around the fountain until Niccolo in little more than a whisper asked, 'Who was it, Totto? Who dared to come into her chamber and...'

His brother held Niccolo close until the sobs had subsided. 'Oh Nicco, I have feared this ever since you were married – feared that Baccia would be in danger because of the many enemies you delight in making. Any one of them could have done this deed. It seems no one saw his face. All the servants know is that they observed a Dominican friar leaving...'

'Fra Roberto!' Niccolo leaped to his feet. 'It was that sanctimonious, womanising...' He plucked the poniard from his belt and ran across to the outer gate. 'Fra Roberto! Within the hour he dies!'

'Niccolo, wait!' Totto hurried after his brother as he stepped out into the street. 'Wait... You do not know...'

But the demented fool was not to be stopped. He rampaged through darkened streets like the riderless horses which used to be set loose in Florence for the St John the Baptist Day celebrations.

How different Niccolo Machiavelli's life would have been if the eyes of reason had not been plucked out by anger and lust for vengeance. He who boasted his knowledge of the ancients had learned nothing from them. Like Alcibiades, who forgot all he had gleaned at the feet of Socrates when he turned in fury against his own Athenians for their perceived treachery, so passion now overmastered this young philosopher. A few hours of patient thought would have discovered to him the truth of Baccia's death and saved him from several months of agonised quest. As it was ... well, I see him now, beating his fists against the oaken portal of St Mark's convent and bellowing imprecations at the top of his voice.

Three times the gatekeeper spoke to Niccolo through the grill, admonishing him to go away and stop troubling the sleeping house, but the distracted hell-raiser only clamoured the louder. At last Niccolo was admitted to a small, bare chamber where, within minutes, the sub-prior, a spare little friar, came in rubbing sleep-reddened eyes.

He glared at the young man who refused to kneel for a benediction and must have looked in the guttering lamplight like a wine-frenzied late-night reveller. 'Who are you and what do you mean by disturbing us at this hour?'

'Deliver to me Roberto Attavanti and I'll be gone instantly.'

'How dare you come here in the middle of the night making such demands. Be off with you!' The sub-prior gathered his dignity around him and turned to leave. 'See this fellow out,' he ordered the gatekeeper. The next second he let out a yelp as his visitor grabbed him by one shoulder, spun him round and pressed the point of his dagger to the friar's nose.

'How dare you fob me off?' Niccolo shouted. 'My wife has been ravished and murdered by one of your crew and I want him here, now, or by God...'

There is no telling what that berserk demoniac might have done in the next few moments – in all likelihood some desperate act that would have brought him to the scaffold. He was saved by the terrified porter, who rushed from the room screeching 'Help! Assassins! The sub-prior's being murdered!' Immediately, Niccolo heard banging doors and running feet in the corridor. In his headlong rush to the convent he had given no thought to what he would actually do when he gained admittance. Now he stared stupefied at the press of men who filled the doorway wide-eyed and open-mouthed in horror.

Suddenly their ranks parted and Girolamo Savonarola was in the room. He brought with him a calming authority, a presence radiating outward like silent music. 'Brother Niccolo, this is an unconventional hour for a call.' Was there humour, mockery or reproof in the level voice and the grey eyes that gleamed in the dim light? 'Obviously some urgent errand brings you here. How may we be of service?'

Niccolo dully repeated his demand. 'I'm here for Roberto Attavanti.'

'Then you will have no further need of my sub-prior. Please, may I have him back?'

The young man lowered his poniard and the little friar collapsed against the wall.

The prior waved a hand at his brethren. 'To your cells, all of you.'

The doorkeeper, still trembling, protested. 'Brother Prior, the man is dangerous. We dare not leave you alone with him.'

'Brother Paolo, our friend needs our help. He has suffered a great wrong and is in deep distress of spirit. He is more peril to himself than to me. Now, leave us.' When the room had emptied he drew a stool from the wall and sat down. 'Now, my son, tell me what is troubling you.'

For the first time Niccolo had to find words for the tragedy. Savonarola listened without interruption to the account which came, disjointedly and punctuated by sobs. Finally the distraught man repeated his demand that Fra Roberto should be produced.

'And why are you convinced that he is the man you are looking for? Has someone identified him?'

'The murderer was a Dominican and there is only one of your number who hates me enough to have done this thing.'

The prior shook his head. 'You are quite convinced, without any enquiry, that this wretch came from my house?'

'He was a Dominican.'

Savonarola's beak of a nose twitched. 'Hm, possibly. What time did this appalling event take place?'

'Around nine o'clock, according to the servants.'

'We were at compline then – all of us, including three visiting friars, here to use the library. And before you ask, I can assure you that I would have noted any brother absent from the office.'

'Oh, no, it was a Dominican sure enough. Of that there can be no doubt.'

'It seems to me that there is a great deal of room for doubt. Brother Niccolo, you are a very intelligent man. I will not say that I approve of all your verses – oh yes, I have read several of them. As I say, I don't necessarily approve, but I recognise the sharp mind behind them. That mind is now dulled by grief.'

'Not so dulled as to be charmed by a smooth-tongued preacher. Not so dulled that it cannot see how desperate you are to protect your own.'

'Think, my son! Think!' It was the first time Savonarola had raised his voice. 'If someone in this house had done this terrible thing do you not suppose that I would be even more determined than you to discover his identity? A soul so steeped in sin would corrupt our fellowship. It must be helped to confess and do penance.'

'Don't talk to me of souls. I'm looking for a filthy, lascivious Dominican animal and when I find him I'll despatch him straight to hell! Now, will you produce him or must I ransack this place to find him myself?'

Savonarola sat immovable, fixing his visitor with unblinking eyes. There was something inescapable about that look. Niccolo felt held as though by chains. 'You will not believe me when I assure you that no one from this house was abroad tonight. Very well, then listen instead to the voice of reason. This assailant was clever enough to win Signora Machiavelli's confidence and gain access to the house when you were absent. None of your servants saw his face.

Does this not suggest a high degree of cunning?' He went on without waiting for an answer. 'And what more guileful than to masquerade in a deep-cowled friar's habit which would conceal his face *and* set his victim's husband on a wrong scent?'

Niccolo reacted with bitter amusement. 'Too subtle by far. Roberto Attavanti is the man and I shall be revenged on him – with or without your help.'

The prior shook his head. 'Fra Roberto is wrestling with many demons. When they are in control he might just possibly be capable of such a cardinal sin…'

'Then yield him up…'

'But he is not the man you seek.'

'You're trying to protect one of your own.'

Savonarola's face screwed itself into a deep frown. 'Fra Roberto is not your man because he is not here.'

'I don't believe…'

'He is unruly, a disruptive influence, especially among the younger brothers. Ten days ago I sent him to our mother house in Rome.'

Like princes, lesser men must take pains to learn whom to trust. Since everyone, friend and foe alike, has his own interests to serve, what he says may not invariably be taken at face value. At some times and in certain situations it may be necessary to put faith in no one, to seek the lies lurking in sworn truth and the treason concealed by sage advice.

Niccolo left St Mark's in confusion. Savonarola, in the pulpit and in private converse, appeared to blaze with white-hot sincerity. Yet even as he did so he was making himself master of Florence and revealing himself to any who took the trouble to penetrate his clouds of pious oratory as a man of prodigious guile and ambition. The further he distanced himself from the lodestone of the prior's over-powering presence the more Niccolo reinforced his own conviction that the worst wickedness of all is that which cloaks itself in religion. And were not friars the worst examples of hypocrisy with their feigned poverty, their hawking of heavenly bliss for hard cash, their seducing of silly women and their preaching against those sins of which they were themselves the most adept exponents?

Over the remaining hours of darkness his aimless meandering brought him to the Ponte alla Rafraia. There, leaning against the parapet and staring down into the rippling grey silk of the Arno, he assembled his thoughts into a sequence that possessed seeming coherence: the overthrow of the Medici had left a power vacuum in Florence, one that Savonarola had filled. The preacher had become politician, with a mission – heaven-breathed as he said – to turn the city into a holy republic, dedicated to pure living; a beacon of godliness for the world. His power depended on Florentines believing in his moral crusade and fearing another visitation of divine wrath if they wandered from the paths of righteousness. What would happen if the corruption at the heart of his own community was revealed? The prior of St Mark's could not permit the slightest blemish to be seen on the glistening fruit of Dominican sanctity. Therefore he would hide Fra Roberto, probably smuggle him out of the city. Well, he would find Niccolo Machiavelli an obstacle to his plans, a barrier which would not only halt Fra Roberto's lecherous career but might also stop Dominican rule in Florence.

By the time dawn discovered Niccolo being admitted by a sleepy servant to Totto's little house on the Via Calzaiuoli and flopping exhausted into an armed chair beside the grey ashes of yesterday's fire he had talked himself into a heroic role as the saviour of Florence. Later in the day, when he was surrounded by consoling friends, he shared his vision with them. They indulged the afflicted man's fancies and nodded to each other when they thought he was not looking. When he asked them to help him track down Fra Roberto they smiled and told him that time would heal. Except Totto and Francesco Bardi; they humoured Niccolo to the extent that they promised to make discreet enquiries about the vanished friar.

The result was not what young Machiavelli had hoped to hear. Several people reported seeing Roberto Attavanti leave Florence at about the time that Savonarola claimed to have despatched him. The party of four friars had passed over the Ponte Santa Trinità, along the Via Maggio and had left Florence by the Porta Romana. They attracted more attention than they might otherwise have done because they were on horseback. Observers speculated that they were carrying urgent messages for the pope. According to the guard captain in charge of the towers and gates south of the river, the group had returned six days later but without Fra Roberto. Niccolo's reaction was to announce his immediate departure for Rome.

Totto and Francey were appalled. They spent three dismal autumnal hours one afternoon trying to dissuade him. I can see their earnest faces now and hear the chatter of gossiping women and shrieks of children playing in the courtyard, which the house on the Via Calzaiuoli shared with neighbouring dwellings. Niccolo had moved in with his brother, unable to face his own home where Baccia's female relatives wept and moaned to each other, and her father made arrangements for a lavish funeral. Guido Vernacci was already infirm of body; this tragedy almost destroyed his mind. He convinced himself that, somehow, Niccolo was responsible for his daughter's death. When the grieving husband had returned to the Via del Proconsolo he had found Vernacci already there and taking command of the situation. The old man had railed at him, waving his stick and tearing distractedly at his flowing beard until Signora Vernacci had drawn him into another room to calm him. Niccolo had left. In truth, he was content to leave Baccia's obsequies in the hands of her own family.

'Nicco, this is madness,' Totto protested, perching on a pile of stones builders had once brought there for repairs and never taken away. 'What do you think to achieve in Rome?'

'I'll find out whether or not Fra Roberto is there. If he is, I'll choke the truth from him before I do to him what he did to Baccia. If he isn't I'll go on searching till I find him.'

'Haven't you listened to a word we said?' Francesco drew a hand across his brow. The lightest effort or anxiety always made him perspire. 'Fra Roberto wasn't here. Lots of people saw him leave the city.'

'Exactly,' Niccolo explained carefully as though to children. 'That's how I know he is guilty. Oh, he is cunning. He would not have dared his crime without some stratagem to throw me off the scent. So, he leaves Florence, as you say, in full view, cowl thrown back from his face, riding a horse.'

'And then?' Totto asked.

'He goes to Rome with his obliging escort who will swear before any magistrate that they left him in the Dominican priory there. Days later he leaves the convent, returns to Florence as an anonymous friar, does what he came to do and slips out of the city once more. Perhaps he goes back to his kennel in Rome, perhaps not. That is what I shall find out.'

Totto's thin face wore that dejected bewildered frown it always assumed when he was trying, unsuccessfully, to play the older, wiser brother. 'And supposing you *do* find him and supposing he refuses to confess to the crime, what will you do then – murder an innocent man and a man in the habit of a holy friar?'

'There's nothing innocent or holy about Roberto Attavanti.'

'Wait, Nicco.' Francey always looked like a hungry, hopeful puppy when he was cajoling. 'Leave it a few days. Till after the funeral. Perhaps by then you'll see things in a different...'

'No!' The poor fool was several leagues beyond reason. 'I'm going *now*. I have to. I can't face the funeral and the Vernaccis don't want me there. Totto, you can represent me.'

'Why do I always end up doing the things you don't want to do? It's always been the same, ever since we were children. "Nicco's too small to do this"; "Nicco's not strong enough to do that"; "Nicco can't possibly go all the way over there"; "Totto will do it."

The funeral – that's what all this is really about, isn't it? Something else Nicco doesn't want to do, so Nicco runs away and leaves it to big brother.'

The outburst took both of Totto's companions by surprise. They were silenced for several moments and Niccolo felt the pang of what he might have recognised as guilt had he allowed himself to reflect on it. He did not. 'Totto, I *can't* wait around here. You know what's happening with these swaggering French soldiers. Everyone knows. Any day now they'll be moving on to Rome. They're all boasting about how they're going to pillage the pope's city – the palaces, the goldsmiths' shops, the churches.'

Francey's face showed his horror at the prospect. 'The holy father has summoned all his vassals and allies to send troops to his aid. They...'

'Will be able to do nothing. Charles and his mercenaries will walk straight in. The Borgia* won't be able to stop him. It will be chaos. My chance of tracking down Fra Roberto will be gone if I wait till then.'

Totto jumped to his feet. 'Oh, well, do as you please. You always do!' He strode

*Editor's note: Rodrigo Borgia, Pope Alexander VI

angrily out of the courtyard and good-natured Francesco stared after him with an expression of profound sadness spread over his wide features.

Rome was an abomination. Not in the sense that these modern heretics use the word – though, of course, they are right, too. I mean the place itself, the wreck of great Roma the city of Nero's Golden House, the Forum lined with temples and palaces faced in Cappadocian marble, the Circus Maximus where heroes raced their chariots, the theatres where actors delivered the liquid lines of Plautus and Terence, the wide streets through which Trajan paraded the captives and treasure brought in triumph back to the capital. This wonder of the world had become a midden, an open quarry from whose ancient monuments men pillaged stone to build their mean, cheek-by-jowl houses. Mounds of rubble lay along the banks of the turgid, stinking Tiber and the disintegrating pile of St Peter's basilica was about to join the ruins. Had you seen Rome in those days you would have thought it beyond hope. That was before Pope Julius began the new St Peter's and Pope Leo determined to restore beauty and grandeur to the centre of Christendom. May his labours be blessed with success.

If Niccolo had not been depressed already his arrival in Rome would have dampened his spirits. He approached the city, attended only by Timeo, on a grey afternoon when a cold wet wind was blowing from the direction of Ostia and the first thing he noticed as he drew near along the Via Cassia was a commotion around the Cassia Gate. Men, women, carts and pack animals were crowded around the city entrance apparently trying to gain entry while a press of equally determined travellers was forcing its way through the throng in order to get out.

Niccolo reined in on the edge of the crowd and asked the red-faced driver of a vintner's dray about the hold-up. The man spat expertly into a puddle. 'It's the guards. Over-officious. Taking ages checking everyone in. I don't know what's come over them. They all know me. I've been coming in and out this gate for fifteen years. Always go through on the nod. Not today. Today it's "Wait your turn, Aldo, and be ready to state your business." State my business! Tchch!' He spat again, with more vehemence than precision. 'Bloody obvious what my business is, isn't it? Got customers waiting for this lot, I have. They're going to try knocking something off the price if I deliver late. Bloody guards – nothing better to bloody do than make bloody difficulties for honest tradesmen. I tell you this, mate, I don't fancy your chances of getting in before they close the gate.'

'You mean they'll shut us out?'

'Too true, mate. As soon as it starts to get dark they ring the curfew bell and bang go the gates. Them as is in is in and them as is out is out.'

Niccolo wheeled his horse away through the suburbs and made for the Flaminia Gate, but there a similar scene greeted him. At length, he turned away from the city and found a *locanda* a few kilometres down the Via Flaminia, where he and Timeo lodged for the night.

After a passable meal he beckoned the innkeeper away from his other full tables to share a jug of Montefalco – brought down specially, the host assured him, from his brother's Umbrian vineyard. Niccolo asked what was going on in Rome.

'Chaos,' the man announced with an expressive shrug of his broad shoulders. 'Worse than the height of the pilgrim season

– except that now it's folk rushing to get out of the city, not in.'

'It looked to me as though people *were* trying to get into Rome,' Niccolo suggested.

'Well, I grant you some *do* have to get in – let me explain the situation as I see it.' He emptied the jug. 'Another draught?'

Niccolo nodded and the innkeeper bellowed to a sluttish blonde creature, already rushed off her feet, to fetch more wine.

'Tell me, Sir, you're from Florence; you've seen this French king?'

'Yes.'

'Will he come to Rome?'

'He is not best pleased with the pope for refusing him free passage through his territory.'

'So he will come, as I thought.' The innkeeper nodded sagely over his beaker. 'I've told them so – my friends in the city. Some of them can't believe it. Holy Rome to be ransacked by barbarians from across the mountains? Impossible! No one would dare. God would strike down an invader for such presumption. There are some who agree with me – as more and more alarming stories reach us from the North. They are the ones who are shutting up their houses, putting their valuables on wagons and leaving for the hills.'

'And causing congestion around the gates?'

'Partly. Careful, girl! Do you think I pay you to throw my Montefalco all over the table?' This to the flustered wench who spilled a few drops of wine as she clumsily set down one of the three jugs she was carrying. The host turned back to Niccolo raising his eyebrows towards the ceiling but easily resuming his narrative. 'Of course, most people don't know what to do. They run to their neighbours' houses and ask "Will he come?" They rush from stall to stall in the markets and tell each other, "Surely he will not come." They waylay their priests in the church and the street. "You have friends in the Vatican," they say. "You must know whether he will come."'

'Then why are so many people trying to get into Rome?'

The host chuckled. 'One man's war is another man's business opportunity. Soldiers rich on booty have lots of money to spend. So city merchants are stocking up on oil, wine and grain, and farmers with nothing else to sell are trundling their daughters into town; and their fair-faced sons – it takes all sorts, eh?' The man treated

Niccolo to a leering wink.

'So, there's plenty of to-and-fro traffic. That doesn't account for all the congestion round the gates.'

'Security.' The innkeeper leaned across the table, the whispered words borne on a gush of stinking breath. 'The unholy father – so I'm told – is like a fat hen in a farmyard when the fox is prowling near; running this way and that not knowing what to do. They say he's twice summoned troops from the Romagna to defend the city and twice cancelled the order for fear of upsetting the French with a show of resistance. He's shut himself up in the Castel Sant'Angelo and he's given orders that no one's to be allowed into Rome without a special permit. So the guards have to check all visitors thoroughly and issue their little bits of paper if they're satisfied. Of course, they're making a fine profit from it. I believe today's rate for a permit is one ducat. Still, that won't prove a problem to a fine young gentleman like yourself, I'm sure. What did you say brought you here?'

'I didn't.' Niccolo had no intention of revealing his business to a gossiping tapster. On the other hand, the man's information was useful. 'I have to meet someone at the

Dominican priory. Perhaps you can tell me how to find it?'

'Dominican?' The innkeeper's fleshy nose crumpled in a sneer. 'Excuse me, Sir. Another customer calling for me.' He raised a hand as though to acknowledge a summons from the other side of the room behind Niccolo's back. 'Coming, Sir, coming,' he called out, lumbering to his feet. One word had apparently damned up the flow of the fellow's garrulity.

The next morning Niccolo was up before dawn in order to be among the first applicants for a passport into the city. Timeo had the horses ready saddled in the stable yard and Niccolo was just mounting when a tall stranger wandered up and called his name.

'Signore Machiavelli.'

Niccolo turned to see a man not much older than himself whose thick travelling cloak, over a silk doublet and boots of finest calf, suggested someone of more than average means. 'That is my name,' he responded. 'I assume you have had it from our host. However, I don't think...'

The man gave a slight bow. 'Alberto Reggio. I have the honour to be of his holiness's household. Permit me, in his holiness's name, to welcome you to Rome.'

'You are very gracious, Signore Reggio,' Niccolo replied cautiously, 'but I doubt whether Pope Alexander either knows or cares about my presence in his city.'

Reggio laughed a deep-throated, genuine laugh. 'Perhaps not, but I, his humble servant, do.'

'And why should that be?'

'My family come from Florence. My mother and sisters live there still. As a boy I was placed in the household of my uncle Cardinal Reggio and he eventually recommended me to his holiness.' He shrugged. 'So there it is; the story of my life in a pounce pot. Will you permit me to be of service to a fellow Florentine? Perhaps we may ride together?'

As they made their way through a drizzling early morning Niccolo warmed to his new companion. He and Reggio discovered several mutual acquaintances in Florence about whom they could swap stories. The courtier was eager for news of how his home town was faring since the overthrow of the Medici and Niccolo was pleased to have details of life in Rome. It seemed that what the innkeeper had told him, while highly coloured, was substantially true. Reggio did nothing to conceal the anxiety which pervaded the papal court.

When they reached the Porta Flaminia there were already twenty or thirty fellow travellers clamouring for admission. Reggio urged his horse through the throng, ignoring the protests and shouted curses, and Niccolo and Timeo followed in his wake. In the gateway the guards had erected a table which blocked half the entrance. Two pikemen were regulating the flow of applicants and a seated captain was laboriously checking credentials. The narrow space remaining had to serve the people making their way in against a steady stream of citizens pushing their way out with wagons, laden mules and handcarts. As Reggio rode right up to the table the captain looked up and smiled his recognition. He stood up to clasp the courtier's hand. Then, after a brief exchange, he motioned his men to allow Reggio and his companions through.

'Where are you staying?' the elegant guide asked as they reached the comparative calm of a small piazza.

'I've nothing arranged,' Niccolo admitted.

'Then we must arrange it for you. This is no place for the unwary. I'm afraid the Romans have centuries of experience in fleecing pilgrims and there are certain areas of the city you should certainly keep well away from.'

Reggio led the way through the narrow streets until they emerged onto a clear strand beside the river close to San Girolamo's Hospital. There, of course, they had a clear view of Ponte Sant'Angelo and the fortress beyond. The monstrous, bulbous bulk of the pope's stronghold was reflected in the steely water and Niccolo shivered involuntarily.

Suddenly there was an explosion, which set the horses skittering over the rutted street. A swirl of dust and smoke obscured the far end of the bridge.

'What is that?' Niccolo exclaimed.

Alberto stared, wide-eyed in the direction of the castle. 'I didn't think he really would do it,' he muttered, half to himself.

'That who would do what?'

'His holiness... Before I went away ten days ago there was some talk of destroying all houses close to the Castel Sant'Angelo to make an open space, perhaps even a moat. At the time it seemed like panic talk. Now...' He shook his head as if banishing unpleasant thoughts. 'Come, we must find your lodging.'

The party crossed the river at the Ponte Sisto and entered the cosy township of Trastevere. Although Niccolo had been in Rome before as a boy he had never visited that little world of alleys and courtyards where bankers', jewellers' and booksellers' fine houses crowded together with the more modest premises of lower-class courtesans and pastrycooks. It was before a pastry-cook's shop with its stall of loaves, honey cakes and *biscotti* that the guide came to a halt and jumped from his saddle, calling out 'Maria'. A fiftyish woman with untidy fair hair and a flour-spattered apron answered the summons. As she appeared from the shadow of the back premises Niccolo fancied that a look of alarm flitted over her features before she arranged them into a smile of welcome.

'Signore Reggio, what can I do for you today – more of his holiness's favourite quince tarts?'

'No, Maria, I want you to take very special care of a friend of mine, Signore Machiavelli from Florence.'

The woman faltered. 'Oh, Signore, the room … it is not…'

'It will only be for a couple of nights, Signora,' Niccolo explained. 'As soon as I have attended to a little business here in Rome I shall be gone.'

Any reluctance was rapidly overcome by the production of some coins from Niccolo's purse and Maria Fortinari (as she was now introduced to Niccolo) led the way to a clean upper chamber furnished with one large bed, a cassone, a prayer desk, a crucifix and a truckle bed in the corner by the door. Maria made a vague, deprecating gesture and apologised for the room. Niccolo said it was charming and would suit him admirably.

While the woman went away to attend to a customer Alberto said, 'Maria will look after you excellently. Her cooking is superb and wait till you see her daughter – very beautiful in a wild, rustic sort of way. Between them, Maria and Lucia will take care of all your needs. Tomorrow you must join me and some friends for the evening. I'll arrange it. Now, I must get back to the Vatican.'

Niccolo thanked his guide and, as he turned to leave, he asked for directions to the main Dominican convent. Alberto registered slight surprise but gave the information readily enough. After the courtier's departure Niccolo wasted no time before setting out to complete his mission. The journey had in no way diminished his hatred. Asleep or awake, imagination evoked miscellaneous scenes of vengeance in which he made Fra Roberto suffer a variety of exquisite pains and torments before finally killing him. He had no idea how he would ever lure the friar into a place where he could carry out the executions he planned. Nor was there any subtlety about the approach he now made.

He negotiated the fish market whose stalls sprawled across the piazza in front of the Pantheon and found his way to Santa Maria sopra Minerva and the adjoining grey bulk of the Dominican convent. He asked the brother who came to the door whether he might see Fra Roberto Attavanti. The man went away and after ten minutes another, presumably more senior, took his place and asked Niccolo the nature of his business. Niccolo explained that he had a private matter to discuss, which had been interrupted by Fra Robert's sudden departure from Florence. The friar listened impassively, then replied that Fra Roberto was not available. 'He is here, then?' Niccolo asked. 'Yes, he is here but he is incommunicado; he is allowed no visitors.'

'You mean, you are protecting him from me!' Niccolo shouted angrily.

'We are protecting him from himself. He is serving a penance.'

Niccolo was convinced that he was being put off but he had not come this far to be thwarted by little men in black. 'And how long will this "penance" last?'

The friar began to close the door. 'That is for father prior to decide. Good-day to you, brother.' Niccolo found himself facing the massive studded oak.

The slamming door jolted him back into the world of reality he had vacated after Baccia's death. Blind emotion had brought him thus far. Now he realised, not before time, that he would actually have to do some thinking if he were ever to have justice. More by fortune than design he made his way to the Forum, that graveyard of civilisation so aptly called the Cow Field by locals. He wandered among the shattered pillars, broken triumphal arches, weed-grown walls, tumbled statuary and piled rubble, and found the desolation suited his mood. He called to mind the passage in Livy where the author describes the sack of Chiusi. You will recall that the barbarians were admitted to the city by one Aruns in order to be avenged on the ruler, Lucumo, who had violated his sister. A whole populace pillaged to efface one family's shame. Excessive? Possibly; possibly not. If Fra Roberto's order stood in the way of retribution then it would share the responsibility for whatever happened. For the first time Niccolo began to put together something approaching a coherent plan of vengeance.

Ideas were still revolving in his head when he arrived back at the pastrycook's. He was surprised to notice that, though it was not yet midday, the stall was empty and the shop premises deserted. He climbed to the first floor. The first thing he saw as he entered the guest chamber was Timeo lying on the main bed. He opened his mouth to shout at the lazy servant, then noticed the sword point held to the terrified man's throat. In the next instant a hand grabbed him and yanked him through the doorway. There were four intruders in the room and one wore a Dominican habit. Before he had wit to shout out or struggle, Niccolo's wrists were fastened behind him and his weapons deftly removed. He now realised that the ruffians were papal guards and that the friar was in charge of them. He ordered Niccolo and Timeo out into the street. There, more soldiers were waiting. They formed up in two ranks with their prisoners between them and set off at a brisk march.

'What's the meaning of this?' Niccolo at last found words to protest.

He received no answer, except a sharp shove from behind and the order to 'keep going'. The little cohort moved rapidly through the streets of uninterested, unsurprised people. After fifteen minutes it reached the Castel Sant'Angelo.

IV

The cell was above ground level – Niccolo should be thankful for that, so one of his gaolers, an inordinately cheerful little man, told him. Some prisoners were kept in two tiers of damp, dark chambers below, he recounted with relish, and few of them survived long without warmth or light. Scarcely a week passed when he and his colleagues did not have to 'parcel up' (that was his utilitarian turn of phrase) a cadaver and take it the short journey to the Tiber. So the young Florentine gentleman should thank the holy father's clemency for allowing him the tiny square high up in the wall through which he could see the sky and, if he watched patiently, an occasional passing bird. Furthermore – and this was represented as a concession of archangelic magnanimity – Niccolo was allowed the ministrations of a servant who might come and go, and bring in whatever delicacies the prisoner craved, which, of course, had to be shared with his guardians – that was only right and proper, seeing what good care they took of their charges and how poorly they were paid. This little speech, with only minor variations, was delivered every time the guard came into the cell so that Niccolo very soon began to relish his long periods of isolation.

They gave him time to think – to jostle the facts of his situation into some kind of order. Not that there *were* many facts. Several questions but few answers. Who was responsible for his incarceration? Why had he been thrust into this oubliette? How long would he be detained? Until he ended up stitched into a sack floating down to Ostia?

Niccolo's first action as soon as he had recovered from the shock of his arrest had been to despatch Timeo in search of Alberto Reggio. The servant had gone to the bakery to ask Maria Fortinari how she might find the courier but she had been too terrified even to speak to him. He had presented himself at the main gate of the Castel Sant'Angelo, only to be sent packing by the guards. He had made his way through the slums of the Borgo di San Spirito to the Vatican palace but no one there had heard of Reggio, or so they claimed. After Timeo had spent two days in fruitless quest

Niccolo instructed him to wait by the Ponte Sant'Angelo in the hope of catching a glimpse of Reggio coming or going.

But, then, perhaps Reggio was the reason he was in prison at all. Niccolo recalled how the elegant young man had gone out of his way to make his acquaintance and then to find him lodgings. He remembered Maria's reluctance to take him in. Perhaps she knew that Reggio was laying a trap – the sort of trap he had laid before, in all likelihood. But why? What possible reason could the pope have for wanting to incarcerate him? Perhaps Reggio was not working for the pope at all? Or perhaps his arrest had nothing to do with Reggio. Niccolo remembered the silent Dominican who had been in charge of his arrest. More likely this was all a plot by the friars to protect one of their own. If they had been warned in advance that Niccolo was coming to Rome they would have had plenty of time to make their plans. But then, how could they have known where he was staying? Only Reggio had that information. Every avenue Niccolo explored arrived at the same destination – Albert Reggio – but still he did not want to believe in the courtier's duplicity.

It was on the third day of his captivity that

some answers began to present themselves – answers so bizarre that he would never have arrived at them after months of pained thought. In the middle of the morning two footmen of the papal guard fetched him from his cell, marched him up stairs and along bare, curved passageways to a high-vaulted chamber strewn with rushes and sweet-smelling herbs. At the far end three high-backed chairs were set behind a long table. To the right of them stood a smaller table where a young priest sat, sharpening a quill. He looked up as the prisoner was marched to the centre of the room and there restrained by the guards who took up positions on either side of him.

'Signore Niccolo Machiavelli of Florence?'

'Yes.'

'Hm.'

The scribe stood up, knocked at a door behind his desk and went through into the room beyond. Minutes later he emerged, followed by three robed ecclesiastics. Niccolo recognised the friar who had arrested him. Of his two companions, one, the obvious president of this tribunal, wore the purple of the cardinalate and the other had a white tabard embroidered with papal arms over his black habit. They took their places and the leader, after scrutinising the prisoner for several seconds with pale, blue-grey eyes, announced, 'This is an ecclesiastical court, established under the authority of His Holiness Pope Alexander VI for the trial of enemies of the holy see.'

The words stung Niccolo into response. 'I'm no enemy...'

'Silence!' The word snapped from the Dominican's thin, cracked lips. 'You will only speak to answer questions.'

'But I don't know the answers to any questions you could possibly ask.'

Niccolo felt the blow of a fist in the small of his back that sent him sprawling. Rough hands jerked him to his feet.

'Signore Machiavelli.' The cardinal's voice was smooth, hard and sharp, like a Toledo blade. 'It is in all our interests that we complete our business here as quickly and painlessly as possible. Years of experience have proved that such proceedings as this reach a swift conclusion when prisoners confess their crimes fully and honestly, and don't try to conceal things. Therefore I urge you, as you must answer to God, reply to all our questions truthfully. Do you understand?'

Niccolo nodded. Since he was still gasping for breath it was all he could do.

'Good. Now, your name is Niccolo Machiavelli, son of Bernardo and Bartolommea Machiavelli?'

'Yes.'

'Yes, Eminence,' the friar growled.

'Yes, Eminence.'

'And you have recently travelled to Rome from Florence?'

'Yes, Eminence.'

There was a brief silence disturbed only by the scratching of the scribe's pen.

'Bearing a message from Prior Girolamo of St Mark's in Florence to his agent here, Brother Roberto Attavanti.'

Niccolo gasped. 'No! No! ... Eminence.'

'Yes, yes, Signore Machiavelli.' It was the member of the papal chapel who spoke for the first time. 'Don't waste our time with denials. On your arrival in Rome you went straight to the Dominican convent and asked to speak to Fra Roberto, didn't you?'

'Yes ... Sir.'

'And shortly before you left Florence you had a long, secret meeting with Prior Girolamo, under cover of darkness.'

'That is true ... but...'

'You are doing very well, Signore Machiavelli.' The cardinal leaned forward, resting his chin on his many-ringed hands. 'Now, all we want to know is what message the prior gave you for the spy he had planted here.'

'Eminence, I know nothing of spies or messages. My visit to St Mark's was on a private matter.'

The friar sneered. 'So, you paid a call on Prior Girolamo in the middle of the night to discuss a matter so urgent that it could not wait till a more civilised hour?' He turned to his colleagues and there was a look of pleasant anticipation on his face. 'Your Eminence, I fear we are going to have to use other methods to get at the truth.'

If ever young Niccolo had known terror he knew it now. He had heard tales of the ungodly machines, the guard dogs of Catholic truth, kept in their prisons for dealing with heretics. 'Eminence,' he blurted out, 'this is all a mistake...' Again came the pain below the rib-cage that crumpled him to his knees.

When he had once more been hauled to a standing position and was swaying before the table, the cardinal addressed him. 'Signore Machiavelli, you must not doubt that we will obtain the truth from you by one means or another. It is for your own good that we do so. The sins of deceit and plotting against the holy father are grave and will most assuredly carry your soul to hell. Your only hope of salvation lies through confession and penance. Now, we are merciful and we desire to bring you into a state of grace as gently as possible. Therefore I am going to send you back to your cell to reflect on your situation and I will do two things to help you. First I will explain to you the absolute futility of any further lies.'

He sat back in his chair and ran his hands over the silver hair which flowed from beneath his skull-cap and curled luxuriantly over his ears. 'You see, we know about your master's plans. Prior Girolamo is a man of overweening ambition. Not content with ruling his own cloister, he seeks the sovereignty of an Italian state. And why only one? After Florence why not Siena, Milan, Venice? The holy father sought in his mercy to bring this arrogant friar to his senses. He ordered him to remove to Lucca. And what was Fra Savonarola's response? You know well what it was, Signore Machiavelli: he denounced the pope as Antichrist.'

At this the priest sitting in the speaker's right crossed himself, turned his eyes heavenwards in pious anguish and breathed the word 'Heretic' from between trembling fleshy lips. Heretic? Niccolo knew that men called the Borgia pope much worse than that – and with good reason – but such reflection was far from his thoughts at that moment. He could only feel the pain in his body and the pain in his mind confusing into one agony of fear and incomprehension as he tried to understand what it was he was being accused of.

The prince of the Church droned on in aggressive calm: 'He sends his accomplice, Charles of France, against us with an army and he plants his spies in our midst – men like Fra Roberto. But, God be praised, there are those in our Dominican house here who have a discerning nose for treachery.' He turned to the friar on his left who nodded with sombre piety – self-righteous bag of shit! 'As soon as Fra Roberto was exposed, all we had to do was wait for the Satanic friar to send his messenger.' His smile of triumph churned Niccolo's stomach. 'So you see how pointless any protestation of innocence would be.

'And now.' He rose and the others, as one man, stood also. 'I promised you two incentives. Brother Andreas here has something to show you. When we send for you again I expect to find you in more co-operative mood.' He waved a hand dismissively.

One of the guards grabbed Niccolo and turned him round. He was marched from the room onto the downward spiral of steps and corridors that soon left behind the light of day for a Stygian realm where the torches clamped to the walls struggled to burn in the palpably sodden air. The friar, Fra Andreas, led the way with self-assured steps, which indicated that the journey was to him a familiar one, until the final staircase debouched into a wide chamber smelling of dampness and death. Water dripped from lengths of rusted chain hanging from the ceiling. A central table was laid out with a selection of whips and scourges. Congealed blood streaked the walls and the floor was foul with pools of slime and faeces.

The first visit to such a place must be a chilling experience for any man. For Niccolo, convinced that he was to be left there to contemplate his non-existent sins against the pope, it was spirit-crushing. He looked round at the six cells which opened off this ante-room of hell. A custodian shambled out from a room beside the staircase and Fra Andreas pointed towards one of the heavy doors. When it was opened the friar called for a torch and went in. Niccolo followed, pushed by his guards. The space was tiny, but adequate for what it contained: a man's naked body suspended by the wrists from a ceiling hook, his feet swinging several centimetres above the flagstones. Weeping lacerations across his back glistened in the light from the flare Fra Andreas held up towards the prisoner's head, which lolled forward on his chest. Only when the friar prodded the torso with a long extended finger, causing it to turn slowly, did Niccolo with a sudden shock recognise the man he had pursued from Florence.

'Is he...?'

'Dead?' Fra Andrea shook his head. 'Not yet.'

'How long has he been here?'

'Only two days.'

Niccolo stared at the man he had taught himself to hate and felt no pleasure at the sight.

The friar obviously did. 'Seen enough?' he enquired.

Niccolo nodded and Fra Andreas marched out of the cell. Much to Niccolo's relief he led the way back up the staircase.

Minutes later Niccolo was lying on foul straw in his own cell and feeling almost glad to be there.

Great God in heaven! What a naïve wretch was this innocent, now making his first acquaintance with the regime of the Prince of Peace, as maintained by his earthly representative. I recently had a letter from our friend Francesco Guicciardini. 'It is not possible to speak more evil of the Roman court than it deserves,' he writes. 'It is an abode of infamy, an example of all that is most vile and shameful in the world.' Well, we would all say 'Amen' to that but even Francesco cannot conceive how bad things were a quarter of a century ago.

The truth certainly came as a shock to Niccolo Machiavelli – the more so because the young fool considered himself so worldly wise. He did not feel so clever now, as he lay shivering in that cell in the Borgia castle-prison. No subtle rhymes or ribald epigrams came to his mind to make light of his predicament. Like some political virgin in the labyrinth of Minotaurus, he cowered from unseen fears and the incomprehensibilities of fate. Only one thing seemed certain: he was going to die, either slowly from fever and neglect or more rapidly and painfully at the hands of Fra Andreas's minions. As to why this mistaken fate was about to engulf him or whether there was anything he could do to avert it, he could not reassemble his broken wits to consider such mysteries.

The ancients used to beat drums and burn black beans to drive away the *Lemures,* the terrifying spirits of the dead. I do not recall how long it took the tremulous prisoner to create a sufficient clamour inside his own head to chase away the paralysing apparitions congregating there – it may have been days or hours. When he was thinking clearly again he sent Timeo for writing implements and composed, very carefully, a letter to his inquisitor setting out, with grovelling servility, the sequence of events that had brought him from Florence. He made a copy of this epistle for Alberto Reggio and instructed his servant to try by all means possible to get the two documents to their respective addresses. When he had done his best in that matter Timeo was to make haste to Florence and return with Totto who would be able to corroborate the truth.

Timeo made a tearful departure two days later, having paid five ducats to a minor court official who assured him that the messages would reach their destinations. The downcast young man could hardly bear to tear himself away from Niccolo's cell. He clung to his master's hand promising not to rest or eat until he had completed the return journey and interspersing his vows with wailing that he would never see Messer Machiavelli again. So distraught was he that he almost forgot to impart the latest important news from the outside world: the French were in Rome. Niccolo pressed him for more details. Well, he replied, some said the troops were behaving themselves, others that they were breaking into houses and taking whatever they fancied. Timeo had heard that one of the Swiss mercenaries had been strung up for looting on the orders of his own captain but he could not vouch for the truth of it. What he did know was that all of Rome was angry with the pope for staying shut up in the Castel Sant'Angelo and not meeting King Charles to make a settlement so that he and his soldiers would go away.

Without Timeo's comings and goings Niccolo's loneliness was complete. Yet at least he had not been dragged back to face the unknown cardinal and his gruesome lieutenants. Perhaps they had forgotten about him. In the current crisis they must have many more important things on their minds. With any luck it would be several more days before they had time to continue his interrogation. By then Totto would be here to back up his story and then his accusers could check it by torturing the truth out of Fra Roberto. If he was still alive.

For the first time since his incarceration Niccolo found himself thinking about what had brought him to Rome. And, also for the first time, he began to ask the intelligent questions against which grief and rage had locked his mind. Was he right about Fra Roberto? Could it be that Savonarola had correctly divined the truth – that Baccia had been murdered by someone *posing* as a Dominican? Was Fra Roberto in reality not a recalcitrant friar but a trusted agent of the new master of Florence? It seemed unlikely, Niccolo reflected, that he would ever know the truth. Even if the naked prisoner in the cells survived his ordeal he would not leave the Castel Sant'Angelo alive. In all probability he was dead already.

'No! No! No!' Niccolo stood in the centre of his cell and screamed his anguish and frustration at the square of blue high up on the wall. He would not abandon his quest for Baccia's killer. He saw her again, golden hair cascading around her lifeless body.

Sobs burst from him in an unstaunched bloodletting. And he knew that he would either die in that place or devote his restored freedom to seeking that truth which alone would set Baccia's soul at rest – and his.

According to the marks he had scratched in the mould on the wall, Niccolo's incarceration had lasted nine days when the door was thrust open by the duty gaoler to admit two papal guards. The prisoner staggered wearily to his feet, half fearful half glad that the uncertainty and waiting were at an end.

Once again he was escorted along the castle's bare stone corridors. But this time the silent soldiers stopped at a heavy door, which one of them opened with a massive key. Beyond was a different world. The walls of the large vestibule were panelled, the floor planked. Men in papal livery hurried to and fro, entering and leaving one or other of the six chambers opening off the spacious ante-room. Guards in part-armour and plumed helmets sentinelled the two arched portals at either end.

His captors marched him across to the door directly opposite. One of them knocked and opened it. When Niccolo had stepped through, they closed it, remaining on the outside. The room was small but sumptuously appointed, the kind of chamber men of sophistication now call a 'cabinet'. The walls were hung with paintings, mostly, it seemed, of religious subjects. Another stood upon an easel where light from a tall window fell upon it. A central table had a turkey carpet thrown casually over it on which reposed, among a scattering of papers, three small bronze sculptures, an open portfolio of drawings and an ivory crucifix. Round the table were three cushioned armed chairs but the only other occupant of the room was not seated. He stood before the easel, gazing in rapt concentration at the garishly contemporary piece resting upon it. It was Albert Reggio.

He turned and looked Niccolo up and down appraisingly. 'My dear Signore Machiavelli, you do look a sight. We shall have to smarten you up for your new job.'

V

Niccolo's knees almost buckled with relief. He leaned his weight against one of the chairs. 'Signore Reggio, you got my letter; thank God!'

The courtier stared back, uncomprehending. 'Letter? No. Nothing has been delivered to me ... unless my secretary...' He rummaged among the papers on the table. 'No, there doesn't appear to be...'

'Then how did you know? ... Ah, I see, it is as I suspected; you were the one responsible for my arrest and imprisonment. How stupid I was to be taken in by that act – the friendly stranger, solicitous for my welfare. Now, I suppose, you've brought me here to gloat over my misfortune.'

'My poor Machiavelli!' Reggio's long auburn hair danced as he shook his head, laughing. 'Do sit down and let me get you some wine.' He poured from a chased ewer into goblets of solid silver as Niccolo dropped thankfully onto one of the chairs, enjoying its softness. As he set a cup on the table before his guest Reggio continued, 'Perhaps I may modestly claim to have taught you the first lesson a visitor to Rome needs to learn – trust no one.'

Niccolo drank deeply. The wine tasted like nectar after days of stale water. 'But why me? What have I done to deserve...'

'The second lesson,' the courtier interrupted, 'is not to expect to understand everything that happens here. The Vatican is a ball of hopelessly tangled threads. Everyone intrigues against everyone else and with everyone else. You're not alone in your bewilderment; none of us here can say for certain at any one time who is a friend and who is an enemy.'

Niccolo struggled to keep on the same mental level as the other man. 'Then the sooner I quit Rome the better – or am I still a prisoner?'

Reggio pulled a chair over to the window and propped himself against an arm. He returned his attention to the canvas resting on the large easel and spoke without looking directly at his guest. 'Well now, as to that, we are looking at another of the Vatican's ambiguities. Perhaps I should try to put your present position in some sort of context. My job here is to catalogue the growing collection of paintings, bronzes, marbles, ivories, medals and so on and, to a certain extent, to advise his holiness on additions to the collection. You've no idea how many artists besiege the Vatican with their works. Everyone with talent, and quite a few with none, want the pope's patronage, so it's quite a job sifting the gems from the pebbles – and, of course, any decision is political as well as aesthetic. Take this picture. Come and tell me what you think of it.'

To humour the man who was probably the architect of his woes and now appeared to be his only saviour Niccolo walked round the table and inspected the canvas. He saw a wild landscape of jagged, tumbled rocks whose shapes echoed the chaotic clouds of an impending storm. On a hillock in the middle distance stood three crosses, lit by a shaft of lightning bisecting the black sky which filled the top right-hand corner of the composition. If the painting was meant to be a crucifixion it was quite unlike any he had seen before. 'Weird,' Niccolo commented.

'You find it troubling?' Reggio asked.

'Yes, I suppose I do.'

'That, I imagine, is what the artist intended. He wants us to see the death of Christ, as a cosmic event involving the whole of nature. It's daring; it's new; but will it catch on? That's what I have to decide. If his holiness buys this work, encourages the artist, perhaps even commissions more pieces, will it enhance his holiness's reputation? And then there are the political considerations I referred to. This is by a young artist called Giorgione – "Big Giorgio" as his friends call him – from Castelfranco – Venetian territory. So, how are relations between the pope and the doge? Do they need cementing or encouraging? Might it be a useful gesture to buy this picture and present it to one of the churches in Venice? These are the sort of considerations I have to weigh up.'

'Very interesting, Signore Reggio, but what…'

The courtier ignored the interruption. 'Of course, I have to travel a great deal in my job – to all the courts and cities of Italy. That means that my usefulness to the holy father extends beyond making lists of paintings and sculptures.'

'A spy?'

Reggio shrugged. 'A gatherer of information. A man trained to keep his eyes and ears open.'

'And that, I suppose, was how you heard about me and Fra Roberto? You linked us together with Prior Savonarola and came to totally the wrong conclusion. As a result I've been shut up in a hell-hole down below and the lecherous friar has been tortured to death.'

Reggio frowned. 'Not to death. At least, I don't think so. Fra Roberto was released into the care of his brethren two days ago.'

'What!' Niccolo blazed in sudden rage. 'You knew you had made a mistake, you let the friar go and yet you left me to rot in your accursed prison!'

The young courtier was unmoved. 'Do sit down, Signore Machiavelli. I'll send for some dinner and I do hope your hurt pride will not prevent you joining me.' He rang a bell and the door was instantly opened by a guard. Reggio gave curt orders, then drew up a chair to the table and sat facing Niccolo across it.

'I understand your anger; of course I do. You think yourself outrageously treated. But what are a few days' discomfort for one individual weighed against the fate of Italy? You know full well what is happening to our country; while we squabble among

131

ourselves over little bits of land – Venice with Ferrara, Florence with Milan and so on and so on – France and Spain are fighting over possession of Italy. And now the unthinkable has occurred: Rome itself invaded by Charles VIII's paid troops; mercenary dogs prowling the streets of the centre of Christianity while the pope is forced to skulk in this gloomy fortress. Is that a state of affairs you want to see perpetuated, Signore Machiavelli?'

Before Niccolo's gaze the languid courtier had become transformed into an ardent patriot whose eyes flamed with passion. He shrugged. 'My opinion is of no importance.'

'Every intelligent Italian's opinion is important.' Reggio hammered the table to emphasise each word.

'What I mean is that I am not a political animal.'

Reggio sat back with a laugh. 'That's not what I heard in Florence.'

'Ah yes, Florence.' Niccolo grasped the opportunity to divert his host from rhetoric to more pertinent matters.

At that point servants arrived bearing covered dishes of food. When space had been made on the table, the meal laid out and the bearers departed, Niccolo fell to with an appetite honed by days of privation. Reggio ate more fastidiously and explained how, because of his contacts, he had been sent to Florence to discover what he could about Savonarola's plans. Any religious house, he observed, was a good place to gather information because it was bound to be split by factions. That was certainly the case at St Mark's, where some of the brothers were very nervous about the prior's defiance of the pope. Reggio had learned of Fra Roberto's departure for Rome, of Niccolo's nocturnal visit to the convent which, his informant told him, was in some way connected with Fra Roberto. Thereafter, the pope's man had kept a covert watch on Niccolo and followed when he set off for Rome. On arrival, having deposited his quarry at the confectioner's, he reported to his superiors and they had decided that Niccolo and the friar must be questioned. 'You see,' he concluded, 'that I would have been neglecting my duty if I had not investigated you.'

Niccolo dipped his fingers in a bowl of rosewater and wiped them on a napkin. 'And having investigated you have discovered my innocence.'

'We established that there was no conspiratorial connection between you and the Dominican. Fra Andreas's men are very professional. If you and Fra Roberto had been plotting anything they would have found out.'

Niccolo pictured the naked unconscious friar. Surely under torture he must have revealed the truth about Baccia's death. 'What did the friar say about me?' he asked.

'Very little. He seemed puzzled by our interest in you. He said he'd met you once and had little reason to love you.'

'That was all? Nothing about my wife?'

Reggio shook his head. 'I was sorry to hear about Signora Machiavelli.'

'You know about that?'

'Everyone was talking about it in Florence.'

'Did anyone say who had killed her?'

'Some black-robed friar or monk – that seemed to be all anyone knew…'

Reggio's eyes narrowed. 'You thought … Fra Roberto… That was why you followed him to Rome?'

'Is it such a fantastic idea? The man has a reputation and as he said, he has no reason to love me.' A sudden thought struck him. 'Look, Signore Reggio, you obviously have a lot of influence here. Can you get me access

134

to Fra Roberto? His superiors at the convent will never let me near him.'

'I suppose I could.' The courtier paused while he poured more wine. 'But I think you will be too busy for a while to pursue private vendettas. I have some work for you to do.'

Niccolo laughed. 'And what makes you think that I would wish to enter your employ?'

'Three things: I believe you would enjoy what I have in mind and I know that you have the skills to carry it out satisfactorily.'

'And the third?'

'You asked me about your freedom and I remarked that there was a certain ambiguity about it.'

'Oh, now I see. I have a choice between becoming one of your spies or returning to the depths of the Castel Sant'Angelo.'

Reggio laughed. 'I said nothing about spying. Oh no, what I have in mind – what I and certain other parties have in mind – is much more straightforward.'

'I will be the judge of that. What is it that you want me to do?'

'First of all, take this and visit a tailor whose address I will give you.' He placed a bag of coins on the table. 'Signore Fanfossi will see you fitted out with some appropriate court dress. He already has my instructions. Then come back here and I will allocate your new quarters. Later, when you are tidied up and rested I will introduce you to your new employer.'

'And if I simply take this money and disappear?'

Reggio smiled and shook his head. No words were necessary.

Less than a week after leaving a cell in the Castel Sant'Angelo, Niccolo, arrayed in the finest black velvet and white silk with a brocaded cape, found himself pressed tightly against other equally well-dressed members of the papal court in the Vatican palace's magnificent Sala Reale. They were all there to witness the formal ratification of the treaty between Alexander VI and Charles VIII, the treaty by which the French king gained all he desired – recognition of his claim to Naples – in return for a form of words whereby he received the crown as a papal gift. Charles had the pope at sword point and obliged him to eat all the condemnations and anathemas he had thrown against the invader. But all the face-saving diplomatic formalities, of course, had to be observed, which was why, before the foreign army withdrew from Rome, the two leaders came together in a lavish display of brotherhood. Everyone who by right or bribery could gain access to this *commedia* had crowded into the great hall and now lined each side behind ranks of papal guards. Most of them were curious to see the man who had marched his troops into Rome but Niccolo was awaiting his first sight of the pope.

The preceding days had largely been spent in finding his way around the offices and corridors of the Vatican (to which Alexander and his suite had returned as soon as the threat of Gallic violence had passed), discovering how to address the varied ranks of ecclesiastical officials and learning the niceties of protocol. Alberto Reggio still told him nothing about the 'work' which lay ahead of him, but he had made some translations for a couple of the young courtier's colleagues and had the strong impression that he was under scrutiny.

Reggio secured places close to the dais where the papal throne was set. As they waited for the two entourages to enter he explained to his companion, 'I want you to mark carefully the two men I point out to you.' The wait was long. After an hour or so, whispered comments rippled along the ranks of onlookers: there were problems; some last-minute diplomatic hitch. When the papal party arrived Niccolo could read impatience and irritation in their demeanour. He strained his neck to look down the length of the room. Alexander was surrounded by cardinals and the phalanx of red and white moved hurriedly rather than regally. The pope smiled and held out his hand in blessing to the crowd, who knelt as he passed, but his eyes betrayed anxiety.

Niccolo gazed, fascinated, at the Borgia pope, the most notorious man in Italy. Whether Christ's vicar or, as many cynically suggested, the devil's lieutenant, Alexander VI certainly had presence. Niccolo found himself contrasting this churchman with the prior of St Mark's. Both men made an immediate physical impact but, whereas Savonarola's aura was an effulgence emanating from an inner passion, the Borgia's power resided in the splendours of physique and office. He was tall – a head higher than any of his attendants – and his jewelled mitre made him appear even taller. His heavy build was accentuated by the scarlet gold-embroidered cope he wore over his elaborate alb and dalmatic. His face was fleshy and high-coloured, and the eyes that looked out from it were dark and always on the move as though constantly seeking something lost or inaccessible. Acolytes arranged the pope on his throne and the cardinals disposed themselves around him in whispering groups.

One figure, positioned immediately on Alexander's left, stood out as very different from all his holiness's other attendants. He was a small, swarthy man in his mid-thirties and clearly not European. Niccolo had seen Moors before. Lorenzo the Magnificent had kept three as body servants and they had always attracted considerable attention in the streets and piazzas of Florence. But there was nothing servile about this man. His long robe was woven in a most elaborate design and glowed with polychromatic splendour. His beard was perfectly trimmed and his eyes sparkled, only exceeding in lustre by the large ruby set in the front of his turban. Niccolo pointed him out to Reggio.

The courtier leaned across so that his lips were close to Niccolo's ears. 'He is one of the men I want you to pay particular attention to; Prince Djem, brother of the Sultan of Turkey; a walking treasure chest; amazing story – I'll tell you afterwards.

Now, look closely at the person standing on his holiness's right.'

Niccolo scrutinised the young man in cardinal's robes who was leaning forward in earnest conversation with the pope. He was about twenty, athletic of build and doubtless what women would regard as handsome. His face was long, under flowing hair with the lustre of polished walnut. He wore a short beard and the lips beneath his aquiline nose curled naturally into a sardonic, arrogant smile. His eyes moved quickly, constantly probing the assembly even as he spoke with Alexander. Once it seemed to Niccolo that they fastened themselves for several seconds on him. Even at that first encounter with the man who was to play such a large part in his life Niccolo recognised someone of whom it was necessary to be very wary. 'Who is he?' he asked his guide.

'That is the new Cardinal of Valencia, his holiness's second son, Cesare Borgia.'

There is no need to linger overlong in detailing the ceremonial of that public consistory. The king, to drive home the strength of his position, kept his host waiting an hour before entering the Sala Reale at a stately pace, preceded by flustered ecclesiastics and a corps of royal guards, resplendently accoutred and followed by more soldiers and a retinue of French nobles. The terms of the treaty were rehearsed, though only those clustered about the throne could hear them and Charles made obeisance by kissing the papal foot. Then Alexander stood, took by the hand Prince Djem and his son, and delivered them to the king, who ceremonially embraced each in turn. At the end of the formalities the royal party formed up again and made their way from the hall, the only difference being that this time Charles was flanked by the Turk and the Cardinal of Valencia.

Alberto hurried Niccolo away from the dispersing crowd and, when they reached his office, dismissed his staff and drew Niccolo to a pair of stools by the window overlooking the Borgo.

'Now you are in a position to understand what I have to tell you and I must do so quickly because Cardinal Borgia wants to meet you within the hour. This morning's delays have made everything later than I planned, so I can only give you the barest outline of the facts. That little ceremony you have just witnessed was all about the French king taking important hostages in order to hold the holy father to his word. Prince Djem and Cardinal Borgia are to remain with Charles until after he has safely taken possession of Naples. Both these men are very dear to the pope, which, of course, is why the king demanded them. It was a sticking point in the negotiations for a long time but at last our side had to give way. Naturally, his holiness is very concerned for the safety of the hostages...'

'I can understand him being worried for his son but what is so important about the Moor?'

Alberto frowned. 'Please don't interrupt; there isn't time. Prince Djem is worth 40,000 ducats a year to the holy father. Briefly, this is how he came to be here: about fifteen years ago he led an unsuccessful rebellion against his brother, Sultan Bayezit. He fled for his life to Rhodes, where he threw himself on the mercy of the Knights of St John. Naturally they reported to the pope – that was Sixtus IV – and he realised what a powerful bargaining piece the prince was: as long as he was held in honourable confinement somewhere in Christendom the Turk would be in no position to renew the war against us. Well, of course, all the Christian kings wanted to hold this valuable hostage but eventually Innocent VIII managed to get him to Rome where he has been ever since, living in idle luxury, for which his brother pays 40,000 ducats per annum. Well, you can understand how reluctant his holiness was to let Djem go and how concerned he is to get him back again. We all know that King Charles has no intention of releasing the prince once he reaches Naples. We also know that Djem's life is in danger. His brother, naturally, wants him dead. He even offered his holiness 300,000 ducats to have him killed...'

There was a knock at the door and one of Reggio's servants entered with a note. Alberto read it and jumped up. 'Come along, Niccolo; your new master is waiting.'

The apartment the two men entered minutes later might have lodged a general rather than a prince of the Church. Two walls were hung with tapestries presenting the pleasures of the chase and a third was almost filled with a huge painting of a battle scene. On a table there was a collection of swords, some jewelled and decorative, others decidedly not. Otherwise, the ante-chamber was sparsely furnished. The only seating available was on benches and uncushioned stools. The man who lived here, Niccolo reflected, was no soft Roman who valued his comforts. Even the fire which burned on the hearth was a modest pile of logs dwarfed by the immense fireplace that housed it.

Almost immediately Cesare Borgia entered from an inner door. He had divested himself of his cardinal's robes in favour of calf-length riding boots, scarlet hose and a leather jerkin over a cambric shirt. He was buckling on a belt and appeared to pay no attention to the two kneeling figures as he strode across to a cassone and opened the lid. 'This your protégé, then, Alberto?' he asked as he delved inside the chest and emerged with a pair of ivory-handled poniards, one of which he tucked into the top of his boot and the other he fastened to the belt.

'Yes, Excellency. Allow me to present Signore Niccolo Machiavelli of Florence. He is a master of several languages, antique and modern, and writes a very fluent...'

'Yes, yes!' The cardinal turned to face them with an impatient frown. 'You've already sung his praises to me. Have you explained his duties to him?'

'I felt sure your Excellency would do that

far better than I.'

'Smooth-tongued bastard! Can you handle a side-arm, Machiavelli?' He walked to the table, selected two hand-and-a-half swords and thrust one, hilt foremost, at Niccolo. Immediately he lunged, forcing poor Niccolo into a clumsy parry. Cesare made a few more passes, which his inexperienced opponent fended off as best he could. Then, with a sharp, pricking pain, Niccolo felt the point of his assailant's blade against his throat.

'You need practice. Get some.' The young cardinal returned the weapons to the table.

'Excellency, I had not realised that I would be expected to be an expert swordsman.'

'I don't trust that ugly little Frenchman and Sultan Bayezit has paid agents everywhere. We'll have to be ready for any and every kind of treachery.'

'I take it that I am to accompany your Excellency to Naples.'

'You are officially my secretary, for the duration of this journey. It's a simple job and will be paid accordingly.'

'May I ask why Your Excellency has chosen me. There must be many more people here in the Vatican better qualified than I...'

The inner door opened at this juncture and Niccolo gaped as a very young courtesan – probably no more than fifteen – emerged. She smiled uncertainly at Cesare who nodded towards the other door. At that the girl knelt in quick obeisance, then scuttled out.

The cardinal answered Niccolo's question as though the interruption had not happened. 'That's the whole point. You're not part of the Vatican establishment. You're not known – anonymous. With any luck everyone will take you at face value.'

'Whereas, in reality, you want me to be a bodyguard.'

'Bodyguard!' The Borgia roared with laughter. 'My God, if I needed a bodyguard do you think I'd choose you after that pathetic performance just now? Your job is to watch Prince Djem and help me to make sure he gets safely back to Rome.'

VI

We who are old now and who lived through those fearful days – did we rightly judge, did we truly understand the cataclysm bursting upon Italy? We look back over the wasteland of the years between – the broken cities, the wars, the massacres, the destruction of ruling dynasties and the dissolution of political order – and we rightly identify Charles VIII as the seed-sower of all this woe. Were we so wise then? Certainly there were prophets crying out amidst the tumult. I have one leaflet before me now which that other Niccolo must have bought on the streets of Rome:

O Italy, weep!
Sob, wail and cry out!
Your land will see foreigners.
Your own leaders will invoke calamities.
Unmeasured will be the disasters of great
    and small;
None shall be spared the tide of blood.

147

How seriously did the young man plucked from the fear of death to the silken service of the Borgia take such prognostications of long-term evil? 'Not very' is the honest answer.

Oh, he was, of course, shocked by the daily reports of atrocities. Shut up as he was in the Vatican, he saw little of the Valois's excesses but incorporeal rumour penetrated the very stones of the papal palace and sickening scandals were on the lips of every scurrying priest and liveried servant: a farrier branded on the cheek with his own irons for refusing to reshoe a whole cavalry troop free of charge; every member of a Carmelite nunnery violated by Swiss mercenaries; a boy of nine whipped through the streets because he shouted rude names at a German captain; an inn and surrounding houses burned to the ground after a drunken squabble between rival soldiery. This, Niccolo reflected bitterly, was the work of the man lauded by Savonarola as the holy scourge of God, the saviour of Italy. All young Machiavelli could think of, when he deflected mental effort from his own ambivalent situation, was that the French monster must be removed from Rome and, if possible, from Italy with all conceivable haste.

I recall that he sought to impress his new Vatican colleagues and acquaintances with classical comparisons. On the evening following his fateful introduction to Cesare Borgia he was supping with Alberto Reggio and a few of his smart friends when he decided to show off his scholarship.

'The ancient historians tell a story of the arrogant Spartan general, Pausanias. In the polis of Byzantium, which he had saved from the Persian menace, he demanded for his bed the virgin daughter of a prominent citizen. She came to him at night while he slept and, trembling with shame and apprehension, accidentally knocked over a candlestick. Waking suddenly in the dark, Pausanias, who had a well-founded fear of assassination, grabbed up a dagger and plunged it into the heart of the "intruder". Thereafter, until the day of his own miserable death, he received nightly visitations from the girl's spirit, which stood over him reciting the imprecation, "Go to the fate which pride and lust prepare."

'Now, whether Charles VIII's nocturnal slumbers are disturbed by Plutonian shades I know not, but I reckon they should be. Our northern barbarian is a man of the same haughty and lascivious stamp as the

Lacadaemonian general.'

Alberto responded with a cynical smile: 'And is Rome, then, the hesitant virgin into whose breast this latter-day Pausanias has plunged his knife?'

There was general laughter at the picturing of Rome, whose whoredoms brought blushes to the most dissolute cheeks, as an innocent maiden.

A long-faced young priest did not join in the mirth. 'No, there's something very different about this king. My father was a *condottiere;* I know how invading armies behave. But this hell-hound...' He shook his head. 'To bring his troops here, to Rome, the city of God, to commit their murders, rapes and robberies – it is a shout of defiance against highest heaven. It is a deflowering of the Church in its own sanctuary, before its own high altar. It will not go unpunished.'

Alberto shook his head. 'In an ideal world, perhaps. In reality, men like Charles and Pausanias flourish.'

'I disagree,' Niccolo said. 'Father Tomasso here is right – in part at least. Men who pursue their own ambitions and desires – regardless of what others think – are fools. They fail to read the times, to trim their sails to changing winds. Take Pausanias, for example.'

'Yes, you didn't tell us what happened to him,' a tall, sharp-featured man in Borgia livery observed.

'He refused to change his ways and so he made new enemies every day. At last, seeing that his own people were against him, he tried to sell his services to their enemies, the Persians. When his treacheries were discovered he fled to the temple of Minerva followed by an angry crowd. Since they could not kill him in the holy place they piled rocks against the doors and starved him to death.'

'There, you see,' Tomasso added triumphantly, 'punished by heaven for his impiety.'

Niccolo shrugged. 'Possibly. I find it easier to see men as either the victims or masters of fortune. If they labour to understand the times and adapt themselves to contemporary events and movements they will prosper. If they insist on imposing their own wills on the tumultuous affairs of humanity they will, sooner or later, come to grief. So, ambition without wisdom leads to destruction. Consider Alexander, Caesar…'

They considered them at length into the small hours.

151

For two days after Niccolo's first meeting with Cesare Borgia he found himself in limbo. No one informed him what his duties were and when he presented himself in the cardinal's suite he was told to wait with a score or more of suitors in an ante-room. There he whiled away his time talking with servants, courtiers and members of foreign embassies, occasionally playing cards or dice with others obliged like him to kick their heels in bored and hopeful attendance, and gathering what information he could about the forthcoming expedition.

He learned that King Charles was proposing to leave Rome at the end of January. The army was already on the move, making its slow, cumbersome way through the Campagna, along the Via Appia. Despite the treaty agreements covering the behaviour of the French troops as they enjoyed un-impeded passage through papal territory, there was no doubt about the fate of the villages through which the invaders would pass in their southward progress. The king and his attendants, together with Cardinal Borgia, Prince Djem and their respective entourages, would set out later and follow at a more leisurely pace until the Neapolitan border was reached, at which time Charles would take his position at the head of the army and, if necessary, grasp by force of arms that sovereignty he claimed was his by right of inheritance.

What Niccolo could not discover – what nobody would tell him – was exactly what was required of him. He caught not as much as a glimpse of the cardinal during those two days. When he waylaid the major-domo, a busy, buzzing little wasp of a priest who projected aggression with every scowl, gesture and sarcastic retort, he was informed curtly that his eminence would see Signore Machiavelli in his eminence's good time and not in Signore Machiavelli's.

When Niccolo returned to his own small chamber at night it was to lie sleepless upon his bed, pondering the hazardous situation into which he had fallen. To protect a foreign prince? To spy upon those around him? To sniff out possible plots? How was a young gentleman-scholar, unversed in the sinuous ways of state politics, to fulfil such a mission? What would be the price of failure? And how had fortune lured him into this undesired role? All he had wanted to do was take vengeance on Baccia's killer. Baccia! Always his thoughts returned to her – wide-eyed and beautiful, and broken upon the crumpled sheets. How could he fulfil his vow to her if he was marching away from Rome and Florence in the ranks of a south-bound army? Perhaps he would not have to go. Perhaps Cesare Borgia had already forgotten about him.

Niccolo was disabused of this hope in the pre-dawn of the third day when he leaped into wakefulness to see someone standing over his bed holding a flaming torch aloft. He was about to call out in alarm when the blotches of lurid light and caverns of shadow arranged themselves into the face of the cardinal's major-domo.

'You're wanted,' was all the taciturn priest said as he turned and bustled from the room.

Minutes later Niccolo passed through the now deserted outer chambers of the cardinal's apartments. A solitary guard stood aside to admit him to the room where he had first met the Borgia. Its appearance was now very different. A dozen lamps shone upon a scene of great activity. All the furniture had been cleared to the sides, and the central space was occupied by several small iron-bound chests, which three liveried servants were packing under the eye of the major-domo with a variety of the cardinal's personal effects. There were documents, books, bed linen, clothes, silver and gold tableware, jewellery and bags of coin. To the right a padded chair had been placed on top of a large walnut cassone and in this Cesare Borgia was seated, his athletic frame garbed in a long brocade gown. He had a parchment scroll open on his lap and, though he was studying it intently, his eyes frequently flickered over the activity before him.

Niccolo dropped on one knee before his new master.

Cesare, instead of extending a ringed hand to be kissed, jumped lightly down from his perch. 'Signore Machiavelli, good! Come, we have things to discuss.' He cut a swathe through the jumble of men and things, and went through a doorway into the bed-chamber beyond. 'Close the door,' he ordered, as Niccolo followed.

In the middle of the room he stopped and turned. He stood there, hands on hips and surveyed his 'secretary' carefully for several moments. 'How old are you?' he demanded.

'Twenty-five, Eminence.'

'Hm, that puts a gap of about five years between us. No matter, we are much the same build. Go over to that press.' He waved a hand towards the tall cupboard standing against the left-hand wall and leaned against the bed's carved tester as Niccolo opened the heavy door to reveal several shelves on which were laid out a trove of costly garments. There were gowns of silk, velvet and brocade, robes and vestments sewn with gold thread, patterned with precious stones or edged with fur.

'You see the dark blue with the sable collar,' Cesare said. 'Put it on.'

Almost reverently Niccolo lifted down the long, heavy robe of ultramarine velvet, sewn with miniature bulls worked in gold thread, slipped his arms into the wide sleeves and drew it around him.

'How does that feel?' the cardinal demanded.

'Exquisitely comfortable, Your Eminence.'

'Right, now let's see you walk around in it.'

Niccolo took a few self-conscious steps across the room.

'No, not like that. Swagger! Strut! Look as if you're used to wearing such things.'

Niccolo did his best to obey the instructions while the younger man corrected him.

'Head up! Longer strides! Look, like this.'

Cesare strode around the chamber, the very embodiment of arrogance, and Machiavelli tried to copy him.

'Yes, not bad, not bad, but you'll need to practise.'

Niccolo ventured a question. 'Your Eminence, what exactly is it I'm practising for?'

Cesare's face creased into a grin that seemed somehow to express very little mirth. Niccolo was reminded of an evil-looking dwarf that Lorenzo the Magnificent had kept and who amused his master by wandering among the crowds in the Medici's presence chamber pinching, prodding and kicking his master's guests with a similar joyless grimace on his twisted features. 'There may be times on our little journey when I want to be somewhere and would prefer people to think that I'm somewhere else.'

Niccolo felt his knees weaken. 'But Eminence, I could never pass for you.'

Cesare waved the objection aside. 'It will only be necessary to be seen at a distance, to make people believe they have caught glimpses of me. Now, let's find a few more items.' He went over to the press, hauled out three or four other garments and piled them into Niccolo's arms. 'Take these to my man and tell him to show you where they're packed.'

Niccolo removed the blue gown, folded all the clothes carefully and carried them into the adjoining room. The major-domo seemed none too pleased to receive an order from his master's latest protégé but he indicated a black chest in which the garments were laid.

Niccolo returned to the inner sanctum and tapped at the still-open door. 'Will there be anything else, Eminence?'

'Indeed there will, Signore Machiavelli; a great deal of else. Shut the door and come over here.' Borgia was standing beside the bed with the scroll he had been carrying now spread out on the silken coverlet, its corners trapped by books.

Standing beside him, Niccolo saw that the document was a confusing conglomeration of inked lines and blotches. A black splodge at the top was labelled 'Roma' and a similar mark at the bottom was inscribed 'Napoli'. Between the two were smaller black spots with village and town names attached. There were also haphazard squiggles and smudges, and between all these features ran a strong line against which was written 'Via Appia'. He traced its course through the hills of the Campagna shown by erratic undulations down to the coast at Terracina after which it left papal territory and crossed the Neapolitan border. It was a map, hastily drawn, untidy and not in the least like the intricate, multicoloured masterpieces he had seen in the Medici library, but a map nevertheless.

'You know what this is?' the cardinal enquired.

'The French army's route from here to Naples?'

'Good, good!' The young cardinal showed genuine surprise and pleasure. 'Yes, you're right. It was based on maps here in the Vatican library but I have had agents out checking distances, conditions on the road, availability of food supplies – everything that will affect the speed of the march.'

'You want them off papal territory as soon as possible?'

'Naturally. I also want to know the places where the Mohammedan' – he uttered the word with a sneer – 'is likely to be most at risk. The king is not to be trusted.'

'But why would he want to harm the man he is holding as hostage for his holiness's good faith?'

'You think an animal like that needs reasons? His mind's as twisted as his body. Reason enough for him to annoy the pope, especially if he can enrich himself at the same time.'

Seeing the bewilderment on Niccolo's face, the Borgia explained. 'Sultan Bayezit pays his holiness 40,000 ducats a year to keep his brother away from Ottoman territory. The money is very useful and holding Djem enables us to keep the peace between Christian and Turk. It's an arrangement the sultan would give anything to see ended. Whoever would rid him of his dear sibling would be richly rewarded. If the French king entered into an arrangement with the sultan he would be well paid and he would have the satisfaction of knowing that the flow of Turkish gold into the Vatican treasury would stop forthwith.'

'But Eminence, if the king intends mischief he will have ample opportunity. How can we stop him?'

Cesare prodded a long finger at the map. 'We spend the first night – tomorrow – here at Marino. We shall be staying in the castle; the French have commandeered the Palazzo Colonna; the Turks will camp outside the walls – these Mohammedans always prefer their tents to civilised surroundings. I will give a banquet for our French and Turkish *allies'* – again the word was spoken with a sneer of contempt – 'and I will make an opportunity to have you attached to the prince's suite. Once there, you keep your eyes and ears open. The Mohammedan has his own guards, of course, hand-picked janissaries, as they call them. He believes they're loyal and they probably are. Most of them are Christian captives, not treacherous Turks. Djem should be safe enough with his own people. Anyone trying an open assassination would be cut to pieces either before or after the attempt. Anyone falling under suspicion would have the truth torn from him by the kind of tortures of which the infidels are such masters.'

'Then what...'

'Your task will be to watch for the unexpected. Mingle with the servants. Ask questions. See if any strangers enter the camp. Remember that Charles will have to be subtle if his schemes are to work.'

'And if I suspect someone?'

'Get a warning to the prince and get a message to me at the first opportunity. You will be reporting back every evening in any case.'

The cardinal rolled up the map, dropped it nonchalantly on the floor and seemed on the point of dismissing Niccolo. But then he

161

turned to face him and Niccolo was startled to observe a passion burning in the young man's eyes – a passion that might have been love, anger or hate, or a combination of all three.

'Make no mistake, my Florentine friend, we play for high stakes – the highest.' Cardinal Borgia prowled around the room emphasising his words with expansive gestures. 'Think what it means if this barbarian makes himself master of southern Italy. What will fall into his clutches next?' He did not wait for an answer. 'Milan!'

'But Milan is his ally...'

Cesare laughed. 'And why do you imagine that will stop him? Allies and friends are useful as long as they serve a purpose. Your fanatical friar in Florence will discover that soon enough. Savonarola will live to repent his folly of siding with the French and so will Ludovico Sforza in Milan. If this coarse, uncivilised, grasping tyrant is not stopped he will lay hold of Naples, Milan, Florence, Pisa, Genoa – and that will be just the beginning. All the states of Italy will fall like olives from a blighted tree.'

He whirled round and glowered at Niccolo. 'And whom will men turn to then to save them from this menace?' He affected a whining, croaking voice. 'Holy father, save us, save us! The cry will go up in every city from Naples to Verona, from Genoa to Venice. Only then it will be too late. This monster must be stopped *now!*' He brought his fist down with a hollow bang on the lid of a large cassone.

Cesare took two long paces across the room and threw himself down on his bed. 'Now, go, Signore Secretary, and be ready to depart at dawn.'

Light was just beginning to force itself into one of the Vatican's inner courtyards when Niccolo joined the bustle of shadowy figures carrying boxes and bundles to and fro, and loading the asses. The major-domo was shouting orders and reinforcing them with a stout cane. Catching a glimpse of Machiavelli as he hurried cursing from one group of servants to another, he scowled. 'Not here, not here! You've no business with the baggage. You ride with his eminence's party. Mount in the fountain court.' He was gone.

Niccolo ignored him. He had his reasons for inspecting the baggage trains. He was leaving nothing to chance over his own preparations. He checked everything and he was there to locate the black chest. Cesare

Borgia expected orders to be obeyed as soon as they were delivered. Niccolo wanted to be able to find without undue delay the clothes in which he might be expected to masquerade as the cardinal. There were twenty or more mules being loaded and he went from one to another looking for the container he needed.

He found it standing with other boxes in a corner of the courtyard, as yet unloaded. Niccolo knelt down and peered at it closely to make sure it was the right one. He had satisfied himself on that score and was about to walk away when he noticed that its lock was open. Just to double-check he lifted the lid and looked inside.

The black chest was empty.

VII

Either it was the wrong chest or the items from it had been repacked – so this simpleton concluded. He had no time to make enquiries for a sudden hush announced the arrival of the cardinal who emerged from a doorway attended by three pages and followed by others of his personal suite. Cesare strode through the courtyard, exchanged a few words with the major-domo, then marched beneath the archway leading to the fountain court. Niccolo fell in behind and, minutes later, mounted the horse allocated to him. As the sun in a cloudless winter sky enflamed the city's terracotta roofs, the cavalcade clattered down the hill through the Borgo, where tradesmen setting out their stalls stopped to stare, though not, Niccolo noticed, to greet the pope's son with a wave or cheer. Over the Ponte Sant'Angelo they passed and through the waking city to the Porto Appia, the huddled suburbs and, at last, the open country.

It was a slow progress. The procession had

three distinct parts: the French king and his guard were in the van; then came the cardinal's entourage; and finally the Turks – well over a thousand mounted men in all. They travelled at walking pace but where the road narrowed through villages or where bridges over swollen rivers would permit only a few horsemen at a time everything came to a halt until the obstacle was cleared. Thus it was not until mid-afternoon that the fifteen miles to Marino had been covered.

Once the cardinal's party had climbed to the castle the procedure of the morning went into reverse. Cesare and his chamber staff went straight to the principal apartments while servants unloaded the mules and began distributing their contents. Niccolo sought the major-domo – who was, as usual, clutching a sheaf of papers and shouting orders at his minions – to enquire about the contents of the black chest.

The little priest scarcely gave him a glance. 'Black chest? Yes, yes, it will go straight to his eminence's bedchamber... Careful with that, you idiot!' He ran across the yard and cuffed a redheaded boy who, in unbuckling a large bale of tapestry, had dropped it on the dusty flagstones.

Niccolo followed. 'It's just that when I checked this morning before we left that chest seemed to be empty.'

The man spun round. He stared at Niccolo with alarm. 'You opened...? You had no authority!' He recovered quickly. 'I will not have people interfering. My job is hard enough without you prying into his eminence's affairs. The black chest' – he checked his list – 'goes to the bedchamber. That is all you need to know. You, Guido.' He was off again to another corner of the courtyard. 'Get Alessando to help you with that; it's heavy – and valuable.'

Niccolo was about to pursue the argument when a page ran up to tell Signore Machiavelli that the cardinal was calling for him.

Cesare was personally overseeing arrangements for the evening's entertainment. A large hall, more like a roofed-over inner courtyard with a wide staircase ascending one of the walls leading to a gallery running round three sides, had been arranged with a table on a dais at one end and two long tables projecting from it the length of the hall. Servants were decorating the walls with the Borgia's heraldic device of the bull and arranging cloth-of-gold drapes behind the dais.

When Niccolo entered the cardinal drew him to one side. He spoke in a low voice. 'It is as we expected; the Frenchman has placed one of his own spies in the Ottoman camp.'

'Who is it?' Niccolo asked anxiously.

'I haven't discovered yet. That means you must be especially vigilant. Watch for anything at all suspicious and report it back to me. Be watchful at all times. Keep your eyes on the prince and never relax – *whatever happens.*' He emphasised the last words, staring at Niccolo with a disconcerting intensity.

'Tonight,' Cesare continued, 'you will sit here.' He indicated a position half-way along one of the side tables. 'You will have a good view of all that goes on. When I summon you come straight over. That's all.'

'Eminence,' Niccolo began, 'there's one matter I would like to raise...' But the cardinal had turned abruptly and was giving orders for the setting out of the plate.

Later the hall was filled with noise – music from players in the gallery, the clink of silver goblets and ewers, relaxed conversation, raucous laughter and the antics of jugglers, clowns and acrobats. The food was varied and excellent. The wine, from a cistern set

168

up in the middle of the room and draped in the Borgia colours, copious.

Niccolo drank slowly from his beaker. He wanted to keep a clear head so that he could, as instructed, observe everything that happened at the top table. The cardinal played to the full his role of attentive host. He plied King Charles, on his right, with wine and food, and the Frenchman allowed his plate and goblet to be constantly replenished. Before the evening was very far gone he was talking and laughing loudly, reinforcing his words with expansive gestures. Prince Djem, on Cesare's left, was more frugal in his consumption and Niccolo noticed that he and the cardinal spent much time in seemingly serious conversation. Another high-ranking Turk, on the king's right, was far less restrained than his master. He was a tall, older man with well-drawn swarthy features and a flowing beard streaked with grey and white. But for all his nobility of bearing he had plunged deeper than Charles into the well of conviviality. He rocked back and forth in his mirth and his braying laughter drowned every other sound in the room.

Time passed and not once did the cardinal look towards Niccolo. It was just as his eyelids were beginning to droop under the influence of heat and alcohol that he saw the Borgia, once again with his head close to Djem's, point in his direction. The prince looked across the room and nodded, at which Cesare raised a beckoning finger. Niccolo hurried over and dropped on one knee before his patron.

'Signore Machiavelli,' Cesare said, 'I have been telling his highness of your impressive scholarship and many accomplishments. We have agreed that we need men of your intelligence and discretion to maintain a good liaison between our two establishments. You will, therefore, remove yourself to his highness's camp immediately and his highness's vizier, Izmet Zeybek, will appoint someone from the prince's entourage to perform a similar service for us.' He indicated the tall Ottoman who was now slumped over the table amid a debris of dishes and semi-consumed food. Cesare laughed. 'Though it appears we shall have to wait until tomorrow before that matter can be attended to.'

Prince Djem summoned one of his attendants and spoke briefly to him. Niccolo left the hall in his company and within minutes had exchanged the cramped quarters he had managed to find for a spacious, sparsely equipped tent in the Ottoman lines.

The next day the long procession twisted its way through the valleys to Velletri, where the leaders were to be entertained by the cardinal-bishop. As the hilltop town came into view two high French officials rode back along the column on their gaudily caparisoned horses. Niccolo saw them make obeisance to Prince Djem and gesture forward to where the Valois flags were fluttering in a stiff breeze. After a few moments they turned and trotted back the way they had come. To Niccolo's alarm he saw the Turk and his bodyguard disengage themselves from the rest of the entourage and follow the Frenchmen. It was obvious that Charles had invited Djem to enter Velletri with him.

'Vigilant ... at all times ... whatever happens' – those had been Cesare Borgia's instructions. And now, within hours, the French were whisking the prince out of his sight. What could he do?

His reaction was instinctive. He jabbed his heels into his mare's flanks. She leaped forward in sudden alarm and cantered into the dust cloud being thrown up by the janissaries. Someone behind Niccolo shouted something but he ignored the sound. He fell in behind the back rank of the Ottoman guard and hoped no one would challenge him. Fortunately Djem's men all had their eyes fixed on their master and Niccolo was able to watch unobserved as the prince on his magnificent Arab was greeted by the king who had halted by a wayside crucifix. Moments later the ugly conqueror and the handsome captive were joined by Cesare Borgia and the three men turned their horses towards the town.

As the cavalcade climbed the final slope to the walls of Velletri Niccolo jostled his way in among the ranks of the French courtiers. Through the swaying grove of upraised lances he maintained an intermittent view of Charles and his hostage. In a wide space before the town's main gate they reined in their mounts. Before them stood the reception party; the cardinal-bishop in his scarlet robes, attended by a corps of clergy and town dignitaries.

Thus young Machiavelli had his first sight of 'Il Terribile'. He had heard much about Giuliano della Rovere, frequently the subject of whispered conversations in the Vatican. The cardinal was Alexander VI's most passionate enemy. He had challenged

Rodrigo Borgia for election to the chair of St Peter and wielded 200,000 French ducats provided by Charles VIII in support of his campaign. But the Borgia brood had outbid him. Men still spoke with wide-eyed astonishment of the four mule loads of silver sent to the palace of Cardinal Ascanio Sforza to induce him to withdraw from the contest. Della Rovere had taken defeat badly and, from day one of the new papacy, laboured with tireless energy and guile to undermine it. In the Sacred College he had denounced as invalid the election of 'a simoniac, a heathen and a heretic'. Alexander, with no less zeal, sought the destruction of his erstwhile rival and, alarmed by della Rovere's growing support, had sent assassins to remove this irritant. The cardinal had fled to the court of his patron and protector, Charles VIII, from where he had canvassed the wider support of the leaders of Christendom for the deposition of the pope and the summoning of a general council. In Savonarola Giuliano had found his most charismatic acolyte but preachers throughout Europe were chorusing their condemnation of papal corruption. And now this crusader for ecclesiastical purity and reform had

173

returned triumphantly to Italy in the wake of a conquering army.

Niccolo stared with intense curiosity at the tall, spare figure of the cardinal-bishop. He saw a man in his early fifties who looked younger. The fringe of hair encircling his skull-cap was still black, his eyebrows heavy, his nose and square jaw thrust aggressively forward. There was a tautness about all his movements and gestures. Giuliano stepped forward to kiss the king's hand and then to help him down from the saddle. Charles warmly embraced his protégé and Niccolo wished he were in a position to observe Cesare Borgia's reaction. Della Rovere greeted Prince Djem with friendly civility and finally nodded a smiling welcome to the pope's son. Velletri's distinguished visitors dismounted with their immediate attendants and the cardinal-bishop turned to lead them through the gateway to receive the cheers of the dutifully assembled townsfolk.

It was at this point that Niccolo saw something that made him gasp out loud. Among the posse of clergy and religious accompanying della Rovere was a black-habited figure with its hood thrown back from its head – Fra Roberto Attavanti.

Niccolo's immediate impulse was to lunge forward and grab this impious monster whom fate had so persistently kept from his clutches. This was, of course, out of the question. He could only stare as the Dominican turned towards the gateway and was swallowed up in the crowd of courtiers and servants following the cardinal and his guests into the town.

Niccolo chewed his lip in impatience, awaiting the order for the mounted contingent to advance through the gateway. He needed to keep a close watch on two men and both had disappeared from his sight. The turmoil of indecision prevented the lamebrain from thinking clearly. The first formal event, after the allocation of quarters, was high mass in the large church on the centre piazza and Niccolo hurried there as soon as he was free. He reached the west door just as the cardinal and his guests arrived. Bowing, he stood to one side. He looked up to see Cesare Borgia scowling at him. Niccolo was alarmed. What had he done to annoy his new master? As he stood, staring back helplessly, the cardinal, now in his full ecclesiastical robes, surreptitiously flapped a white-gloved hand at him. It took several more moments for the little secretary to interpret this gesture of dismissal. Of course, Cesare was telling him to get on with his job of watching the prince. The one place where Djem would not be was at this piece of ostentatious Christian worship.

Niccolo turned to go in search of the Turk. As he did so he caught his second glimpse of Fra Roberto. The friar was in the press following the cardinal-bishop and talking with a colleague. As Niccolo spotted him the Dominican chanced to look his way. Quickly Niccolo averted his face and walked, with what he hoped was a non-chalant step, along the west front of the church, praying that he had not been recognised, that the murderer would not be startled into flight.

The Ottoman camp had already been set up. Djem's pavilion, resplendent with its red and yellow silk awning and fluttering pennants, stood at the centre of the com-pound, the entrance guarded by two turbaned janissaries. It was encircled by rings of smaller tents, all virtually identical. However, Niccolo had little difficulty in spotting the vizier's; it was the only other one with a guard posted outside. Niccolo approached, but the tall janissary lowered his spear to bar the way. Niccolo embarked on some elaborate sign language in the hope of making the man understand his mission but the Turk stared unsmilingly back. After a sequence of inventive but futile gestures, Niccolo was about to retreat when the flap opened and the vizier appeared, escorting another caller who was just leaving. It was Cesare's major-domo. The little priest treated Niccolo to his customary scowl before scurrying away towards the town.

'Good-day, Signore Machiavelli.' The venerable Turk bowed.

'Good-day, Izmet Zeybek.' Niccolo smiled at the man who seemed now fully recovered from the previous evening's excesses.

The vizier motioned his guest across the tent's carpeted interior and settled him on a bank of cushions. He served him wine and a dish of raisins and almonds.

Niccolo soon established that the prince had retired to his quarters where he would rest until the time for evening prayers, but etiquette demanded that he remain engaging the official in polite conversation. He asked whether Izmet missed his own country.

'The whole world is Allah's country,' his host replied solemnly. 'Where Allah wills us to be, there is home.'

'I wish I could be as philosophical; I have a longing for my home already.'

The Turk looked puzzled. 'But, Signore Machiavelli, this is your home.'

'Ah, no, Izmet Zeybek, I come from Florence, the finest city on earth.'

'I shall never understand you Italians.' The vizier shook his head. 'Your viewpoint is so limited, so restricted. You think of yourselves as men of Florence, Rome, Venice, Milan. Rather than make common cause, you allow a foreign invader like this Frenchman to overrun the land.'

'But you have divisions in your own country, otherwise you wouldn't be here supporting a prince in exile.'

Izmet stroked his long beard and smiled as though explaining something to a small child. He set a bronze tray on the cushions between and scattered a handful of raisins and nuts over its surface. 'A great nation is a mix of peoples and a great sultan can rule over them all with wisdom and firmness. Such a man was Sultan Mehmed, my old master. He was the Prophet's champion and carried the black flag into new lands. For thirty years he held together his growing empire and when anyone rebelled...' He scooped up three almonds and popped them into his mouth. 'He was ruthless with any who opposed him, whoever they were.' To emphasise the point the Turk placed two raisins on his extended tongue and swallowed them. 'But observe what happens when there is a weak sultan.' He separated the remaining almonds and raisins. 'Factions; each seeking to control the new ruler because they want power for themselves. That is what happened when Sultan Mehmed died. Bayezit preferred the luxuries of the court to the glories of the campaign. He let himself be governed by certain powerful men in Istanbul and became a figurehead in *their* struggles against their enemies. They turned him against his brother, Prince Djem, because he was much more like Mehmed. They knew he would not tolerate their ambitions.' His smile broadened. 'They will pay dearly when Djem becomes sultan.'

'And when will that be?'

'As soon as this French king has conquered Naples. He has promised an army to march with us. All the Italian states will have to contribute troops. Venice will provide ships and together we will place a real sultan on the throne.'

Niccolo pondered this political analysis as

he made his way to the quarters designated to him by the vizier. If King Charles had, indeed, made such elaborate promises to the Ottoman prince it was, presumably, to lull him into a false sense of security – assuming that Cardinal Borgia was right about the Frenchman's sinister intentions towards Djem. Well, that was not his problem; he had been charged with keeping a watchful eye on the prince. His immediate problem was fulfilling that function while finding an opportunity to settle his score with Fra Roberto.

It was all, he realised, a question of timing. Soon Prince Djem would be at the Mohammedans' evening prayers. Nothing could happen to him there. At about the same time della Rovere's party would be leaving the church after mass. That would be the time to seek out Fra Roberto. Within minutes he heard the strange wail of the muezzin calling his brethren to the worship of Allah. Going outside his tent he watched as Djem's people congregated in the space before his pavilion, each carrying a rug upon which he proceeded to prostrate himself. The prince himself emerged to take part in the ritual. Niccolo slipped away quickly.

He hurried through the darkening streets of Velletri, anxious lest the mass should be concluded already, but as he reached the church he heard the chant of the choir. Slipping in through a side door, he was in time to see the clergy procession leaving the altar and making for the sacristy. From behind a pillar he scanned the congregation for the friar but in the gloom it was impossible to recognise faces. He saw the standing crowd part to allow King Charles and his entourage to leave, but though he climbed onto a ledge running along the wall he could not recognise Fra Roberto among those following the royal party. For the first time the possibility occurred to him that the Dominican might not be at the service.

With a feeling close to panic he rushed out of the building and round to the west front from where he could watch the dispersing crowd. At last he spotted a black, cowled figure ... and another ... and a third. The three Dominicans were walking together and all had their hoods drawn well forward over their heads. One of them must be his quarry – he urged the fates that it should be so.

The trio entered the complex of narrow thoroughfares that made up the tradesmen's quarter and Niccolo followed. After a few twists and turns they reached the street of the tailors, where Niccolo saw them stop and knock at a stout door, which opened to admit them. So this was where they were lodging, Niccolo thought as he made a mental note of the premises. He hoped the tailor did not have a young wife or any daughters.

That evening Cardinal della Rovere gave a banquet followed by a play in his *palazzo*. The comedy, commissioned by his eminence, was a hilarious and outrageous satire about a priest who arrived in a certain town with his large family and proceeded to take over the place by bribing the leading citizens, seducing their wives and insinuating his children into important offices. He turned the church into a whorehouse and grew exceedingly rich on the proceeds. At length, the people in desperation turned for assistance to a nobleman who lived over the hills and who came to the town to send the priest and his tribe packing. The parallel was obvious and the treatment hilarious – quite worthy of our old Boccaccio. Poor Niccolo had to contain his laughter as best he could: though seated at one of the tables in the lower hall he was in full sight of

Cesare Borgia who stared fixedly at the players throughout the satirical piece. Fra Roberto was not in the audience. Doubtless, Niccolo reflected bitterly, he was performing in his own *commedia*.

Around midnight the entertainment came to an end and Niccolo made his way back to the Ottoman encampment where, having observed Prince Djem retire to the safety of his own quarters, he made his way to his own tent. He had now decided on his course of action. His plan was woefully lacking in subtlety: at first light he would resort to the street of the tailors and wait for Fra Roberto to emerge. Then he would stay close to the wretch, like a fly hovering over rotten fruit, until he had an opportunity to get him alone.

In the event he overslept. He was awakened by the muezzin summoning his neighbours to morning prayers and the camp was busy with the congregating faithful as, still fumbling with the points of his doublet, he ran towards the town.

He never reached the street of the tailors. The piazza municipio was in a state of excited confusion. A curious and chattering crowd was being held back by a ring of French soldiers. Niccolo elbowed his way through to a vantage point and beheld an extraordinary scene. In the centre of the square stood or sat several members of the Borgia chamber staff, all looking dishevelled, dejected and fearful. As he watched, more members of Cesare's entourage were dragged out of neighbouring buildings and, with the aid of kicks and punches, forced to join their colleagues. Scattered around were several of Cesare's chests and boxes. All were open. All were empty.

The central figure in this drama was King Charles. He stamped back and forth across the cobbles brandishing a sword and shouting imprecations, most of which Niccolo had no difficulty translating: 'Dogs! Borgia excrement! Lying, cheating pigs!' He pointed to the cardinal's major-domo and when the trembling priest had been thrown down onto the ground before him he prodded his sword, a large, wide-bladed weapon, at the man's neck. 'You planned this with him!' The terrified official gabbled his denials. 'Liar,' Charles roared. 'All Romans are liars!' He swung the sword in a wild arc and partially severed the priest's head from his body, so that blood spurted over the king's boots.

'What's happened? What's all this about?' Niccolo demanded of his neighbour, an old woman who smelled pungently of fish.

'It's Cardinal Borgia.' She chuckled. 'He's run away.'

VIII

Niccolo did not wait to be identified as one of the absconding cardinal's attendants. He slipped back through the crowd and returned to his tent. To think.

At first he made the assumption that Cesare had broken his pledge and escaped in protest at della Rovere's taunting of the Borgia clan. The young cardinal was not the sort of man to submit meekly to insults. But the briefest reflection revealed the inadequacy of that theory. Niccolo remembered the empty black chest and the other containers strewn around the cobbled piazza. He pictured again the scene in Cesare's Vatican apartments: all those servants frenziedly packing the cardinal's plate, clothes and papers. He recalled the twenty laden mules making their way over the hills to Marino and Velletri. And yet when he had angered the major-domo by prying into the black chest on the morning of departure there had been no sign of Cesare's sumptuous garments. Now it seemed that, as the king's men rifled Cardinal Borgia's rooms, they had found nothing but empty containers. If that were the case the hostage must have left all his treasures in Rome … and that meant…

Niccolo's thoughts were interrupted by a janissary who stooped in at the entrance and beckoned to him. The Florentine was led immediately into the presence of Prince Djem. Robed and turbaned in peacock blue and seated in a padded chair upon a dais, the prince looked more imposing than ever. Izmet Zeybek stood at his right and the two men were flanked by Djem's principal advisers. All were looking intently at Niccolo and they were not smiling. Djem formally acknowledged the newcomer's greeting, then nodded to his vizier.

'Signore Machiavelli,' Izmet began, 'you are aware what has passed here during the night. His highness would be obliged to receive full details of Cardinal Borgia's flight.'

Niccolo improvised nervously. 'I can assure his highness that his eminence's disappearance has taken me completely by surprise. Doubtless, it was a sudden decision and his eminence had good reason…'

'We do not think so.' It was the first time

the Turkish prince had spoken to him directly. The voice was deep and languid, but not a whit lacking in authority.

Izmet explained: 'There are aspects of the cardinal's removal from Velletri, which suggest to his highness careful planning and preparation.'

Niccolo floundered. 'What "aspects" does his highness have in mind?'

Izmet and the prince spoke together in lowered tones for a few moments before the vizier responded. 'Signore Machiavelli, his highness is not convinced by your denial but it may save time if I tell you all that has come to his highness's ears. You will then see the futility of evasion and you will answer his highness's questions.'

Niccolo nodded. There was nothing else he could do.

'Some time in the middle hours of darkness Cardinal Borgia slipped out of the town by the east gate disguised as a groom. In an olive grove on the flank of this very hill someone was waiting for him with a saddled horse. The cardinal was not missed until dawn, when French troops were sent in pursuit. King Charles was, of course, enraged. He ordered the cardinal's staff to be questioned and his quarters searched. It seems that all this revealed was that the cardinal's flight was prepared in advance. He had brought very few possessions with him – certainly not enough for a journey as far as Naples. This suggests to his highness that the escape was planned with the pope who has, therefore, been guilty of bad faith. It would be very unfortunate if his majesty came to suspect that his highness was a party to this plot.'

Now Niccolo grasped what was behind this inquisition: because the Turks believed – surely mistakenly – that Charles VIII was going to help them in their bid for the Ottoman crown, cordial relations were vital and it was essential for Djem to distance himself from Borgia double-dealing. 'I'm sure his majesty would never think his highness capable of bad faith.'

'And if he were to discover that the horse upon which the cardinal made his escape belonged to his highness?'

Niccolo gasped. 'You mean...?'

Djem leaned forward. 'Signore Machiavelli, your surprise looks almost convincing but we are not deceived by it. The day before yesterday Cardinal Borgia persuaded us to agree to your transfer to our household. The arrangement was proposed as a gesture of friendship. In fact, it was an essential part of the escape plan. It placed you in our camp – outside the walls of Velletri and with access to our horses. Last night you stole one of our animals and took it to an agreed rendezvous point. We doubt not that it is now half-way to Rome.'

Niccolo silently cursed Cesare Borgia and all his devious schemes – and fortune which had tangled him up in state intrigues which he did not understand. 'Your Highness, I...'

'Silence!' Izmet roared the word. 'Do not presume to address his highness directly.'

'A thousand apologies.' Niccolo was now trembling and the sweat was standing out on his brow. 'I meant no disrespect. I was alarmed and dismayed that his highness could think I would repay his kindness to me with dishonesty and treachery. I assure his highness that I played no part in the cardinal's plans.'

'Then why was the cardinal so insistent that you should be attached to his high-ness's suite?' Izmet watched closely for Niccolo's answer.

It was a question Niccolo was beginning to ask himself. The poor fool lacked the quick wit for anything save the truth. 'His eminence told me that he was concerned for his highness's safety. He wanted me to be on the watch for any attempts to do him a mischief.' Even as he said it Niccolo knew how unconvincing it sounded.

He read the scepticism in the Turks' faces and steeled himself to withstand their anger. But at that moment one of the guards entered accompanying a herald in the Valois livery. The king's man made his obeisance and informed Djem that his majesty would be grateful if his highness would wait upon him. The prince and his vizier exchanged anxious glances as the herald withdrew. Niccolo knew what they were thinking: Charles was obviously investigating the circumstances of Cesare Borgia's disappearance and intended to discover whether the Ottomans were implicated.

After a hurried conversation with Izmet Zeybek, Djem rose. Everyone present prostrated themselves as the prince made his way into an inner chamber.

As the silken curtains closed behind his master the vizier spoke to Niccolo. 'It seems, Signore Machiavelli, that you will have to explain yourself to his majesty.' He signalled to two of the janissaries and they stepped forward to grasp Niccolo's arms. Once again he was a prisoner.

The little procession that made its way into the town, across the Piazza Municipio and up the steps of the Palazzo della Rovere, consisted of the Ottoman prince with his honour guard of conical-helmeted spearmen, followed by his council and lastly two ranks of janissaries conducting Signore Niccolo Machiavelli. The king received them in the great hall of the cardinal's residence. He was standing with his generals, Cardinal Giuliano and advisers behind a table on which were spread papers, maps, silver flagons, goblets and dishes of cakes and sweetmeats. Niccolo felt his legs sagging beneath him as the column came to a halt. He was shivering and not with cold for a large fire blazed in a marble fireplace some three meters from where he stood. Nervously he peered at the lop-sided, bulbous-nosed face of the French king. He stared hard. Did he misread the irregular features or was Charles actually smiling?

Seconds later there was no doubt. The king affably welcomed his guest, waved him to a chair and had pages offer him refreshment. He emerged from behind the table and strode energetically to and fro, gesturing expressively and pouring out a rapid torrent of French which the prince's interpreter struggled to translate. Niccolo picked up the gist of Charles's remarks.

'Good news, Your Highness, good news. The coward Alfonso, who calls himself King of Naples, has fled. They say he had nightmares and would start up in the middle of the night screaming "The French are coming! The French are coming!"' His laughter was more a cackle than a roar. 'He was right to be afraid, was he not?'

The prince offered warm congratulations.

Charles responded with due modesty. 'We applaud the pretender's wisdom in saving himself and the people of Naples from our just wrath. We are terrible in our anger but magnanimous in our mercy. We detest bloodshed.'

Niccolo recalled Charles's sanguinary display of temper in the town square earlier and shuddered.

The king continued: 'So, Your Highness, this means that we can conclude your business in Naples quickly. There will be no need to impose our will; the people will welcome us with unfeigned acclamations of love and joy now that they are delivered from the Spanish tyrant. And once we have established our government in the South we can settle scores finally with our pretended allies. Little Cesare Borgia has gone running home to his father but the pope will be unable to save him. He will be unable to save himself. Within a year we will have rid the Church of that fat bladder of corruption and St Peter's chair will have a more worthy occupant.' He smiled at Giuliano della Rovere, who nodded and pursed his lips in a grimace of self-satisfaction.

As he concentrated hard to clutch meaning from the torrent of the king's exuberant French Niccolo's dominant thought was how long it would be before Charles noticed him and demanded to know why he had been brought here. But the Valois seemed oblivious to everything except his own plans and good fortune. 'Your Highness,' he continued, 'there is now nothing to delay our march. We will be obliged if you will have your people ready to continue by noon. And now, if you will excuse me; we must despatch our good news to our friends – and enemies.'

The audience was over. Djem's party returned from the town and the order was immediately given to strike camp. Niccolo was escorted to his tent where he gathered his belongings together, then waited, still under guard, while the tent was dismantled.

His overmastering desire now was to escape the sticky embrace of intrigue. He had been used and exploited, lied to and manipulated, threatened, bullied and subjected to so much deception that he, too, had become a deceiver. He wanted no more of it. He wanted his own life back. Above all, he wanted freedom to pursue his vendetta against Roberto Attavanti.

Yes, it is true. This proud student of history and cynical satirist of men in power had had his fill of politics. The dish whose subtle combination of aromas had always been so attractive and enticing proved too piquant in the tasting.

As soon as he was able to attract Izmet Zeybek's attention he remonstrated with him. King Charles had no suspicions about the prince's implication in Cardinal Borgia's flight, he said. Therefore, the Turks had no right or reason to detain him.

The vizier was unimpressed. He stared down at Niccolo, a frown creasing his swarthy face, his fingers playing with the jewelled pommel of the curved dagger at his waist. 'Signore Machiavelli, you have abused our hospitality and his highness has not yet decided on your punishment. For the present he is not disposed to allow you

195

to return to Rome to report to your master to aid him in fresh intrigues.'

'I assure you, Izmet Zeybek, Rome is the last place I wish to go. I...'

The tall Turk turned away. 'The matter is decided. You will remain his highness's hostage.'

When the French king's triumphant cavalcade resumed its journey that afternoon Niccolo was still a part of it and he rode with a janissary on either side. Only one thing slightly sweetened the bitter experience: Roberto Attavanti was also a member of the Naples-bound expedition. Niccolo had seen the Dominican ride out of Velletri in Cardinal della Rovere's entourage.

Niccolo spent the next three weeks in virtually total isolation. Though never alone, he was surrounded by guards with whom he was unable to converse. His confinement was not uncomfortable and there was no deterioration in his food or accommodation, but he was never allowed to leave the Ottoman encampment.

The one advantage afforded by his confinement was the opportunity it provided him to think. To escape his predicament he needed to understand it. To avoid being manipulated he must himself learn to manipulate men and events. I have before me some of the jottings this political novice, emerging not before time from the cradle of innocence, made in those days. They are scribbled in the blank pages of Caesar's *Gallic Wars* and Cicero's *On the Good Life*, and I see him spending dusty days on the road locked inside his own thoughts and evenings in his canvas cell using what daylight remained to make these notes:

Pope Alexander: The most corrupt of St Peter's successors, as all men agree. Prime concern: to create a powerful Borgia dynasty ruling all the lands of the Church. Has a real fear of being toppled by the French in league with enemies like Cardinal della Rovere. Interest in Prince Djem: financial; peace of Christendom? Planned escape of Cesare Borgia? Probably not – too fearful of repercussions.

Cesare Borgia: Ambitious, aggressive, cunning, ruthless, unscrupulous. Prime concern: personal power; creation of a strong central Italian state to withstand foreign threats. Escape: decided before leaving Rome but not planned in detail;

intended to use NM as a decoy before deciding on a simpler plan. Who arranged escape? Collusion with Izmet Zeybek (Why did major-domo visit him?)? Interest in Prince Djem: probably minimal; placing NM in Ottoman camp to help protect Djem an excuse, but for what NM to be a spy? NM to be suspected of helping Cardinal B escape to protect real accomplice?

King Charles: Blinded by the dazzle of greatness and glory. Barbaric and lecherous. He has the dangerous characteristics of the elephant rather than the fox. Prime concern: building an empire to include Italy. Interest in Prince Djem: financial (reward from sultan for killing his brother)? To use him in a crusade against the Turk? To set him on the throne in Istanbul?

Prince Djem: A warrior run to seed. Too many years of indolence and luxury. Prime concerns: self-preservation (the sultan has many agents) and gaining the Ottoman throne. He will show friendship to whoever can help him achieve his objectives. Currently this is King Charles. He will hand NM over to the French if it is in his interest.

Ambition

O spirit insatiable, arrogant, crafty,
  inconstant,
Malignant, iniquitous, violent and savage,

Who, with pestilential venom, armed Cain
  against his brother,
Filling his vitals, his heart, his bosom,
Who ever since prowls the world with
  vicious cronies—
Envy, Sloth, Hatred, Cruelty, Pride,
  Deceit.
I see her now, with that swarm which
  Heaven
At the world's beginning allotted her,
    Flying over the Tuscan mountains.

All these observations tended towards one
conclusion: escape; extricate yourself from
the coils of political ambition, young
Niccolo, before it crushes you and leaves you
in its wake with countless other corpses. Flee
to the safety of mother Florence. But he was
the victim not only of other men's ambition.
His own passion to avenge Baccia's death
was a force he could not resist.

During the continuing southward march
Niccolo caught occasional glimpses of

Roberto Attavanti and was convinced that the friar remained unaware of his pursuer's presence. Within days the royal contingent reached the Neapolitan border where the French army was waiting. Then Charles VIII entered upon his inheritance.

Oh, the folly of the man, the arrogant, bestial folly! He who posed as a saviour of the Italian people from Aragonese tyranny and who could have won the hearts of his new subjects with displays of liberality and gestures of goodwill fell upon the unresisting land like a monstrous leech, intent on sucking from it everything of value, even it's life-blood. Men said afterwards that he came like a conqueror armed with chalk. They referred to Charles's quartermasters who went through town after town, village after village, marking the doors of those dwellings to be commandeered by the troops. Within these houses nothing was safe. Charles's mercenaries occupied the best rooms, emptied the larders and the wine cellars, slaughtered beasts for food (sometimes just for fun) and helped themselves to the Neapolitan womenfolk.

One thing the French did give in return – to Naples first, then to Italy and the world. They brought with them in their generosity

the gift of the shepherd Syphilus of whom
Hieronymus Fracastorius of Verona tells us,

He first wore buboes dreadful to the sight,
First felt strange pains and sleepless
  passed the night.
From him the malady received its name.
The neighbouring shepherds caught the
  spreading flame.*

It was Charles's dirty and lecherous followers who first brought the French disease
to Italy and thousands died of it in Naples
during the spring of 1495. The king himself
might have arranged an epidemic single-
handed. He kept a book of his personal
conquests during the campaign, which subsequently fell into enemy hands. I understand that it ran to several hundred pages.

The rampaging army moved steadily
southwards, drawing in its wake an ever

*Editor's note: Hieronymus Fracastorius of
Verona published *Syphilis sive morbus Gallicus
(Syphilis, or the French Disease)* in 1531 but his
poem describing the mythical origin of the
affliction had circulated in manuscript several
years earlier and a copy had obviously come into
Machiavelli's possession.

lengthening baggage train of booty. Niccolo studied to be an exemplary prisoner, hoping by his compliance to tempt his guards into slackness. Unfortunately, the janissaries displayed exemplary vigilance – until 21 February. That was the day the conquerors came within sight of the city port of Naples. It coincided with the eve of the Mohammedans' holy month which they call 'Ramadan', a period of fasting similar to our Lent. As we have Carnevale, so they precede their weeks of austerity with a great feast. Thus it was that Prince Djem invited Charles and the other notables to celebrate with him at his camp overlooking the sea. Niccolo was not invited to the festivities, though his guards brought him a sample of what the prince's guests were tasting – spiced chicken with almond paste, *maghmuma* made with lamb, onions and herbs, *reahat lokum* (various fruit-flavoured jellied sweetmeats). He enjoyed his meal but the music and laughter coming from the specially erected pavilion prevented him from concentrating on his own thoughts.

The festivities continued long beyond nightfall. After an hour or more of lying sleepless on his bed Niccolo went to the door of the tent to breathe the cool night air.

Across fifty yards of open space shadows moved on the canvas wall of the pavilion. Round the entrance a crowd of Turks had gathered, watching the entertainment within. Suddenly, Niccolo was aware that he was alone. The guard who was always positioned to the right of his doorway was not there. Obviously he had been unable to resist the lure of the lights and the music.

Niccolo looked around carefully. The rest of the camp seemed deserted. He acted intuitively, without careful thought. Pausing only to bundle up his more prized possessions, he slipped out of the tent, sidled around it to the side farthest from the crowd, stepped lightly across the space to the next rank of tents and so on until he reached the edge of the encampment. He looked to right and left. The only sentry was thirty yards away and facing in the opposite direction. Niccolo dropped down to the grass and crawled to an outcrop of rock.

There was a sudden clink of mail. Peering round the side of the boulder, Niccolo saw the sentry stamping his feet and banging his arms with his hands to keep warm. He turned and slithered down the slope which fell away towards the coast road. Reaching it, he ran and ran towards the walls of Naples.

IX

To exchange the life of a prisoner for that of a fugitive was no great bargain but the fugitive did have a purpose and the freedom to pursue it. Niccolo made for the water-front, where he did his best to merge with the life of mariners, dock hands and lightermen. Although Naples was bursting at the seams with Charles's soldiers and camp followers needing accommodation, none ventured to the waterlogged, rat-invested hovels wedged between the ware-houses lining the quay and it was here that Niccolo sought to make himself invisible. He bought himself some seamen's boots and breeches, and a rough leather jerkin, and swiftly changed them for his velvets and silks, which would very soon have attracted the attention of back-alley cutthroats. From a seedy chandler he rented a minute chamber leading off a store-room reeking of pitch and the mould that forms on damp canvas. By the time he had begrimed his face and allowed a couple of days' beard to sprout unchecked he was sufficiently non-descript to wander the city unnoticed. If anyone asked – and few did – he told them he was a coastal trader working out of Livorno. This accounted for his northern accent and Livorno was a port so small that no one was likely to have much contact with it.

Thus disguised, he asked his way to the Dominican convent where he lingered in the lee of San Domenico Maggiore hoping for a glimpse of his quarry. Several of the brothers came and went during the first day of Niccolo's vigil but it was not until the bell was ringing for Vespers that Fra Roberto appeared, hurrying along the broad street known as Spaccanapoli from the direction of the duomo. Having located his prey Niccolo was back at his watching post soon after dawn on the second day. Attavanti emerged in mid-morning after sung mass and made his way back along Spaccanapoli. His journey was a short one. It ended at the Palazzo Sanseverini, a new building whose glistening white façade emphasised its owner's importance.

Niccolo walked around the building a couple of times and had just decided that he could suspend his surveillance long enough to obey his stomach's clamouring for food when a side door of the palace opened and from the courtyard within a group of mounted men emerged – Giuliano della Rovere and his court. Roberto Attavanti was among those, seated on mules, who attended the cardinal. As the party turned left into a narrow side street, Niccolo followed. He had to move quickly and was afraid that he might not be able to keep up, but the centre of Naples was crowded and, despite the two armed men sent ahead to clear a path for his eminence, della Rovere's entourage proceeded at nothing more than a dignified trot. They descended towards the harbour but turned under the great triumphal arch that spanned the entrance to the Castel Nuovo where Swiss guards at the door and the Valois standard fluttering over the battlements indicated that Naple's new master had taken up residence.

For three days Niccolo checked on the friar's movements and found them as regular as the motions of sun and moon. He was not always in attendance on the cardinal when della Rovere left his lodging but every day he left the Dominican cloister after the morning office, returning in time for Vespers. Niccolo became so familiar with the accursed friar and his long-striding, arrogant gait that he no longer troubled to conceal himself. Once he even jostled Fra Roberto outside the convent, daring him to look him in the face. The man showed no sign of recognition.

It was time for the next phase of the plan, a plan that had been maturing for days in his gutted imagination. The waterfront taverns were the haunts of thieves, assassins and ruffians who would undertake any task for an appropriate fee and Niccolo had no difficulty falling in with a pair of men eager to listen to his requirements and even more so to pocket his silver. They were brothers though, for reasons best known to themselves, they elected to be known as Carlo One and Carlo Two – or simply, One and Two for short. They had the same stocky build and wiry black hair but One was the larger and easily distinguished by a broken nose and, indeed, a face which had obviously been through many adventures. He always deferred to his sibling and it was Two who did most of the talking and who struck the bargain.

'A man of the Church, you say,' Two said sharply and spat into the water. 'That'll be extra.'

They had come to a quiet stretch of the quay where, at the moment, no ships were tied up.

'You're squeamish about religion?' Niccolo enquired.

Two sneered. 'Certainly not, but the risks are greater. Your merchant or your nobleman – they can buy information but they don't have the contacts in places where it matters. But your churchmen stick together. They've got a network that's very good at finding out things.'

One leaned back against a stack of crates, whittling a piece of driftwood with a viciously sharp knife and seemed not to be following the conversation closely until he asked, 'You're sure you want him alive?'

'Alive and unharmed,' Niccolo insisted. 'Do you have a problem with that?'

'Much more difficult, isn't it?' Two observed. 'Stabbing someone in a quiet alley and slipping away quickly – nothing to it. Abduction, now that means organisation and more risk.'

'And more money, I suppose.'

Two shrugged. 'Do you have a problem with that, Signore? Only it would be far easier for us to take your money now. These timbers,' he added, stamping his foot on the resounding boards, 'can get very slippery. Men have been known to fall in.'

'I'm not so stupid as to bring money with me,' Niccolo lied, feeling the weight of the heavy purse against his thigh under the loose jerkin. 'Now can we leave threats aside and get down to business?'

They agreed terms and Niccolo took his accomplices to the Spaccanapoli. Having walked twice between the convent and the palace, Two shook his head and pushed his woollen cap to the back of his head.

'Now what's the problem?' Niccolo demanded.

'See for yourself.' The smaller ruffian waved an arm. 'It's a wide street and always busy.'

'It quietens down in the evening.'

'Granted, but there are still people about and it's overlooked by all these smart buildings. Too easy for someone to raise the alarm.'

'So you're saying it can't be done?'

Two shook his head. 'No, just needs more organisation, that's all.'

Niccolo scowled. 'And more money, I suppose.'

'It's you who's making the job difficult, my friend.'

'Look, all I want is the friar delivered to my lodging...'

'What? Are you mad?' One stared down at Niccolo in disgust. 'Leave a trail straight to your door – and ours?'

'He's right,' Two agreed. 'We'll have to take him somewhere else. We'll show you where.'

The brothers went away to make their plans and met up with Niccolo again that evening in the same place, so that he could point out Fra Roberto to them. On their way back to the harbour they outlined to him what they had arranged. It seemed remarkably elaborate but Niccolo had to agree that he could think of nothing better. He certainly was not going to make difficulties now. The taste of revenge was strong in his mouth, a revenge he had waited for and suffered for over four turbulent months. It was, therefore, with a cheerful heart that he parted with a down payment to his hirelings and arranged the fine details of the abduction. That night sleep was denied him by the excitement, bitterness, exultation and anticipation churning inside him. Pictures flashed around his brain – Baccia; Baccia dead; Fra Roberto smug and sneering; Fra Roberto lifeless at his feet.

The following evening he arrived in good time at his place in Spaccanapoli about fifty yards from the convent. Several people were standing about in small groups and others joined them as the light drained from a grey sky. Minutes passed and Niccolo was gripped by sudden anxiety. Was the murderer not coming? Had he chosen this one day to change his routine? Had he been detained by the cardinal? Or perhaps been taken ill?

Then from along the street came a whistled signal; three staccato notes. He crossed to the corner opposite. From the Piazza San Dominico a cart appeared laden with grain sacks and pulled by an ancient, underfed horse. One, who was driving the wagon, gave Niccolo what he supposed was intended to be a grin. The vehicle drew level and began to turn into Spaccanapoli. At the moment when it screened him from the view of passers-by Niccolo fell to the ground.

A woman screamed. The cart jarred to a sudden halt. Running footsteps sounded along the street. Instantly it seemed Niccolo was surrounded by a crowd who stood or knelt around him. Someone shouted, 'He's crushed against the wall!' Another voice said, 'Pull him clear!' and yet another, 'No, best not move him!' One, still seated on the cart, called out 'I didn't see him; he was in the shadow. Is he dead?' Then, not before time, Niccolo heard Two's voice: 'Stand aside, there! Stand aside! Here's a priest – well a friar. Let him through!'

Niccolo did not dare open his eyes but he felt someone kneeling close beside him and, placing a hand on his shoulder, turning him gently onto his back. Then there was a thud, a grunt and Fra Roberto's body fell heavily across him. Niccolo looked now. He saw One jump down from the cart and haul the friar's limp form upright. Two slipped a sack over him and together they lifted it over the side rail. Then One was back in the driving seat and cracking his whip. The vehicle lumbered away along the broad street, the crowd dispersed and Niccolo walked briskly through the back streets towards the western gate of the city. The whole incident had lasted a few seconds.

Niccolo met his accomplices in a grove of trees a quarter of a mile from the city and jumped aboard the cart. He congratulated the brothers on a job well done but Two waved his words aside. 'Save that till we've got this cargo safety stored away.'

They drove on towards Posillipo Hill, a black undulation against the slightly less dark sky. When they stopped beside a wooded cliff, Two thrust a lantern into his hand. 'Here, light this, while we get our friend.'

Niccolo struggled with his tinder box in the gloom but eventually had the oil-soaked wick burning and closed the lamp's glass front. As he held it aloft the others lifted Fra Roberto down and carried him between them to a black indentation in the cliff face which, as they drew closer, became a cave entrance. Going ahead, Niccolo found himself in a tunnel which after a few yards, branched into three.

'Right,' Two ordered. 'Then second left.'

For what seemed several minutes they plunged deeper and deeper into the labyrinth, then stopped in a small cavern where a litter of animal bones, food scraps and tallow candle ends provided evidence of earlier occupation.

'What is this place?' Niccolo asked as the others dumped their burden unceremoniously on the rock floor and removed the sack.

'There are miles of tunnels,' Two explained. 'Some unexplored. They've been here for years – probably dug out by the Romans more than a century ago. I've heard a priest say that some of the Christian saints used to take refuge in here when the Church was being persecuted.'

'Catacombs,' Niccolo muttered.

'Very likely,' Two agreed. 'What d'you want to do with him now you've got him here?' He nodded towards the recumbent figure.

'When he comes to I want to talk to him and then kill him.'

'Reckon we'd best tie him up then. Make your job easier.'

Niccolo nodded and watched as One produced twine with which he and his brother bound the friar's hands and feet.

'We'll be off then, Signore. How long do you want … a couple of hours? Right, we'll come back then and carry the body further in. Finish the job off properly. He'll never be found.'

Two lit a candle stump from the lamp and with its aid he and his sibling departed.

Niccolo could never recall afterwards how long it was before his victim began to move and opened his eyes. It seemed a long time that he sat in the flickering lamplight, the only sounds the echoing drip, drip of water in a nearby gallery and the occasional fluttering of bat wings. All he could ever remember – can still remember – was a feeling of emptiness. For weeks and months he had envisaged this moment or, if not precisely this moment, one very like it, for in his imagination Fra Roberto Attavanti had died a hundred different deaths. He had persuaded himself that the shedding of the murderer's blood would free Baccia's uneasy spirit; that she would be able to find rest. And that he, too, would be released from his anguish. Not until now had any doubt broken through the smooth surface of his conviction. He stared at his captive's face. In the repose of unconsciousness it displayed no emotion – no malice, no anger, no contempt. It was just the visage of a man about the same age as himself; a man with thin lips and thick fair eyebrows; a man with a mole on his left cheek and a smear of blood across his forehead from the abrasion just above the line of his tonsure.

Niccolo shivered, suddenly cold. He busied himself collecting the scraps of candle, lighting them and distributing them round the subterranean chamber. Then he went over to Attavanti and dragged him into a sitting position with his back against a rock.

As he did so the friar began to move. He blinked, shook his head and muttered several incoherent words.

Niccolo sat opposite, the lamp on the ground between them. 'Good-evening, Fra Roberto. No, don't try to move; you are tied hand and foot. And don't try to call out; you could shout yourself hoarse from now to Armageddon and no one would ever hear you.'

The other man clenched and opened his eyes several times, doubtless finding it difficult to focus. Then he stared across the space between them. 'What?... Who?...'

'Ah yes, who? You really don't recognise me, do you, Brother. Here take a good look.' He moved forward, thrusting his face close to the other man's and holding the lamp aloft so that it fell full upon him. 'No? Still mystified? Well, why should you recognise me? I am only the husband of the woman you raped and murdered. A man of no consequence in your life.'

'Dear God, the man's mad!' Niccolo just caught the words Fra Roberto muttered to himself.

The friar composed himself quickly.

'Look, fellow, whatever it is you want, I beg you to think of your immortal soul. Harm me and you will assuredly rot in hell.'

'Assuredly,' Niccolo agreed, resuming his seat, 'and I shall have you for company. But yours I fancy will be the greater torture:

'In the smallest circle, at the core
Of the universe, where Dis[*] in darkness reigns,
Each traitor is consumed for evermore.

'And you are hypocrite and traitor rolled into one, false to your humanity, your Christian profession, your order and your God.'

'So, you quote Dante. Then I see a scholar lurks beneath those rough clothes. Tell me your name. And what is all this about rape and murder?'

Niccolo drew a long stiletto from the top of his boot. 'How dare you goad me with this pretence of innocence! Your time is short and you will need it all for prayer. Don't tempt me to make it shorter.'

In all Niccolo's dreams of vengeance his victim had by this time been crying, grovelling for mercy. Fra Roberto only

[*]Editor's note: Dis = Satan's city; innermost hell

217

breathed a long sigh. 'Signore, whoever you are, you should know that I have suffered at the hands of the Inquisition. If you had faced all that those hell-hounds can do the threat of sudden death would stir no fear within you, as it does not within me.'

'Curse you, you arrogant, false, lecherous…!' Niccolo jumped up, tears starting to his eyes, the pain of months erupting in a lava flow of grief. 'Will you still, even at the moment of death' – he held the dagger point to the friar's throat in a trembling hand – 'deny that last year in Florence you abused and strangled the most beautiful…' He turned away, unable to speak Baccia's name to her violator.

After moments of silence Attavanti spoke softly. 'Signore, you have obviously suffered a most appalling wrong, yet I swear to you by God and Mary and all the saints, and by the memory of your poor wronged wife, that I am innocent of her death.'

Niccolo struggled to bring his emotions under control.

Attavanti looked at his captor more intently. 'All this took place in Florence, you say. Certainly I was there until just before the French came. And there was an incident…' He squinted at his captor in the half-light. 'And, yes, now I think I do recognise you. Was it not you who complained of me to Prior Girolamo?'

'Yes, I am Niccolo Machiavelli and I have spent all the time since then...'

But the friar was not listening. 'Niccolo Machiavelli? You are Niccolo Machiavelli?' He was staring wide-eyed. 'Then it is you who are the murderer.'

'*I* the murderer ... of my own beloved Baccia? For that you *shall* die!' He raised the stiletto above his head.

'No!' Attavanti shouted. 'Not your wife! Prince Djem! All Naples is searching for you for killing the Mohammedan.'

X

Niccolo laughed. 'I give you full credit for ingenuity, friar, but don't imagine your wild inventions fool me.'

Attavanti's demeanour dispelled any suggestion that he was lying. 'The prince died of poison – probably administered during a banquet he gave the evening before we came into Naples. He was in terrible pain for several days and gave up his soul this morning.'

Niccolo considered the news in silence for several moments. 'What's this nonsense about me being suspected? I wasn't at the banquet. I had been nowhere near the prince for days. It is ridiculous to suggest...'

'As ridiculous as it is for you to believe that I killed your wife?'

'A Dominican wormed his way into my house and into my wife's chamber. It was someone she knew; someone who hated me or had a secret passion for her, or both. You are the only man who meets all those conditions.'

'But no one identified this visitor?'

'No, but...'

'And on that slender evidence you have me beaten by Neapolitan ruffians and are prepared to cut my throat? Yet you seriously expect me to believe that you are not a murderer?'

'And what evidence do you have for saying that I killed the Ottoman prince?'

Fra Roberto tried to wriggle his cramped limbs. 'It isn't I who say it; I don't know the truth of the matter and I prefer not to jump to conclusions. The story from the Turkish camp is that you were planted there by Cesare Borgia to facilitate his escape by stealing one of their fleetest horses, that you remained there for the purpose of assassinating the prince and that as soon as you had achieved this objective you disappeared...'

'That's absurd...'

'They claim that you were the agent in a plot concocted in Rome to deprive King Charles of his hostages.'

Niccolo was stunned into silence. The fiction which had just been rehearsed had a certain tidy logic, granted its false premiss.

Attavanti watched him shrewdly. 'So, Signore Machiavelli, what will you do now?'

'Hold your tongue. I need to think.' Niccolo shuffled into the darkness beyond the flickering circle of candles.

'You have a double reason for killing me now,' the friar persisted. 'I am the only person who knows that you are still in Naples. Once that news is out every scoundrel in the city will be searching for you in order to claim the reward.'

'Reward?'

'Didn't I mention it. The king has put a price on your head. A thousand ducats.'

Niccolo gasped. 'A thousand... Then I must get away from Naples immediately.'

'To go where? Florence? Messengers have already been despatched there. His majesty will look for full-co-operation from his "friends" in Florence. Rome? You'll be expected to return to your Borgia masters.'

'They are *not* my masters!' Niccolo shouted. 'They have used me ... for God knows what!'

Attavanti stared at him thoughtfully. 'So you are not an agent of the pope or his vicious son?'

'No, no, no! I went to Rome to find you. Then I was picked up by one of the Borgia officials.'

'What exactly happened to you in Rome?'

Niccolo briefly and dejectedly told his story.

Fra Roberto listened in thoughtful silence, then said, 'These accursed Spaniards, the devil-spawned Borgia must be stopped.' After a long pause he added, 'I'm going to tell you what not even the Inquisition forced from me. When I have done you must decide whether to use that blade of yours to cut my throat or my bonds.

'I come from near Genoa where my family have for generations served the della Roveres. When I was no more than a boy the Lord set his seal upon me and I was accepted into the Dominican order. At school I had good masters and I learned well. I went on to study at Pisa and Bologna, and it was from the university there that I was taken into the service of Cardinal Giuliano. He employed me in certain confidential matters, which I need not go into. When Rodrigo Borgia grasped the papacy della Rovere was devastated and I was scarcely less so. That the Church of Christ should have come to this... Well, there can be only one answer: Alexander is the Antichrist foretold in Scripture and we are in the last days.' The friar's eyes glinted in the candle-light. 'All Christian men are called to resist the limb of Satan.

'The cardinal's opposition very nearly cost him his life but he was under divine protection and escaped to France, where he persuaded King Charles to take up the cause of true religion against this so-called "pope". I was to have joined him but the cardinal decided I could be more use in Italy. So I was placed in Florence under the care of that great and godly champion of righteousness, Prior Girolamo, who was in close contact with the cardinal. When messages arrived that needed disseminating, I carried them to our friends in Rome and elsewhere who were planning the overthrow of the Borgia.'

'And did your mission involve plaguing vulnerable impressionable women?' Niccolo demanded scornfully.

Fra Roberto frowned. 'The reproof is just, Signore. I can only say by way of mitigation that the atmosphere in Fra Girolamo's convent is one of such intense holiness that sometimes some of the brothers go a little too far. I am sorry for any trouble I may have caused between you and your wife.'

Niccolo waved the apology aside. 'Carry on with your story. I'm not saying I believe you but carry on.'

'The cause I was involved in was the Lord's. The work was exciting – but dangerous. Our enemies had agents everywhere but they did not suspect me – until last November when I went to prepare our colleagues in Rome for the invasion. Somehow they traced me to the Dominican house there and, thanks to traitors within the order, I was handed over to the Holy Office for interrogation.'

Memory replayed vivid scenes on the stage of Niccolo's mind – the 'chance' meeting with Reggio, the imprisonment in the Castel Sant'Angelo, his investigation by the Inquisition and the dangling, emaciated form of Fra Roberto. But he said nothing as the friar finished his story.

'The Lord strengthened me with his Spirit and I told my torturers nothing. How close I came to blessed martyrdom only God and his angels know. I longed for it, ached for it, but it was not to be; I was spared for further service. And now, please God, we are close to the triumph of the righteous and the casting of Antichrist into the pit.'

Niccolo listened carefully, trying to cut the flesh of relevant fact from the bones of fanaticism. 'A fascinating story, Brother, but did you really think it would save you?'

Attavanti shrugged. 'I hope the truth will save both of us. Beware of following Vengeance, Signore Machiavelli. He is a blind god and has led many to the precipice. If you kill me you commit a mortal sin for which you will burn eternally. I would be failing in my duty if I did not warn you of that.'

Niccolo tested the dagger's edge against his thumb. 'A just God will understand.'

'Then consider two other matters. In despatching an innocent soul to heaven you do not provide the satisfaction for which your wronged wife's spirit cries out. And in bringing destruction on yourself you render impossible the justice you seek against the guilty.'

'And why should I bring destruction on myself by executing you here in this very secret place? My associates assure me that your body would never be discovered in these catacombs.'

'Do you know of anyone else who can plead your innocence before Cardinal Giuliano or have your case presented to King Charles? Will you remove the one man who believes you guiltless of Prince Djem's death and take your chance as a fugitive never to return to your beloved Florence where, surely, lies the truth concerning Signora Machiavelli's brutal murder.'

Niccolo frowned. 'You say you believe my version of events?'

'I do.'

'Why?'

For the first time the friar smiled. 'Perhaps, because, unlike you, I am not a sceptic. And also because' – and here his tone changed and words reverberated round the chamber – 'I believe that it is not chance that has thrown us together. Consider the remarkable, the bizarre events that have brought us to this moment. Do you not see the hand of God in them? It is he who has led us to the threshold of a wonderful destiny. We can help free Christendom from the Borgia Antichrist and bring in the age of glory.'

Niccolo saw flickers of Savonarola in the friar's smouldering oratory and wondered how many of the ringing phrases were taken directly from sermons thundered in San Marco. But he also realised that there was logic in some of the friar's more prosaic observations.

His knife sliced through the cords binding the prisoner's ankles and wrists. When, shortly afterwards, the two Neapolitan *bricconi* returned, they were puzzled to see executioner and victim seated side by side upon a rock engaged in earnest conversation.

Doubt, not conviction. It was doubt that had stayed Niccolo's hand. He by no means trusted the man he had pursued half the length of Italy but Fra Roberto had planted debilitating tares of uncertainty among his confident dogmas. Fear, too. Eavesdropping on conversations in taverns and market-places soon confirmed that the friar had spoken the truth about Charles VIII's determination to track down the assassin of Prince Djem. That was unnerving. Niccolo fancied that, wherever he went, people looked at him suspiciously. The harbour, where he had sought anonymity in the ever changing cosmopolitan population, now took on the appearance of a closed community in which all outsiders became objects of curiosity. The two brothers he had hired were not slow in spreading the strange tale of the Livorno shipman and the Dominican friar. It was only two days after the confrontation in the labyrinth that Niccolo returned to his quarters in mid-afternoon to find the chandler going through his meagre possessions. There was nothing there to reveal his identity – of that Niccolo had made sure – but as he entered, the man was peering curiously at the handful of books Niccolo had concealed under the straw of his bed place. Fortunately the fellow was semi-literate and would have been able to understand nothing of the great classical authors whose genius made futile appeal from the printed page. He was startled by Niccolo's arrival and muttered words of embarrassed apology. Niccolo raged and drove the chandler from the room, concealing his genuine alarm under blustering indignation. In fact, the incident provided him with an excellent excuse to do what he had already decided upon – leave the area.

But to go where? He wanted to maintain contact with Attavanti but there seemed to be nowhere in Naples that he could hide. It was the friar who suggested the answer – uncongenial but effective.

'You have to melt into the background, merge with the stones of the buildings and the furrowed mud of the streets.' Fra Roberto was seated on a fallen tree trunk in a woodland clearing not far from the city's eastern wall, where he and Niccolo had agreed to meet. 'You need to be just a common part of the townscape; something whose presence people take for granted and therefore ignore.'

'And how do I achieve that?'

'Naples is full of beggars. You've seen them on every corner, outside every church, importuning visitors to the great *palazzi*, foraging among the kitchen garbage thrown into the gutters. Sometimes they enjoy the Christian charity of devout citizens; sometimes they are cuffed and spat upon for their pains; most of the time they are ignored. Join their ranks and no one will pay any attention to you.'

Niccolo shuddered at the thought of the filthy, bedraggled, lice-infested creatures who shambled about the city, thrusting their wooden bowls and canvas bags at respectable Neapolitans. 'Impossible,' he announced firmly.

'It would only be for a few days, until I have had an opportunity to speak to his eminence on your behalf. Once under his protection you will be safe.'

It took several minutes of persuasion before the young gentleman-scholar agreed to descend to the ranks of semi-humanity but once he had accepted the idea the transformation was quickly accomplished. The friar removed all Niccolo's clothes for safe keeping and in their place provided him with a bundle of stinking rags, the sole legacy of a wretch who had recently died in the hospice run by the brothers. He obtained a permit for Niccolo to occupy a pitch close by the convent and a berth in a night shelter run by Franciscans in one of the poor quarters of the city.

No purpose can be served by recording the details of Niccolo's life over the next three weeks, although they were, for him, as salutary as they were demeaning. It is, perhaps, an experience every philosopher should go through at some stage if he wishes to be considered wise about the human condition. When carts spattered him with mud as he sat huddled against a wall, or children prodded him with sticks and taunted him, or he crouched with genuine unfortunates holding out frozen hands over a feeble fire, he tried to comfort himself by reflecting that he shared something with ancient heroes. With the Justinian General Belisarius, reduced to penury by imperial ingratitude holding out his begging bowl to passers-by in Constantinople beseeching them, *date obolum Belisario*. With Diogenes the Cynic, sleeping in his barrel on the streets of Athens, eschewing all possessions and rejecting Alexander the Great's charity with the words 'Get out of my sunlight'. My recollection is that young Niccolo derived little solace from such reflections. They did not warm the bitter winds that felt for every tear in his sacking cloak or soothe the calluses raised on bare legs by hours of kneeling on uneven streets. The consolations of philosophy are apprehended more readily when the impatience of youth has been ground down by experience.

Niccolo had to endure this painful humility for more than the 'few days' suggested by Fra Roberto. Whenever Niccolo asked what progress had been made the friar replied that he was still waiting for a suitable moment to broach the matter with della Rovere. Later he claimed that when he had explained Machiavelli's plight to the cardinal his eminence had replied that he would need time to think about it. Niccolo did not fully trust the procrastinating friar and if he could have conceived any other means of escape from his predicament he would have employed it. He had, in fact, finally reached the conclusion that Fra Roberto had played him false when, arriving at their usual rendez-vous, the friar announced that he had 'good news'.

'The cardinal wants to see you.'

Niccolo laughed. 'What's "good" about that? He'll simply have me arrested and hand me over to the king. It will be quite a triumph for him to say that he has captured the assassin.'

'I don't think he'll do that.'

'What you think is very far from being good enough.'

'Yes, I imagined you would say that. Let's walk a bit.'

They strolled in silence to the edge of the wood. It was a radiant April day. Beyond the roof-tops of Naples a sea of intense, throbbing blue lay between the mainland and distant Procida. In the shadow of the tree the air was cool.

Roberto breathed it deeply and appreciatively. 'As we agreed, I told his eminence that you would need a promise of security before you came out of hiding. He quite understood.'

'And?'

'His main interest is getting the king to concentrate on the deposition of the pope. There is support for this all over Christendom. Mobilising it all behind the French king's leadership requires an enormous amount of diplomatic activity.'

'And he has little time to devote to the fate of a Florentine gentleman falsely accused of murder.'

'It is not high on his list of priorities, certainly.'

Niccolo tore the tattered cloak from his shoulders and threw it to the ground. 'Then we can put an end to this play-acting!'

Attavanti held out a restraining hand. 'Not so hasty, I beg you. Whatever the cardinal thinks about the mystery of Djem's death, it is a matter of increasing importance to the king. He is not popular in Naples...'

'That shouldn't surprise him. He lets his men plunder, butcher and rape at will.'

'Yes, and he has upset the nobles who helped to oust Alfonso by allocating all the most coveted offices and titles to Frenchmen. To add to all that, it is being rumoured that Charles is responsible for the Mohammedan's death.'

'He probably is.'

'He insists not. I have seen him and I can tell you that he is genuinely furious that this crime has been committed against someone under his protection and that he's determined to prove his innocence.'

'By fixing the blame on me!'

'Charles will arrange a public execution so that he can show the world that the King of France honours his obligations. It doesn't matter to him whether the person who features in that execution is the culprit or a scapegoat.'

'Very comforting,' Niccolo observed wryly. 'And you told me you had good news.'

'The good news is that, to please the king, the cardinal wants me to find out the truth.'

'And how will you do that?'

'I very much hope with your help. You were in the Ottoman camp. You saw who came and went. You observed the routine surrounding the prince; indeed, you were put there for that very purpose.'

'I wasn't at the banquet.'

'No, but I was. Possibly I can remember something that may be important. The cardinal has excused me from other duties for a week and we will have the king's authority to question whomever we wish. If we pool our memories and talk with others who might know something we should be able to uncover the truth... And that will mean Signore Machiavelli will be able to resume his own life.'

Niccolo gazed down at the harbour. A two-masted coaster had just slipped her moorings and was standing out into open water, her speed increasing as the crew hauled sails into place. Where was she bound – Sardinia, Sicily or northwards to Ostia, Livorno, Genoa? For the first time he dared to allow his imagination to picture himself on board such a vessel, disembarking on the Tuscan coast, arriving in Florence, walking the familiar streets and squares, the gasps of astonishment from servants, embracing dear Totto, sitting in his own garden and recounting his misadventures to wide-eyed friends.

The vision was smashed by Roberto's next words. 'You may remain incognito for a week but then, whatever the result of our enquiries, I am to take you to the cardinal.'

'I see. And the cardinal will hand me to the king. And the king will...'

'Believe me, Niccolo, it was the best bargain I could strike and my vow of obedience compels me to abide by it.'

'I would have been better off taking my chance on the run.'

'Don't give up so easily. Trust God. We have seven days... Starting now.'

XI

'I suppose,' Niccolo suggested, 'that we should start with the question, "Who wanted Djem dead?" We know that the sultan had offered a considerable sum to have his brother removed.'

Fra Roberto nodded. 'Then there are the Borgias. The pope was careful to keep the prince alive as long as he was under his control in Rome, but once he was in the Frenchman's clutches the attraction of Ottoman gold must have become much more compelling.'

A group of merchants' wives came into view, laughing among themselves and attended by a couple of servants as they slowly climbed the slope. The beggar and the friar withdrew into the cover of the trees and ambled along a path still overlaid with the previous autumn's leaves.

Niccolo raised an objection. 'I'm not convinced about the pope. He was still receiving regular payments from the sultan, even though the prince was a temporary hostage with King Charles.'

'But he knew full well what Charles meant by "temporary". Djem, whether he realised it or not, was on his way to Paris and would never see Rome again. Therefore he was of no more use to Alexander and Alexander wanted to be sure that he was of no use to Charles.'

'You think the assassination was planned before we left Rome?'

'Yes, just as Cesare's escape was obviously agreed upon. The two must go together.'

'Hm, I wonder.' Niccolo shook his head. 'Cesare went to a lot of trouble to place me in the prince's entourage to watch for any sign of foul play.'

'Bluff.'

'Possibly. I agree we must not rule the Borgias out. By the same token we should not reject Charles as a suspect.'

Roberto laughed. 'But it's the king who has put up a reward for the arrest of the culprit.'

'More bluff.'

'But surely...'

'Think about it: you said yourself that he is only concerned with clearing his name. He either started the rumour about me or encouraged it to deflect attention from himself and his agents.'

'Perhaps we ought to concentrate on the agents. If we can find out who administered the poison we should discover whom he was working for.'

When they were well inside the wood they stopped and sat on the ground. From a knapsack Roberto produced baked fish, some bread, some goat cheese and a flask of wine. To Niccolo it seemed like a feast and he fell to vigorously. 'How sure are we that the poison was administered at the banquet?' he asked through a mouthful of food.

'The prince was taken ill an hour or so afterwards with severe stomach pains. He was in agony for four days with vomiting, diarrhoea and a high fever. He was attended by Charles's French physicians – among the best in Europe – but his condition worsened steadily and the end was … distressing.'

'The body was examined, presumably?'

Roberto shook his head. 'In Mohammedan customs burial follows death within hours. The prince's own people took care of the final rites the very next day.'

'How very convenient for the murderer. So we are back at the banquet. Can you remember anything useful from it?'

The friar took a long draught of wine and passed the flask to his companion. 'The festivities went on for about five hours and you know how lavish the hospitality of the infidels is. A great variety of delicacies were served. Naturally, I wasn't seated near the prince but I probably watched him more closely than most.'

'Why was that?'

The Dominican sneered. 'Much of the time we were eating, several of their women were performing lascivious dances. Of course, I averted my eyes from such lust-provoking displays and that enabled me to observe the prince and his guests of honour.'

A burst of laughter broke from Niccolo's lips.

'Something amuses you?' Roberto enquired.

'The thought of a Dominican friar so pure that he cannot look on a woman's body is difficult to entertain.'

'Only because vulgar comedians delight to tell ribald stories about "the abbot and the courtesan",' Roberto observed somewhat haughtily.

'One doesn't need tavern bawdy – or visits to Rome – to be aware of what supposedly holy men get up to. "Do as I say, not as I do" is the motto of most of our clergy.'

'Such behaviour is much exaggerated. Being out in the world as you are, you can have no idea of the earnest prayers uttered daily by every true religious that God will keep us chaste and strengthen us against women, those most potent weapons used by the devil to breach the sanctified bastions of our souls.'

'Spare me the holy claptrap, friar!' Niccolo retorted with sudden vehemence. 'You forget that one of your order, so far from resisting temptation, deliberately violated and murdered my wife.'

'That's as may be,' Attavanti responded. 'But do you want me to tell you about the Mohammedan's feast or not?'

Niccolo nodded and the friar continued. 'Well then, I can picture the scene clearly. Djem sat cross-legged on a bank of cushions and rugs, with the king on his right and the cardinal on his left. His chief minister...'

'Izmet Zeybek?'

'Very possibly – tall, imposing–looking figure. He hovered behind the prince all the time. As servants brought the dishes this fellow took them and offered them to Djem's taster, a scrawny little man who looked as though he needed a good meal rather than nibbles from his master's table. When he had sampled the food he handed it back to this Zeybek, who laid it before the prince. The prince proffered each course to his principal guests before helping himself.'

Niccolo nodded. 'Yes, that was the way things happened at all meals. The prince was very cautious. The same routine was followed with the drinks, presumably.'

'Almost; these Mohammedans are supposedly prohibited fomented beverages but that doesn't seem to prevent them consuming copious draughts of wine. Except Djem: he apparently took the teachings of the Prophet more seriously. While everyone else was served with wine, he drank something different from a special flagon. However, that, too, was tasted before it approached his lips.'

'Still, that looks like the only way the poison can have been introduced. If it was in the food the king and the cardinal would have eaten some as well. Can you remember exactly what happened when the prince was served?'

Roberto closed his eyes in concentration. 'A servant brought the flagon from where it stood on a table at the side of the pavilion.

Zeybek took Djem's goblet – silver gilt with enamel decoration. He held it for the servant to fill, then he handed it to the taster, who drank and returned it, and Zeybek set it down before his master.'

'You're sure that's everything? You haven't left anything out of the sequence?'

The friar looked thoughtful for several seconds. 'No, that's what happened: Zeybek holds up the cup; it's filled; he hands it to the taster; he receives it back; he wipes the rim and sets...'

'What?' Niccolo interjected sharply. 'He wipes the rim? What with?'

Roberto looked puzzled. 'Just a clean napkin. I think he had a little pile of them. These Turks seem to be obsessed with cleanliness. Not like the French; some of the king's courtiers...'

Niccolo interrupted. 'That action of wiping; could it not have concealed slipping something into the goblet?'

The friar shrugged. 'Conceivably, but ... are you suggesting that the prince was killed by his own chief minister and in full view of a hundred or more witnesses?'

Niccolo jumped to his feet and took a few paces up and down the track, thinking hard. '*If* Djem was poisoned at the banquet – and we don't know that for sure – and if you have remembered accurately what happened, then no one else had the opportunity to tamper with the prince's food or drink.'

'But if it was this Zeybek fellow,' Roberto objected, 'why did he choose that night? He had plenty of opportunity every day to kill his master. To do it so publicly... Well, it just seems a very foolish risk to take.'

'Not necessarily. You yourself said that everyone with less purity of mind than you was watching the voluptuous dancers. Who would pay any attention to the routine of...?'

'The dancers!' Roberto was suddenly excited. 'One of them could have done it.'

'How?'

'There were moments when they came very close to Djem and his guests. They would approach with their obscene gestures and even sit beside them.' The friar's nose wrinkled in revulsion. 'The prince and the king sometimes fed them titbits from the dishes before them.'

'But did it happen the other way round? Did any of the women give the prince something to eat?'

The friar's face clouded with doubt. 'I don't ... I'm not ... I didn't watch them closely ... shameless whores! But they could have done.'

Niccolo shook his head. 'Pity. I really thought we'd discovered how the murder was committed.'

Roberto repacked his knapsack in silence. Then he said, 'But we have two possible approaches, surely.'

Niccolo thrust a hand inside his tattered shirt and scratched his stomach where the insect population were gorging themselves. 'Not really. There is no way to get to the prince's women; they're kept firmly under lock and key. As for Izmet Zeybek, what can we do with him; go up calmly and ask him if he killed his master?' He began to walk despondently back along the path and the friar fell in beside him.

Suddenly Niccolo stopped. 'Unless ... the first time I met the vizier ... I wonder.'

He explained to his companion the scheme that was shaping itself in his mind. As he did so he watched the friar's face register bewilderment, disbelief, apprehension and finally a scarcely convinced acquiescence. 'Do you really think it will work?' he asked at last. 'I don't know that I'll be able to persuade him to co-operate.'

'And I don't know that I'll be able to

stomach masquerading as a Dominican but with only seven days at our disposal we'll both have to sink our natural aversions.'

At the edge of the wood they parted and each made his own way back into Naples.

Niccolo waited impatiently for news that Fra Roberto had succeeded in putting the first part of their plan into operation. Two days passed and most of a third. At times he could almost feel the noose round his neck. But he had plenty of other thoughts to occupy his mind. From his memory he dredged a miscellany of impressions – things he had seen, heard, overheard since his arrival in Rome. Some he knew, were relevant, some not – but which was which? And if he could select those happenings which had a bearing on Djem's death, how could he arrange them into a meaningful sequence?

It was dusk on the third day and Niccolo was just preparing to leave his pitch close to the convent when Fra Roberto emerged. The friar stooped to place a coin in the beggar's bowl and muttered, 'Vicolo Santa Margareta, ten minutes.'

The alley between the church and the back of a row of artisans' houses was so narrow that Niccolo could touch both walls simultaneously. By the time he reached it it was almost pitch dark. He stumbled half-way along it before he heard his name called and the figure of the friar emerged from the gloom.

Attavanti held out a bundle. 'Here, put this on.'

Niccolo unrolled the Dominican habit and with Roberto's expert help pulled it over his head. This was followed by the scapula and cowl. Then, by feel rather than sight, he fastened a pair of sandals to his feet. Moments later a pair of black friars emerged into a wider thoroughfare and walked briskly towards the city centre.

'It's all arranged,' Roberto reported. 'He was very reluctant but when I pointed out that the request came from the king (not strictly true, of course) he realised he had no choice.'

'How did he seem?'

'Almost in tears over Djem's death. Quite a good act, I thought.'

'It might be genuine.'

'I don't think so. For one thing he doesn't seem very worried about his future. Several of the others are very distressed. They dare not return home but they cannot stay here, particularly after Charles has returned to France.'

'No, anyone connected with the king is likely to be lynched. Yet you say Izmet has no worries on that score?'

'He speaks of taking ship to Izmir, which is what they now call ancient Smyrna, and going into business.'

'He has money, then.'

'So it seems.'

'Not that that proves much, I suppose. No one was better placed to raid the prince's treasure.'

'I doubt that he had much chance for that. As soon as the king heard that Djem was ill he sent guards to take the prince's belongings into his royal "protection".'

'Then we must find out where the vizier's sudden wealth has come from.'

Roberto pointed along the street to where a hanging sign showed a white star on a dark ground. 'We're almost there. You'd better give me about an hour before you come in.'

They parted company and Roberto entered the tavern, one of Naples's more respectable drinking houses much frequented by lawyers, churchmen and courtiers. Niccolo took up station on a corner opposite from where, several minutes later, he observed the tall figure of Izmet Zeybek stoop in at the doorway. For the next hour he walked the streets in mounting excitement, turning over and over in his mind the questions to which he needed answers. Could the Turk be induced to provide any?

When he returned, the White Star's un-shuttered windows were gleaming invitingly in the darkness. Cautiously Niccolo entered at the open doorway. The *locanda* was busy, more than half the tables occupied with customers, and there was a loud babel of conversation and laughter. Niccolo spotted Roberto seated in the middle of the room facing the door with the Turk opposite him. Niccolo looked around for a place, saw a vacant bench immediately behind Izmet Zeybek and located himself there, the cowl concealing his untonsured hair.

But what was necessary for his disguise also impeded his hearing. He leaned back, turning his head to one side, in an effort to catch the conversation behind him. It was almost impossible. The background noise was loud and Izmet's speech was already uncertain and fumbling. Niccolo was in an agony of frustration.

Then he heard his name called. 'Brother

Niccolo, is that you? Won't you join us?'

He looked round quickly at Roberto. Had the man gone mad? Izmet would be sure to recognise him if he got a close look at him.

The friar was insistent. 'Brother, do come and drink with us. There's a seat there beside my friend.'

Niccolo stood up and grimaced at Roberto from behind the Turk's back. The other man smiled and made an undulating gesture with his hand indicating that his guest was well into his cups. Looking down, Niccolo noticed the unsteady way Izmet lifted the beaker to his lips. Carefully and with the cowl covering most of his face he sat down next to the vizier.

Roberto introduced him. 'Izmet, this is my good friend, Brother Niccolo. Brother, this is Izmet Zeybek. He came to Naples with the Turkish prince; you know, the one who was so tragically killed.'

Izmet waved a hand vaguely in the new-comer's direction but did not turn to face him.

Roberto prattled on cheerfully. 'Niccolo – now that's a coincidence. Isn't the man they want for Prince Djem's murder called Niccolo? What a desperate fellow he must be. I suppose you knew him well, Izmet.'

The Turk waggled his head enthusiastically. 'Borgia spy,' he slurred. 'Nasty Borgia spy.'

'Really? A Borgia spy?' Roberto smiled encouragingly. 'How did you find that out?'

Izmet drained his beaker and belched loudly.

'How did you know this fellow was a spy?' the friar persisted, pouring more wine for his guest from a large carafe.

'Watching ... always watching ... and taking notes ... but I knew anyway... They told me...' The large man swayed back and Niccolo felt the shared bench almost tip over.

'They told you he was a spy, did they? Who was it who told you?'

The Turk shook his head violently. 'No, no ... secret.'

'That's all right, Izmet, you can tell us. We're old friends, isn't that so, Brother?' Roberto had obviously decided it was safe to bring Niccolo into the conversation.

The vizier turned, peering at his neighbour. 'Know you,' he muttered, wagging a finger within an inch of Niccolo's nose. 'Know you very well.'

Niccolo was alarmed. Was the alcoholic fog not thick enough to conceal the truth.

'That's right,' he bluffed. 'I'm Brother Roberto's friend. We all know each other very well. You can tell us who warned you about this spy.'

'Spy?' The Turk's brow went into ridges of concentration. 'I'm a spy ... but no one must know.'

Niccolo feigned astonishment and admiration. 'You're a spy! How very clever you must be.'

Izmet nodded. 'Yes, no one fools old Izmet Zeybek... Not the sultan, not the prince, no one.'

'I'm sure of it,' Roberto observed with solemn conviction. 'I suppose it was the sultan you were spying for.'

The Turk yawned and again rocked so far backwards that he almost toppled over and Niccolo had to put an arm round him to steady him. 'So you were spying for the sultan on his own brother and the prince never knew,' he said. 'How very clever.'

The vizier's thick lips opened in a smile that extended right across his face. 'Would you like to know what the sultan said to me?'

'Yes!' Niccolo and Roberto exclaimed in chorus.

Izmet leaned forward and beckoned his

companions to bring their heads close to his. 'Sultan Bayezit said to me...' There followed three or four sentences in fluent Turkish.

Niccolo sat back, deflated.

His companion was more persistent. 'So the sultan wanted you to kill Prince Djem.'

Izmet stared back, shook his head and explained in a stream of more elaborate Turkish.

The interrogators tried more questions but their victim's mind had crossed the language frontier and there seemed to be no way to recall it. In exasperation Roberto asked directly the question that lay at the heart of their investigation. 'Tell us exactly how you killed the prince.'

At this the Turk became very voluble, though still in his native tongue. Roberto and Niccolo listened intently, trying to pick out any word or phrase that might tell them something. There were only two Italian names that stood out from the torrent of Turkish – Manfredo and Velletri – and Izmet uttered both of them more than once. In his agitation he swayed more energetically and this time he did topple. He fell backwards, taking the bench and Niccolo with him. Both men landed in a heap on the floor, drenched in wine from the full beaker Izmet was still grasping.

With difficulty, because of the unfamiliar heavy habit, Niccolo extricated himself and clambered to his feet to face a circle of laughing bystanders. The Turk, however, lay prone and motionless, his features locked in a contented grin. It took Roberto, Niccolo and two others to drag the large man to a standing position but he remained limp and unconscious. It was obvious that he was going to go nowhere in his own strength and also that the two 'Dominicans' could not handle him alone. While they were still debating what to do next the innkeeper hurried up and made it abundantly clear that he wanted the trio off his premises – immediately. So eager was he to see the back of them that Roberto was able to make a deal with him. Thus it was that minutes later two cowled men could have been observed wheeling through the streets a handcart upon which reposed a bizarre figure who occasionally lapsed into consciousness and shouted Turkish obscenities into the night.

It was agreed that Roberto would take their charge back to the convent with some story of having found the inebriate lying in

254

the street. As he ruefully admitted, this act of spontaneous charity to an infidel would not please father prior but he would be unable to refuse Christian hospitality to the unfortunate. Niccolo removed his Dominican garb and, having agreed to meet his co-conspirator next day, he returned to the meagre haven of the Franciscans.

The next day he was up early and walked to the wooded hilltop that had become his regular rendezvous with the friar. Thus, aided by the fresh morning air, he was able to spend more than an hour in solitary thought before Roberto arrived. He cast his mind back to the beginning of the sequence of events leading up to Djem's death and tried to slot in the few details that Izmet had let slip.

'How's our friend?' he asked, as the friar strode into the clearing.

'Uncomfortable.' Roberto laughed. 'The infirmarian gave him something for his headache and he went off muttering that the Christian dogs had poisoned him.'

'Did he know how much he'd given away last night?'

Roberto sat down on a moss-covered bank. 'No, he was utterly confused. He insisted that two Dominicans had got him drunk although I assured him that he and I were alone.'

'Fortunate for us that he has no head for strong drink. The Mohammedans are denied it in their own country so I suppose Izmet had little experience of it in his early years.'

'He's certainly making up for it now. He'd have drunk wine by the bucketful last night if he'd had the chance.'

'I knew his weakness,' Niccolo said. 'That's why I thought we might loosen his tongue if we could get him drinking.'

'So, what have we learned?'

'Well, Izmet as good as confessed to having poisoned Djem.'

'Of course, he would deny it when sober, so that may not help us much, and we're still left with the questions of who was behind the assassination and why it was carried out at that particular moment. No one had better opportunity than him to despatch the prince at any time.'

Niccolo nodded in agreement. 'The more I think about it, the more convinced I am that the timing is the vital element in this whole puzzle. Did anything happen at the banquet that might explain why it was necessary to get rid of the prince quickly?'

Roberto made an effort of concentration. 'Of course, I don't know what he and the king were talking about. They did make a couple of speeches – the usual sort of thing, boring and insincere pledges of eternal friendship. Charles confirmed his promise to set Djem on the Ottoman throne.'

'Well, that certainly would not please the sultan and we now know that Izmet was the sultan's man.'

'And yet last night the only thing that seemed clear from that confusing torrent of Turkish was that the sultan did not arrange for his brother's death.'

Niccolo said, 'Well, that brings us to whatever he was saying about Velletri. Something important happened there and it involved a man called Manfredo. Does that name mean anything to you?'

The friar shook his head. 'Manfredi is a family name up in the Romagna, around Faenzi. I don't know anyone from that region. But I wonder if we're not making it too complicated for ourselves.' He lay down on top of the bank, gazing up through the fresh green leaves bursting on the branches overhead. 'If we discount the sultan as Izmet's paymaster that only leaves the Borgias. They certainly had no intention of letting King Charles use Djem as the figure-head for a Christendom-wide crusade. Now, it was at Velletri that Cesare de-camped. He could have contacted Izmet before he left – perhaps even supplied him with the poison. Can you recall any contact the vizier had with the cardinal that day?'

Niccolo thought hard and into his mind came images of Cesare Borgia's steward, the little priest: annoyed and flustered because Niccolo had pried into the black chest; surprised and annoyed again to be seen emerging from Izmet's tent. He told Roberto about these incidents.

The Dominican sat up suddenly. 'Well that's it, then!' he said with a look of triumph on his face. 'That's how it was done: Cesare sent the poison to Izmet via his major-domo with instructions that it was not to be used until he was safely out of the way. Now all we have to do is track the man down and force a confession out of him.'

'That will be rather difficult,' Niccolo observed. 'Charles executed him personally in a fit of rage.'

Roberto was only momentarily crestfallen. 'Still,' he said, 'this fellow must be the link we've been looking for. I can make enquiries about him.'

Niccolo was doubtful. 'But why should Cesare Borgia arrange to have the prince killed and at the same time station me in the Ottoman camp to prevent him being killed?' He pummelled his temple with his fists. 'Nothing in this whole wretched business makes any sense. And time is running out.'

XII

The Lazaret of St Luke was adapted from what had once been a post-horse stable, close by one of the city's smaller gates, and little had been done to render it more suitable for human than animal habitation. Its wretched inmates were accommodated in narrow stalls which received a weekly layer of fresh straw. That and a blanket were the only comforts provided to the miscellany of unfortunates who cast themselves upon the charity of the Franciscans. At nightfall the brothers dispensed vegetable pottage from a large cauldron and handed out a dole of rough bread. At daybreak those who could walk, limp or stagger were ejected onto the streets of Naples to beg or steal their 'sustenance' – which for most meant the wine or aqua vitae which kept them in a tolerable semi-oblivion.

Niccolo's sojourn in this abode of misery was hard. His first two nights there were long and sleepless, unconsciousness denied by the babel of moans, snores, grunts and raucous song assailing him from all sides. Scarcely less disturbing to him was the fact that on the third night he *did* sleep – very soundly. Did that mean, he asked himself, that he was growing accustomed to this level of existence? Was it so easy to descend to semi-humanity? How many of the lazaret's *habitués* had once been men of education, culture, perhaps even noble breeding? After four days Niccolo realised that he no longer worried about the growing population of fleas in his coarse clothing, the citizens who hurried along the street past his out-stretched, supplicating arms, hands to their noses, the rats which foraged among his bedding straw all night long and the hospice's distinctive *mélange* of smells – sweat, urine and vegetable stew. As the week allotted by the cardinal drew towards its close the hostel assumed an aura of luxury compared with the looming alternative. If he could not extricate himself from the threat of a gallows death nothing would be left him but flight and the life of an outlaw.

Day five began with a sandalled foot poking him into consciousness. Niccolo rolled over stiffly on the straw and stared up into the face of a young Franciscan, which bore an expression of pained self-sacrifice.

'Prime in ten minutes,' the friar announced, before continuing on his tour of duty. The brothers' guests were always invited to attend the morning office. Some inmates availed themselves of the opportunity of another half-hour's security and relative comfort but most of the beggars ventured straight away onto the streets. Niccolo, having no interest in the Franciscans' devotions, was among the majority. Quite why he changed the pattern on this occasion he never knew. He simply found himself crossing the Via San Pietro to the small complex of buildings which were an outstation of the Franciscan house in the city centre. He stood at the back of the church with a tiny group of Neapolitans while the brothers filed into the chancel and began to chant the service. He was too concerned with his own plight and earnest prayers for deliverance to follow the liturgy. Though not wrapped in divine contemplation, he was, nevertheless, deeply preoccupied. Therefore he was just as startled as the religious professionals at the sudden noisy interruption.

Niccolo was positioned close by the west door when it was thrust open violently. It crashed back against the wall, sending discordant echoes through the building. He spun round to see three men –carpenters or stone masons to judge by their aprons and the tool bags slung over their shoulders – struggling to carry a fourth between them. They laid their burden down on the flagstones, then straightened up, wiping their brows and stretching their arms.

Niccolo hurried over. 'What's the matter?'

One of the bearers – a little redhaired fellow – stared disapprovingly at the ragged questioner but decided to explain. 'We found him round the corner. He's in a bad way … dying most like.'

Niccolo stared down at the figure on the floor. He was a big man, a soldier with a breastplate gleaming beneath his cloak. Then Niccolo saw the fleur-de-lys on the shoulder of the cloak and realised that here was a member of King Charles's bodyguard, one of the swaggering braggarts who had been intimidating the city ever since their arrival. But he did not look so domineering now. His black hair was matted with blood. His face was streaked with red and was a mess of lacerations and purpling bruises.

Niccolo stepped and pulled back the cloak, searching for other wounds. It was then he saw something that made him gasp.

'What's all this, then?'

Niccolo was scarcely aware of the brittle, agitated voice.

'You, fellow, what are you about; looking for a sickman's purse? Come away, do you hear!'

Niccolo looked up at the portly figure of the sub-prior. 'There's a stab wound here, in the thigh. He's lost a lot of blood.' He pointed to the dark, soaking stain covering the skirt of the blue garment, which protruded from beneath the breastplate. The garment with the frayed edge where it had been cut down from something longer. The garment of ultramarine velvet. The garment strewn with little bulls sewn in gold thread.

The Franciscan was not listening. He was extracting their story from the three Samaritans. Not that there was much of a story. The carpenter-carvers were on their way to the cathedral to commence another day's work on the new clergy stalls when they had come across the obvious victim of a nocturnal robbery lying in the narrow gap between two houses. It was a common enough sight and the craftsmen would have ignored it had one of them not heard the poor fellow moaning. Realising that he was still alive, they had decided to bring him to the convent to see if the brothers could do anything for him. And now that they had done their Christian duty the redhaired man pointed out they must go. They were already late for their work and the cathedral chancellor was a stickler for punctuality.

Niccolo ignored the instruction to leave the wounded man's side. He scanned the Frenchman's face for signs of movement and bent down to listen for any whisper of breath. Desperately he wanted the king's guard to live. Niccolo had to know how Charles's man had come into possession of Cardinal Borgia's gown.

He had discerned that the soldier was just about alive when the sub-prior's foot against his shoulder sent him sprawling.

'I told you to be off,' the friar hissed. 'All of you!' He glared at Niccolo's hostel colleagues who had clustered into an inquisitive semicircle.

As the bystanders drifted away towards the church door, Niccolo picked himself up and shuffled after them. But he had no intention of leaving as long as there was any chance of extracting vital information from the stricken man. He slipped behind a pillar and watched as the sub-prior returned to where his chanting brothers were simultaneously singing their office and craning their necks to see what was happening at the back of the church. He observed the officious little man engage some of his brethren in whispered conversation. Four of them then left their places in the choir and converged upon the recumbent figure. Between them they lifted him and carried him across the empty nave to a side door in the far wall.

As soon as they had disappeared Niccolo followed, grateful that the alignment of massive pillars partially obscured the view from the chancel. The door gave straight into the cloister and as Niccolo cautiously closed it behind him he saw the friars diagonally crossing the enclosed courtyard towards an archway in the far corner. The pursuer flitted round two arcaded sides of the cloister and reached the opening just in time to see the Franciscans manoeuvring their burden through the entrance to a separate building, which he guessed was the infirmarium.

What to do now? He could pursue his quarry no further – certainly not dressed in his beggar's rags. There was no time to give the problem leisurely thought: the sound of approaching voices obliged him to make a quick retreat. In the doorway to the church he almost collided with the procession of brothers returning from their worship. He scuttled past them into the street and, via a maze of byways, reached the Spaccanapoli and took up his accustomed position close by the Dominican convent.

He crouched cross-legged in his allotted spot glancing every few seconds at the small door used by the friars, willing Roberto to appear. He had to see him; had to work out some way of gaining access to the Franciscans' patient. Then it began to rain. Within minutes he was huddling against the wall facing an unremitting bombardment of water, which seemed to be aimed exclusively at him. It splashed into his begging bowl. It streamed in miniature waterfalls from the roof above. It ran in rivulets along the cart tracks in front of him. Everyone else was quickly driven from the street and Niccolo sat, soaked and alone. He pulled the woollen cap down over his ears and pictured Fra Roberto warm and dry in his cell, caring nothing about Niccolo Machiavelli's fate. It was all very well for the friar, he brooded; his life was not under threat; there was no price on his head. Well, if Roberto was abandoning him to his fate he would have to work out for himself some way of obtaining the information he desperately needed. He had to think – think hard and think fast. And he could not do that sitting in a puddle.

Niccolo stood up and shuffled, squelching, along the street, in search of somewhere dry and secluded. He had gone only a few paces when he felt a hand on his arm and heard Roberto's urgent voice: 'Quick, my friend, this way.'

Turning, he saw Roberto and knew by the droplets falling from the front of his hood that he, too, had been walking in the rain. The friar steered him back towards the little door in the convent wall. It led directly into the cloister. Roberto hurried him around it, along a corridor, ignoring the curious glances of the two or three other brothers encountered *en route*, and spoke no word until he and his companion had reached his cell.

Then, throwing back his hood and dabbing his face with a towel, he announced, 'I've just come from the cardinal's with great news.' He stared at the dripping, dejected figure before him and smiled. 'But first we must get you out of those soaked rags.'

Thankfully Niccolo stripped off the

saturated shreds and dried himself with the towel offered by Roberto.

From under his narrow bed the friar produced a bundle of Niccolo's own clothes. 'And now Signore Machiavelli can make his reappearance,' he stated with beaming confidence.

'But why … how… Tell me what's happened.' Niccolo sat on the bed to draw on his own, but strangely unfamiliar, hose.

Roberto, too, was changing out of his wet habit. As he pulled a fresh garment over his head he explained: 'I told the cardinal we needed to find out about someone who was part of Cesare Borgia's household. He said that the king was still holding some of the Borgia officers in prison in case they could be useful in his bargaining with Rome. He wrote out a pass so that I could get into the dungeons of the Castel Nuovo and interview any of the prisoners.'

He knotted the cord round his waist. 'It all sounded very easy: I just had to walk in, find the right person and quiz him about the Borgia major-domo until he let slip some vital piece of information that linked him with the Ottoman camp. By all the saints, I couldn't have been more wrong! It took me all of yesterday – hours of brain-numbing interrogation in that slimy hell in the bowels of the earth.' Roberto shuddered. 'Too reminiscent of another oubliette deep below the Castel Sant'Angelo.'

Niccolo finished fastening his points and stared at his companion, frowning. 'You'll forgive me if I say that the narrative of your discomfort holds little interest for me. What happened at the Castel Nuovo? What did you find out? In God's name, tell me!'

'Nothing.'

'Nothing! Then what...'

'Calm yourself, Niccolo.' Roberto held up his hands. 'Let me tell it my way and you'll see just how important my visit was.' He sat down on the bed, slipped off his sandals and dabbed his feet with the towel as he explained: 'There were two people there who I hoped would be able to tell me what I wanted to know: a boy called Giuseppe who was Cardinal Borgia's favourite page and a wizened greybeard, Paolo Barbarado, his butler. Both of them were reluctant to speak. The old man was stubbornly loyal to his master and unwilling to say anything to the Borgia's discredit. As for the lad – he was just terrified of being questioned at all... At least, that's what I thought first of all.'

'Get to the point, man!' Niccolo jumped up and glowered at the loquacious friar.

Roberto ignored him. 'It was very odd: they were both quite relaxed in talking about themselves and the workings of the cardinal's household. They even spoke happily about Cesare's escape, which, apparently, took them completely by surprise. But whenever I brought up the subject of the cardinal's steward it was as though someone had sewn their lips together. So you see what I mean when I say they told me nothing.' He looked up at his guest triumphantly. 'And that in itself confirms what we suspected.'

Niccolo shook his head despondently. 'I don't see the king being very impressed with the story of two frightened prisoners. If you've raised my hopes just to tell me...'

'No, no, Niccolo, listen. There *is* more. Young Giuseppe did tell me something vitally important. He didn't know that what he was saying was significant but it was. It was absolutely crucial.'

'Well?'

'He referred to the major-domo by name.' Roberto leaned back against the wall, a smile of exultation radiating his face. 'Manfredo Manfredi.'

When Niccolo failed to respond with excited jubilation the friar was crestfallen. 'Don't you see it? That establishes the link between Borgia and Prince Djem's treacherous vizier.'

'Yes, but it still doesn't explain...'

Roberto clapped a hand to his head in exasperation. 'By all the saints! What's the matter with you, man? Why must you worry yourself about what you *can't* explain. All that matters is that we can lift the blame for the prince's death from your shoulders. I've told Cardinal della Rovere everything. He will report to the king and all that Charles has to do is arrest Izmet Zeybek, examine him and Borgia's servants under torture, and the whole story will come out. His eminence is quite convinced about this. He wants to meet you so that he can tell you himself that you are no longer under suspicion. I am to take you to him straight away.'

'What's to stop him simply delivering me to the king?'

'But why should he? He asked me to find out the truth.'

Niccolo sighed. 'For men like della Rovere, Borgia and Valois truth isn't a treasure to be ardently sought and highly prized; it's a coinage to be acquired and then hoarded or disbursed according to convenience. Charles's only concern is to show the world that he has discovered and punished an assassin. He can as well make that demonstration by executing me as by exposing the real murderer. You said yourself that he would as cheerfully hang a scapegoat as a culprit.'

Roberto weighed the objection. 'That may well be true of the king but his eminence is different. You'll realise that when you meet him. Believe me,' he added, seeing that Niccolo was still dubious, 'I've known him a long time. He is a man of his word.'

Niccolo stretched out on the creaking bed, forcing his tired brain to think. 'But della Rovere's only concern is to fasten this crime on the Borgias.'

'But that's exactly what we've done!' Roberto raised his voice in exasperation. 'We've linked the murder to Cesare – indisputably.'

'Hm, I wonder.'

'And what does that mean? Are you refusing to come with me to the cardinal's?' He glared down at the figure whose eyes were now closed. 'I suppose you'd rather stay in hiding. You know that will only appear to confirm your guilt.' Again there was no response. 'Well, if you're just going to lie there after all I've done for you...' Roberto paced the narrow strip of floor between the bed and the wall. 'I thought you'd be pleased. Instead of that all you want to do is cling to your doubts. I tell you this: if you're going to do nothing to help yourself till you've understood every twist and turn of this business you'll still be puzzling it out on the gallows. Well, I can't do any more. The cardinal granted me seven days...'

Niccolo was not listening to the tirade. He was staring in his mind at a blue velvet gown sewn with golden bulls. A gown that was supposed to have been packed in the Vatican was, according to the French, deliberately left behind by the scheming Borgia and yet subsequently turned up in the loot of one of the French king's henchmen.

He swung himself into a sitting position. 'Roberto, I want you to come with me to the Franciscan convent. There's someone there I must talk to.'

The Dominican scowled. 'I promised his eminence I'd be back within the hour.'

'It's very important, Roberto, and it will only delay us slightly, I swear to you.'

It was the other's turn to be unconvinced. 'A black friar will scarcely be welcome in a Franciscan house and anyway, what is so vital that his eminence must be kept waiting?'

Niccolo jumped up, hope now banishing lethargy. 'I must shave and make myself respectable for this cardinal of yours. Then, as we go, I'll explain.'

Half an hour later they entered the narrow street where the Franciscan house was situated.

Roberto, to whom Niccolo had described the events of the morning, was still raising objections to their mission. 'But what do you hope to get out of this royal guardsman?'

'I want him to tell me how and where he came into possession of Cardinal Borgia's gown and what other booty he has.'

'And how will knowing that help?'

'The official story is that Cesare Borgia planned his escape before leaving Rome and that most of his chests of personal belongings were empty. The king made a great show of discovering this deception at Velletri. If, in reality...'

They had arrived at the main gate of the friary. Roberto banged on it with the heavy iron knocker. It was opened instantly by a lay brother who looked askance at Roberto's black habit and enquired their business. Roberto explained that they had come to visit the poor unfortunate who had been brought to the convent that morning. 'I was one of the men who found him,' he lied, 'and I am most anxious to see how he is.'

After consulting a superior, the porter let them in and another brother conveyed them to the infirmary. They were left outside the door until the infirmarian was ready to see them. When he did appear – a studious, gaunt-faced brother smelling strongly of some pungent herbal remedy – he eyed them gravely. 'You have come to see the Frenchman?'

Niccolo repeated his mendacious explanation for the visit.

The Franciscan shook his head. 'I fear you come too late. Capitano Gautier died about half an hour ago. Mercifully, he was conscious enough to make his confession and be shriven by father prior.'

Roberto crossed himself and Niccolo hastened to follow suit, though his thoughts were far from the repose of the French soldier's soul. The infirmarian raised his arms in a well-practised gesture of sympathy and resignation.

As he turned to retreat into his domain Niccolo said suddenly, 'May we see him, please ... and ... er ... pray for him?'

The Franciscan nodded and, ignoring Roberto's angry frown, Niccolo stepped through the doorway. Gautier was laid upon a bed at the far end of the room. As they gathered round, the infirmarian explained in a whisper, 'I haven't cleaned him up yet – just cleared away the blood. He was very badly beaten. I gather he and his companions became involved in a brawl at a nearby brothel. Some of the local men turned on them. They're not bad at heart but I fear the strangers have stirred up a great deal of resentment. The rest of them escaped but this poor fellow was not so fortunate.' He gazed down at the swarthy, black-bearded face – once fearsome but now pathetic in its lack of either menace or composure. 'There were many lacerations and bruises, some broken ribs and, I am sure, bad internal injuries. There was very little we could do for him.'

Niccolo smiled reassuringly. 'He can't have been in better hands. May we have a few moments?'

The solemn ascetic nodded and glided

noiselessly away. Niccolo knelt at the bedside but his attention was directed not at its occupant but at the neatly folded pile of clothes on the floor beside him. Carefully he laid aside the breastplate and the blood-soaked shirt, and lifted up the blue gown. He felt the soft cloth and ran his finger over the fur collar. There was no doubt. 'Here,' he whispered, thrusting the garment at Roberto, 'tuck this under your scapula!'

The Dominican looked shocked. 'What are you thinking, man? I can't...'

'Don't argue. Do it!' Niccolo folded back the blanket covering the naked body. The left hand was decorated with two heavy rings; one an irregularly cut ruby, the other an opal of exquisite shape. Niccolo eased them from the stiff fingers, examined them briefly and returned the one with the red stone. The other he slipped into his purse.

Behind him Roberto hissed his outrage. 'In God's name, Niccolo, robbing the dead is a mortal sin!'

'Not when it's done to protect the living, Brother.' Niccolo straightened up and replaced the blanket. 'Now it's time to go.' He took Roberto's arm and drew him, still muttering protests, from the sick-room.

Outside in the street the rain had stopped.

After a few paces Roberto halted and pulled his companion into a doorway. 'And now, by the mass, you *will* explain! How dare you involve me in this crime.'

Niccolo faced him squarely. 'I'm sorry, Roberto, but I had to have proof. The gown definitely belonged to Cardinal Borgia.'

'And the ring?'

Niccolo took the small gold band from his purse. 'Look at the inscription.'

Roberto held up the ring to catch the light and read aloud the Latin words engraved on its inner surface: *'Factus Sum Pro Ludovico Borgia'*.

'You see?' Niccolo drove his point home. 'It's a family jewel looted from the cardinal's baggage train – the train that King Charles insists contained nothing but empty boxes.'

'But what has all that to do with the murder of the prince?' The friar began walking again with quickened steps.

Niccolo shook his head as he fell in beside him. 'I wish I knew. There were two men who could have told us and they're both dead.' Into his mind flashed the vivid image of the furious French king whirling a heavy sword to despatch Father Manfredi in the market-place at Velletri. He laughed out loud and leaned against the wall. 'Of course!

Of course! Thersites and Agamemnon.'

His companion stared at him in amazement and irritation. 'Would you mind telling me what's going through that tortuous mind of yours now?'

Niccolo gave him a radiant smile. 'The truth, my friend, the truth.'

From a nearby church a clock chimed the hour.

'Time is pressing,' Niccolo observed brightly, 'and we mustn't keep his eminence waiting. But first we have to hide our trophies.' He set off briskly along the street, leaving Roberto staring after him in bewilderment.

XIII

The two men made a detour to the Dominican convent where they thrust under Roberto's bed the two items taken from the dead soldier. Then they strode – almost running – along Spaccanapoli to the Palazzo Sanseverini. Despite his companion's breathless entreaties, Niccolo offered no explanation for his sudden change of attitude.

At the cardinal's residence, while his companion was summoned to the exalted ecclesiastical presence, Niccolo was told to wait in a wide hall whose tapestried walls recounted scenes from the *Aeneid*. He tried to quell the anxieties bubbling within by walking from panel to panel and identifying characters and events in the stirring story, but though he urged himself to be calm it was all he could do to stop fears and fantasies chasing from his mind the details of what he had decided to tell della Rovere. He knew the cardinal would question him closely and that he would have to be clear and consistent in all he said. Everything depended on his performance – escape from the world of Inquisition dungeons, bewildering intrigue and degrading beggary; return to Florence and some sort of normality – everything, even life itself. At the end of the interview he would either be walking from the *palazzo* a free man or under escort bound for the Castel Nuovo. Yet again he banished from his consciousness the prospect of failure and its consequences.

When, after what seemed like an hour but was less than half, Roberto returned, he looked as nervous as Niccolo felt and the reassuring smile with which he tried to cover it failed to convince. 'I've told his eminence that you will tell him whatever he wants to know; that you'll answer his questions honestly and accurately,' he said.

Niccolo nodded. 'Of course.'

Roberto looked intently into his companion's face. 'For both our sakes you won't say anything about the gown or the ring, will you?'

'Certainly not,' Niccolo replied with a slight smile.

Roberto regarded him quizzically but said nothing. He turned and led the way through two interconnecting chambers to a door at which he tapped, then opened. The *camera* which the two men now entered was small and high-ceilinged. It was also crammed with treasures. Rows of paintings occupied the walls and Niccolo was immediately reminded of Alberto Reggio's Vatican domain. At the far end, between two tall windows, stood an elaborately carved cabinet of drawers and cupboards whose fronts were inlaid with panels of different coloured marbles. In the centre was a wide, almost square, table covered with sheets of paper and it was these that the standing figure of Giuliano della Rovere was scrutinising, bending his tall frame to peer at them with the aid of a pair of eyeglasses.

He looked up immediately, his square face impassive. 'The elusive Signore Machiavelli! Are you aware how much trouble you've given everyone?'

Those were the first words Niccolo heard from the man who was to play such an important part in his life. He fell on one knee and kissed the ringed hand held out to him by the cardinal. As he stood again he found himself overpowered by della Rovere's sheer presence. The man generated power. His eyes stared unblinking from a face whose contours might have been roughly chiselled in stone. He was dressed simply in a long gown of brown trimmed with grey fur and he needed no impressive clothes in order to impress.

There was no trace of humour in his voice as he said, 'Prolonged anticipation generates increased curiosity, Signore Machiavelli. I trust you will now satisfy that curiosity fully.'

Niccolo mumbled a reply.

Della Rovere seated himself in a cushioned chair and regarded his visitors across the expanse of table. Niccolo he left standing in the centre of the room and Roberto hovered by the door. 'Now let us establish the facts as succinctly as possible. You are in the employ of the Cardinal of Valencia, are you not?'

'I was, Your Eminence – briefly – but I no longer consider myself as servant of one who has treated me so poorly.'

The cardinal nodded. 'And how did you come to be in his pay?'

Niccolo gave a truncated account of what had happened to him in Rome.

'So, the Cardinal of Valencia' – Niccolo noted that della Rovere could not bring himself to speak the name 'Borgia' – 'goes to great trouble to secure the services of an obscure young Florentine for an important assignment. Did that not strike you as odd?'

'Very, Your Eminence, but I was in no position to demur.'

'And the task assigned to you was nothing less than the assassination of a foreign prince.' It was a statement rather than a question.

'No, Your Eminence!' Niccolo put all the force he could muster into the denial. 'I would never have agreed to that.'

'But you were in no position to demur, were you? Refuse the cardinal's blood money and you would be returned to a slimy oubliette in the depths of the Castel Sant'Angelo. Most men would agree to anything rather than face that prospect.'

Niccolo steeled himself to return his interrogator's withering stare. 'Your Eminence, I freely admit that I was part – an unwitting part – of a diabolical plan. That plan, as I now know, was as devious as it was wicked.'

'But the Cardinal of Valencia had you placed in the entourage of His Highness Prince Djem, so that you could take the best opportunity to strike at our honoured guest. There was nothing devious about that.'

Niccolo hoped that della Rovere could not see the perspiration he could feel breaking out on his brow. 'The truth is that I was being used as a decoy. The Cardinal of Valencia affected to believe that the Ottoman prince was under threat from King Charles and my role was to watch for anything suspicious in his highness's camp.' Before della Rovere could interject, Niccolo hurried on: 'As we now know, it was the accursed Borgia himself who was plotting the death of Prince Djem and he used another agent; not me.'

The cardinal seemed quite unmoved but he now leaned forward, elbows on the table and hands folded beneath his chin. 'Fra Roberto has expounded his *theory* of how his highness came to his tragic end. Have you anything to add to it, Signore Machiavelli?'

'The good brother will have explained how we questioned the Ottoman vizier. He revealed the scheme to kill the prince. It was financed by the sultan and executed by the pope and his son. Their agent was the cardinal's steward, Father Manfredo Manfredi, who, by the justice of all-seeing God, has already paid the price for his crime.'

'Interesting, Signore Machiavelli.' Della

286

Rovere raised his gaze to the ceiling. 'But since, as you say, Father Manfredi is no longer available for questioning, what proof can you offer of his complicity?'

'Manfredi came to the Ottoman camp at Velletri and gave Izmet Zeybek the poison he was to administer to his master.'

'You saw this yourself?'

'Yes. I happened to enter the vizier's tent when Manfredi was there. The Turk was holding a phial of white powder the steward had just given him and I heard Manfredi say, "Be sure to wait until the cardinal has left." That night, as Your Eminence knows, the Cardinal of Valencia absconded. If his majesty were to arrest Izmet Zeybek and put him to torture he would soon discover the truth of what I am saying.'

Della Rovere was silent for several seconds and Niccolo sensed the smooth and rapid functioning of the mechanism behind the cardinal's shrewd eyes. At last he said, 'His majesty is an impatient man. I am just wondering why he should go to the trouble of seeking out this Turk when he is firmly convinced that the assassin of the prince is none other than Signore Machiavelli of Florence.'

Niccolo feigned a light laugh. 'His majesty

knows the delight with which the pope and his son would react to my arrest. It would distract attention from Manfredi and they could disclaim all responsibility. As you have said, Your Eminence, I am but an obscure young Florentine and not a trusted servant of the Borgias. Since my employment by the Cardinal of Valencia was secret they could deny any knowledge of me. I was, they would say, merely a court hanger-on. On the other hand, the truth – about Manfredi and Izmet Zeybek – would be very damaging to the Vatican – very damaging indeed.'

Della Rovere appeared abruptly to lose interest. He placed the glasses back on his nose and bent over the papers which Niccolo could now see were architectural plans and drawings. After some moments Niccolo turned to his companion with a quizzically raised eyebrow. With a frown and a raised hand, Roberto counselled patience.

'Of course, it might prove impossible,' the cardinal said quietly without looking up, 'to find this Turk. What would happen then?'

'Alas, Your Eminence, I suppose the perpetrators of this terrible crime would go unpunished.'

'Signore Machiavelli of Florence would

not consider it his solemn duty to publish what he knew?'

'He would know that his duty was to be guided by Your Eminence.'

'To speak or not speak as I directed?'

'Even so, Your Eminence.'

'Hm. Come over here, young man. What do you think of this?' He pointed to the plans before him and, as Niccolo looked at them, he explained: 'His majesty has a hunting lodge at Fontainebleau, near Paris.' He pointed to a drawing of an impressive old building. 'Being a man of taste, sensibility and breadth of vision, he is resolved to extend it into something more in keeping with his regal state. He has asked me to advise him and I have commissioned two of our best Italian architects to produce specimen plans. These' – he planted his right hand on a sheaf of papers – 'propose an edifice that is simple, elegant but perhaps lacking in sophistication. These' – he indicated the other set of plans with his left hand – 'are for a building that is elaborate, grandiose and would make his majesty the envy of Europe's rulers. But the expense! If the king chose this he might find himself unable to complete the enterprise. Tell me, Signore Machiavelli, which do you think I should recommend?'

Niccolo bent over the papers and pondered his reply carefully for several moments. 'I feel sure that his majesty would prefer the one that expresses his greatness and intelligence. He has abundantly proved himself a king who is not afraid to take risks.'

Della Rovere laid aside the eyeglasses. 'I think you are right. I had almost decided the same thing myself; you have helped me make up my mind.' He sat back in his chair and permitted himself the faintest of smiles as he looked at Niccolo. 'You may be an obscure Florentine now but I prophesy that you will not remain so – not if you learn carefully from your experiences.'

He beckoned the friar to the table. 'Fra Roberto, I mentioned earlier that I have certain despatches for Prior Girolamo Savonarola in Florence. You will stay and help me to prepare them and you will leave at first light tomorrow. I will have horses and an escort waiting for you here. You had better take Signore Machiavelli with you.' He waved a hand in dismissal at Niccolo as though he had completely lost interest in him and the reprieved young man bowed himself out of the room.

In a soft, clear dawn that gave promise of great heat to follow the gentleman and the friar rode northwards from Naples following two of the cardinal's own personal guard. It was the first opportunity they had had to talk together since the previous day's interview and Roberto was bulging with questions.

'Why didn't you tell me you'd seen Manfredi pass the poison to the Turk?' he demanded as soon as they were clear of the suburbs.

'Because I didn't,' Niccolo replied nonchalantly.

Roberto gasped. 'You lied to the cardinal! By all that's holy, do you know what a risk you took? You could have got yourself – and me – into the most appalling trouble.'

Niccolo gazed out over the soft blue of the motionless sea. 'I don't think so; I told his eminence what he wanted to hear.'

'That the Borgias organised the assassination of Prince Djem?'

'Oh, no, no!' Niccolo shook his head and smiled. 'I told his eminence that King Charles organised the assassination of Prince Djem.'

'What!' This time Roberto was so startled

that he involuntarily pulled back on the reins so hard that his mount came to a surprised halt and had to be urged forward again.

'Well, that's not strictly true. Della Rovere, of course, knew all about the prince's death, though I suspect he didn't approve of it. Too much Thersites about the French king and not enough Agamemnon.'

The friar flung back the hood from his head in a gesture of exasperation. 'Niccolo, I haven't the remotest idea what you are rambling about. Either you're mad or I am.'

'Mad?' Niccolo shuddered. 'I think I very nearly *did* go mad working out the truth. It was so complex. Not just a case of secret intrigue: plans were carefully laid; some were improvised; some were changed at the last moment.'

Roberto grimaced. 'Would an explanation be out of the question?'

Niccolo's brow wrinkled in concentration. 'There are still bits and pieces that don't fit neatly but this is the story in outline. The pope was very worried at having to entrust his son and Prince Djem to the care of King Charles. He had no choice, of course, but he believed they were in danger. Cardinal Borgia shared this concern but being a young man with overweening self-confidence he thought he could take care of himself. He made his own secret plans and they involved securing the services of someone unknown to the scores of spies and informants who lurk in all corners of the Vatican. His agents found an "obscure young Florentine" – to use Cardinal della Rovere's words – who could easily be coerced into doing his bidding. I was to perform a dual function: keeping an eye on the prince and, when the time came, masquerading as Cesare Borgia himself while he made his escape. The only other person with whom he shared his plans was his major-domo, Father Manfredi.'

'But,' Roberto objected, 'he is the one who passed the poison to Izmet Zeybek; we know that. So it must have been the Borgia...'

'That's what I thought for a long time – until I realised that Manfredi was the French king's man. Somehow, at some time, he had been bought and maintained as an agent at the very heart of the Vatican.'

'But that's ridiculous! Charles killed Manfredi – personally. You saw it yourself.'

'Yes, the little priest was cruelly rewarded for his service. It was remembering that

scene accurately that confirmed my suspicions – but I'll come to that later.
Naturally, Manfredi reported back to his
master my appearance on the scene and this
brought about an impromptu change in the
Valois's plans. He realised that I provided a
perfect scapegoat. He could still use his paid
accomplices – Manfredi and Zeybek – to
murder the prince but now he could load
the blame onto the man Cesare Borgia had
insinuated into the Ottoman camp. He put
the first phase of his new scheme into
operation as soon as we reached Velletri. It
was all hurried and there was no time for
meticulous organisation. Manfredi was sent
to Zeybek with the poison. I didn't see him
hand it over but I was there when he sidled
out of the vizier's tent and I'm quite sure
that's what he was doing – and also telling
the Turk how to implicate me in Cesare
Borgia's escape, because at the same time
the cardinal was panicked into flight; probably Manfredi told him some story of an
imminent attempt on his life.

'All this led up to that extraordinary
display in the marketplace at Velletri. Like
you, I could make no sense of that very
public execution of royal wrath – especially
as Charles had already heard of the flight of

Alfonso from Naples, which put him in a very good mood.'

Roberto, who was listening to all this with a sceptical frown, observed, 'The king is of a changeable nature.'

'True, yet I couldn't get out of my head that what I saw at Velletri was a *performance*. What was it meant to impress on the audience?' Niccolo answered his own question. 'That Borgia had planned his escape before leaving Rome; that his fake baggage of empty chests and bales was proof of this; and that Manfredi was the principal agent in the deception.

'When Lorenzo de'Medici ruled Florence leading citizens were sometimes invited to his court for theatrical spectacles. They were very impressive affairs – gorgeous costumes, painted scenery and bombastic speeches. We were all stirred by them. It was only on reflecting afterwards that one realised how absurd they were. That was how I felt about the Velletri affair – more theatre than drama.'

'That was why you were excited to discover some of Cardinal Borgia's possessions among the dead guardsman's effects.'

'That was the proof – the hard, tangible proof – of what I already suspected. The

Borgia apartments *had* been plundered and the loot shared out by the king with members of the royal guard. That's exactly what one would have expected.'

'Why were you suspicious before that?' Roberto asked.

'First of all, because I didn't think Manfredi was stupid. If he had aided Cesare Borgia's escape and been a prime mover in an escapade that made the French king look ridiculous he would not have stayed around to face Charles's anger. He would surely have fled with the cardinal. That was a basic flaw in the plot and it kept on nagging at my brain. I felt sure that there was also something wrong in the staging. It wasn't until yesterday that I realised what it was: the sword.'

Roberto shook his head. 'Sword? What sword?'

'The sword King Charles used to hack poor Manfredi's neck. It was a heavy, two-handed weapon, not at all like the lighter blade he always carries. It wasn't even like the arms issued to his personal guard. But it *was* like the headsman's sword favoured by French executioners. The audience at Velletri were meant to believe that Charles killed the priest in a sudden burst of anger.

In fact, the act was planned and the appropriate props ready to hand.'

'But *why?*' Roberto almost shouted. 'Why kill his own agent?'

'It may have been sheer brutality. Manfredi was the only person who could link Charles to the plot against Djem and the king decided to make sure he could never tell what he knew. A spy who had turned his coat once might do it again. But there is another possibility: Manfredi may have told his patron that I had seen him in the Ottoman camp. That would certainly have alarmed Charles and sealed the priest's fate. Whatever the details, the fact is that with Manfredi out of the way the king could feel safe. The assassination of Prince Djem could go ahead. I would be arrested and swiftly executed. And all the blame would be laid at the door of the perfidious Borgias.'

'And then you escaped.'

'Yes and that created problems for Charles: how much did I know and what use would I make of what I knew if I were not recaptured? On the other hand, my predicament was just as bad: I was a fugitive and a branded assassin. The situation was what chess players call "stalemate" – it means that neither opponent can win and the game must be abandoned. I could see this – but could the king?'

'I don't imagine Charles Valois is the sort of man who plays chess.'

'No, but Giuliano della Rovere is. He is the brains behind Charles's brawn. But what was he thinking? Could I trust myself to him? You know how reluctant I was to walk into the cardinal's *palazzo* with no guarantee of coming safely out.'

'I told you that his eminence would give you a fair hearing,' Roberto protested.

Niccolo laughed. 'My friend, you have rendered me many services but convincing me of della Rovere's disinterested quest for truth is not among them. You created the circumstances in which the cardinal would listen carefully to what I had to say and decide how best he could use the information. You also showed me the wretched existence to which I could well be doomed if I did not take the risk of reaching some sort of accommodation with your patron. But right up to almost the last moment I did not know really what I would say to the cardinal or how I would say it.'

'I could see how anxious you were,' Roberto recollected. 'I was scarcely less so myself. Then, suddenly, after we left the Franciscan house, your mood changed. You were muttering something about "Thersites and Agamemnon" and you could scarcely get to the *palazzo* fast enough.'

Niccolo breathed deeply the soft morning air and luxuriated in the feel of the sun on his back – the back of a free man. 'There's nothing new in the world,' he said. 'History repeats itself over and again. Philip of Macedon was a conqueror and a tyrant who overran the whole of Greece. He was a by-word for cruelty and treated his vanquished foes with contempt until one day, when an Athenian confronted him bravely with these words: "Why do you, O King, act the part of a Thersites, when you could represent the elevated and dignified character of an Agamemnon.' He was referring to the Trojan War, and the contrast between the magnanimous Agamemnon and one of his captains who brought dishonour to the Greek cause by his needlessly vindictive behaviour. There is a parallel here with our conqueror. Charles makes himself more unpopular every day by his merciless exercise of power. I could not believe that della Rovere approved the king's impolitic behaviour. I thought that if I could show him that the king had nothing to gain from relentless pursuit of an innocent scapegoat he might counsel a more intelligent course of action. That, at least, was my only hope.'

'And that was why you put the blame on the Borgias even though you knew they were guiltless of this particular crime.'

'What I told his eminence was that I knew how Prince Djem was murdered, that I knew who was responsible for that murder, that it would be possible to spread the story of Borgia culpability and that I would never reveal what I knew without his eminence's approval. I hinted that a truce would be better for the king's already damaged image than his continued persecution of an innocent man. Fortunately he agreed.'

After a long silence Roberto said, 'I see how right his eminence was. He remarked after you had left yesterday that you had an extremely sharp mind and would go far in the service of some prince.'

Niccolo laughed. 'Well, in that at least he was wrong. I am too lazy to seek public fame. I would never have worked out the truth if my life had not been in danger. And now I go to Florence determined on returning to the obscurity whence I came. I have had more than enough of state politics to last me a lifetime.'

Was the young ingenue seeking to persuade himself or fortune? Either way, one thing is clear: the fates were laughing.

XIV

Such, then, is the truth about what really befell the sultan of Turkey's brother. Within days of the events I have just recorded it was given out by the king of Naples that his physicians had minutely examined the body and concluded unanimously that Prince Djem had died of a quotidian fever. Guided by Cardinal della Rovere, Charles had come to realise that attempting to fix the blame on Borgia agents would only keep the issue alive and encourage the sceptical to speculate. Official statements, of course, never stifle men's fascination with conspiracy theories and over the years questions have sometimes been asked about what really happened on the road from Rome to Naples in the early months of 1495. Well, now you know.

As for young Niccolo, who had so narrowly escaped death in his first embroilment with interstate politics, he craved peace with an ardour more common in men twice his age. But, as is her wont, she eluded him. She was not to be found within, nor in the spring country of budding vines, dusty roads and village walls throbbing with reflected heat. Certainly, she did not stand with welcoming arms on the banks of the Arno as the reluctant wanderer came within sight of home.

The relationship between Niccolo and Roberto was an unconventional one. It would not be accurate to call them friends and yet the remarkable adventures they had shared had created between them a bond akin to friendship. During the ride from Naples each learned much about the other as they shared personal experiences, ideas and ideals. However, conversation became gradually sparser as the companions neared Florence. On the last afternoon it ceased entirely. Niccolo was a tournay of conflicting emotions. The first glimpse of the city's towers and cupolas through the haze of an unseasonably hot April day sent a thrill of joy and pride through him, and this did not diminish as the riders put the heights of Certosa behind them and joined the cavalcade of horsemen, pedestrians, carts and carriages making their way into the city. Niccolo ached for familiar sights and sounds. Not just the magnificent and the beautiful attractions of which Florentines justly boast – the great competing *palazzi* along Via Tornabuoni, the white and green marble baptistry, the wide, paved Piazza della Signoria where the citizenry assembled for occasions grave and gay – but the everyday features of life in Florence, familiar only to its inhabitants – the cracked bell of Santa Trinità, Marco Conti's packed tavern across the square from the Palazzo della Signoria, the one-eyed vintner on the Ponte Vecchio whose idea of selling his wares was to yell ripe abuse at potential customers who failed to stop at his stall.

He longed above all for the dear faces of family and friends. But how would they receive the Niccolo who had left them so abruptly five months ago and disappeared? Five months? Dear God, it seemed more like five years. He knew how much he had changed in that time. Even if loved ones welcomed and supported him there could be no slipping back into the old life. For there was no Baccia. He had failed her. Her killer was still walking the earth a free man and here was her husband happy at the prospect of returning home to carry on living in Florence – her Florence. There were times when he had an overwhelming desire to turn away his horse's head from the painful memories that lay ahead; away from the restless spirit of Baccia, which would be rustling in every shadow; waiting for him in every place where they had shared happiness and love.

Beside the Franciscan church of San Salvatore al Monte the little group reined in their horses. Before and below them in the greying afternoon lay the city, huddled within its ancient walls, its two parts linked across the river by its four bridges and by the ferry that plied downstream beyond the weir.

It was Fra Roberto who broke the long silence. 'Niccolo, don't let the past become an anchor or a drag chain.'

Niccolo sighed deeply. 'She has a right to be avenged and I no right to deny her.'

'Do you not believe that your lady's murderer will be punished and with a torment far more horrible than you can inflict?'

Niccolo urged his mount down the winding hill towards the Porta San Miniato. 'I don't know what God will do. Who does? I know only that I must find this violator, confront him, see the terror in his eyes when he knows he is about to pay for his vile sin and then send him to the greater judgement the Church boasts about. Do you find that so difficult to understand?'

Roberto considered. 'To understand? No. To condone? Yes. It is my duty to remind you that vengeance belongs to God. I have certainly never known any good come to anyone obsessed by a lust for revenge.'

'Well, now that you've done your duty perhaps we can continue in silence.' Niccolo stared fixedly ahead down the road.

'How do you propose to go about your investigation?' his companion persisted. 'Memories become blurred over time. No one will be able to tell you much now.'

They went into single file to pass a cart with a broken wheel whose cargo was being laboriously unloaded so that it could be repaired. Roberto found himself talking to a hunched and unresponsive back. 'One thing you can be sure of: your culprit is not a Dominican. You do realise that, don't you?'

Again there was no reply. 'It is absolutely forbidden for any of our order to expose himself to the temptation of lust and that certainly includes being alone with a lady in her chamber.'

'It has been known.' Niccolo could not resist the cynical jibe.

'Very rarely,' Roberto declared defensively, 'and usually when the brother in question has been seduced.'

'Absolute nonsense,' Niccolo retorted. 'And Baccia would never have invited an unknown friar to her room.'

'Exactly. So we can discount that possibility. Whoever wormed his way into your house was masquerading as a black friar.'

'I had managed to work out that possibility myself,' Niccolo retorted.

'And have you, then, made a list of likely suspects? Whoever it was must have been driven by intense hatred for you and your wife, and I assume you haven't made all that many bitter enemies.'

Niccolo turned as Fra Roberto drew alongside once more. 'A moment ago you were catechising me about the sin of vengeance. Now you're counselling me how to go about it.'

'I have a very vivid memory of finding myself at the wrong end of your poniard and only saving you from a mortal sin by some very fast talking. I wouldn't want you to blunder into another hotheaded mistake.'

'Well, you needn't trouble yourself about that. I know exactly how I am going to track down the assassin.'

It was a lie; the proud and confused young fool had only the haziest of ideas of what he was going to do now that the time for action had come. As for suspects, he had not, despite Roberto's reasoning, rejected the idea of a renegade Dominican. Beyond that the only name that occurred to him was Doffo Spini. He had often recalled his lucky escape from the leader of the Compagnacci and Spini's vow to get even 'when you least expect'.

The light had begun to fade when Niccolo, shouldering his few belongings wrapped in a bundle, walked slowly along the Via del Proconsolo. He had said goodbye to Fra Roberto and left his horse with the mounted escort. There were few people about and none cast a curious glance in his direction. He might have been invisible. Perhaps, he thought, it would be better if he were. He could then go, undetected, to the little house near the far end of the street – the house still leased in his name, though what might have become of it in his absence he knew not – could watch and listen to the servants, the neighbours, to his friends if they still called, and discover what they said about him. Then he could either reveal himself or slip quietly away. Apprehension dragged at his heels but at last he stood before the arched portal with its green-painted door. The latch which he had meant to have fixed was still loose. He unfastened it and pushed.

He caught his breath and stood as though rooted to the threshold. The lamps were already lit and the room was exactly as he remembered it. The mingled smells of beeswax and floor herbs was painfully familiar. A fire burned in the hearth and a chair – his chair – was drawn up in front of it, its back to the door. Someone was seated in it and after a few moments the someone called out sharply, 'Timeo, you worthless lout, shut the door. Do you want to give me an ague?'

Recognising the voice, Niccolo rushed forward. 'Totto!'

His brother leaped from the chair as though prodded. He stood facing Niccolo, his mouth opening and closing but no sound coming.

Niccolo hurried to embrace him, laughing. 'No, Totto, it's not a ghost. It's really me.' He felt the tremors vibrating through his sibling's body.

'But how...?' Totto gasped into speech. 'I

thought ... we thought ... Timeo came back and said you'd been taken by the Inquisition. We both hurried to Rome ... but we could find no trace... No one would tell us anything.' He stood back. 'How are you? You look well... Not like a man fresh from the torture chamber.'

'Oh, Totto, it's a long story and one you'll find hard to believe. I can scarce credit it myself. But that can wait till later. How are you and our parents, and Paolo and Francesco? Is he still hanging on the mad friar's every word? I see you're keeping an eye on this house.' Niccolo looked round approvingly at the familiar room.

Totto gazed sheepishly at his feet. 'The Vernaccis pestered me to take on the lease and when you didn't come back... Of course, I'll find somewhere else now that you're here. I'm sorry ... I don't want you to think...'

'Dear Totto, there's nothing to be sorry about. I'm glad you were able to make use of the house.'

A sudden silence fell between them; the sort of silence that occurs when two people have much to say and neither knows how to start.

It was broken by the arrival of Timeo who,

on seeing his master, broke into a tearful frenzy of joy, dropping to his knees, grasping Niccolo's hand and kissing it over and again while babbling incoherent self-condemnation about deserting him in Rome. Detaching himself at last, he hurried into the back premise to tell the other servants. They, too, had to come in to shriek their excited welcomes. Then a neighbour looked in at the open street door to see what the commotion was about and immediately added to it. He rushed off to spread the news and within minutes the little house was overflowing with people, crowding in to shake Niccolo's hand, slap him on the back and kiss him.

It was a couple of hours before Niccolo was able to escape with Totto, Francesco, Paolo and a couple of other friends to Marco Conti's tavern. There, wedged into a corner of the crowded hostelry, consuming pasta, Signora Conti's famed poultry pie and several celebratory rounds of wine, his astonished companions listened to the adventures of their returned Aeneas.

'And now, my friends,' Niccolo asked when he had, at last, satisfied all their questions, 'what of you – and Florence?' He turned to Francesco. 'What has your ugly little Dominican been up to in my absence, Francey?'

Paolo Valori, slightly drunk, giggled. 'You mustn't call him "Francey", Nicco. It's "Consigliere Bardi" now.'

Everyone laughed as the stocky Francesco reached across the table to punch his friend playfully in the chest.

It was Totto who explained lugubriously: 'Florence is now a republic with an uncrowned king. Prior Savonarola has handed down to us a new – divinely ordained – constitution. There is a Great Council made up of all the *beneficiati* over the age of twenty-nine and that includes our exalted friend, Signore Bardi, since he was able to find in his recent ancestry someone who had been a magistrate.'

'And about three thousand others,' Francesco added. 'Prior Savonarola has created a true republic in which all responsible citizens have a voice. There are so many on the Maggior Consiglio that he is having a new hall built for our meetings.'

Niccolo frowned sceptically. 'That sounds to me like a recipe for chaos and interminable argument.'

'Ah, but the Great Council don't debate; they just vote on issues and elect the

Ottanta, the Council of Eighty, who make most of the executive decisions,' Francesco explained enthusiastically.

Niccolo was not convinced. 'According to Plato…'

There was an alarmed outcry around the table. 'Hush!' Paolo whispered. 'Don't even mention the name. Florence is a godly, Christian commonwealth; there is no room here for the old authors. Their books are confiscated whenever the prior's men can find them.'

'Don't worry,' Totto said in response to Niccolo's obvious alarm. 'No one will discover your library; I've destroyed it.'

'You've what!'

Totto was not shaken by his brother's look of pain and outrage. 'I didn't think you were coming back and I didn't want anyone to discover incriminating books in the house, so I put them in a sack with a large stone and threw them in the Arno late one night.'

Niccolo gaped at this shocking revelation. 'Has Florence gone mad?'

'Aye,' Francesco said, a radiant smile across his wide features, 'with a divine madness. The city is being purified. We were all chastened by the coming of the French king. It proved that Savonarola was right and that we all needed to repent. Holiness has swept through Florence like a cleansing fire. There is a citywide fast twice a week. Crowds of people attend sermons at the Duomo and try to amend their lives. The whores – "meat with eyes" Savonarola calls them – keep within doors – those who have not taken the veil. Bands of children – "Savonarola's Angels" – roam the streets singing hymns and urging the proud and overdressed to emulate their simplicity and innocence.'

Niccolo listened with mounting dismay as the transformation of Florence was described to him: ancient festivals and public games cancelled, extravagant fashions forbidden, balladeers forced to clean up their ribald wares, pious citizens hastening to throw out gaming boards, cosmetics, lewd pictures and other such 'devices of Satan'. He reflected on the corruption that fouled Christian Rome and the fanaticism that gripped Christian Florence, and wondered why human affairs had to be dogged by such religious extremes.

Eventually the conversation drifted to the future. When Niccolo's friends asked what his plans were he said that his first priority was to search for his wife's killer. The company fell silent until Paolo gave voice to what Niccolo suspected his companions were thinking.

'Better to let it rest, Nicco. Look for another bride. There are many fathers who would be happy to bestow their daughters on you.'

Niccolo looked around at the circle of faces – all sympathetic, all displaying nothing but concern for his welfare. 'That's easy counsel to give, Paolo, but would you, or any of you, feel the same if it was your wife or sister who had been violated and slaughtered?'

No one answered and it was eventually Totto who asked, 'Where will you start, Nicco? Have you any ideas where to look?'

Niccolo had to admit that all he could do was make guesses. 'I do have a few enemies – Doffo Spini for one.'

'He's in Venice,' Francesco said. 'He fled there with his master, Piero de'Medici.'

'When was that?' Niccolo demanded urgently.

Francesco shrugged. 'About the time that the French arrived.'

'Yes, but before or after?' Niccolo insisted. 'It's crucial. Baccia was killed that very day. If Spini was still here, he or his minions probably carried out the murder before he left. He'd promised to revenge himself on me and that was his last chance.'

One of the company said, 'I don't think he waited long after the people turned against the Medicis. According to mariners, when a ship is stricken the first occupants to be aware of danger and leap overboard are the rats. It's the same with politics.'

Niccolo clung desperately to his only lead. 'It should be possible to find out exactly when Spini left and whether any of his henchmen stayed behind.'

'I suppose I could make a few enquiries,' Francesco offered.

'Be a friend and do that,' Niccolo urged. 'And all of you.' He looked around the table. 'I beg you, if you remember anything about that day that might be of any help, please tell me.' When there was no immediate response, he went on. 'It seems that all we know definitely is that some man, dressed in a black habit, was seen leaving my house about the time Baccia was killed.'

'Or woman.'

Everyone stared at Totto who quietly made the suggestion.

'What do you mean?' Niccolo demanded.

The stern-faced elder brother explained in

an expressionless monotone: 'Baccia and her cousin Bianca were planning a little surprise. Knowing how you felt about Savonarola and Fra Roberto they had decided to perform a short play, a burlesque making fun of the black friars. They went to your house that afternoon to rehearse their performance and try on their costumes.'

'No one else knew about it except Totto and me,' Francesco added.

Niccolo was stunned by this revelation. 'Totto, why in heaven's name didn't you tell me this before?'

'I tried, Nicco. I really tried. But you were in no mood to listen. You went rushing off to St Mark's, convinced that one of Savonarola's men was guilty. In your state of blind grief and fury no one could have stopped you.'

Niccolo weighed his brothers words. He cast his mind back to the dinner at the Vernaccis' – the last occasion on which he had seen his wife alive. There she was again, laughing and sharing whispered secrets with her cousin. Now he knew what it was that she was so amused about. And if it had been Bianca in Baccia's chamber that afternoon that explained what had always been a puzzle: why his wife had admitted someone in a black habit. But if this explanation answered some questions it raised others. 'Where did the habits come from?' he asked.

Totto lowered his eyes and his voice. 'I stole them.'

'You?' Niccolo stared in disbelief at his staid brother.

'Well, not exactly me. I paid a couple of boys to take them from the washing line at the convent.'

'So, the two women were in Baccia's room that afternoon trying on the costumes.' He endeavoured to picture the scene. 'And you think Bianca left in hers.'

Totto shrugged. 'I just suggest it as a possibility.'

'But you're not seriously suggesting that Bianca murdered her cousin?'

Totto looked shocked. 'No, of course not. But she may have seen something or someone. Perhaps there was a man outside, waiting until Baccia was alone in the house.'

'Yes, Totto, I see what you mean. If he had been following the women he would have known that the servants were away watching the French army and enjoying a holiday.'

'Isn't there another possibility?' Paolo suggested. 'If the assassin surprised Baccia

removing her habit it would have been easy
for him to throw it on over his own clothes
after he had killed her. There was a disguise
waiting ready to hand.'

Francesco added, 'That would have been
an amazing stroke of good fortune.'

Niccolo smiled. 'You have no idea how
good it is to be back among friends. I thank
you all for your support and your under-
standing. You've given me at least a glimmer
of hope that I can find out what happened
to my wife and put her tragedy behind me.
I must go and talk with Bianca tomorrow
and I hope that if any of you think of
anything else that may help you'll come and
tell me.'

'But not tonight,' Francesco called out,
slamming his beaker down on the table.
'Tonight we're celebrating and that means –
more wine!'

Niccolo woke late and with a thick head. It
took him several moments to realise where
he was and to remember why he was there.
Hazily he recalled being brought back to his
own home by Totto and Francesco, and
being helped up to his chamber. His brother
had insisted on Niccolo's taking the great
bed while he slept on a truckle bed by the

wall. Raising himself on one elbow he glanced across the room, dimly lit by the sunlight that filtered through chinks in the shutters. Totto was still sleeping soundly.

Gingerly Niccolo swung his feet over the edge of the bed, stumbled across to the window and threw wide the shutters. The dazzle of mid-morning light attacked his eyes and he hastened to a table where a bowl of water lay ready. He splashed his face, then took deep breaths of the fresh air tumbling in at the casement. He turned back into the room and saw Totto sitting up and stretching his arms.

'What time is it?' the elder brother asked.

'It must be at least ten o'clock.'

Totto yawned and struggled from the blankets. He walked unsteadily to the door. 'I'll make sure Timeo has breakfast ready.'

Half an hour later, washed and shaved, and with bread and cheese and raisins filling his stomach, Niccolo felt able to face the demands of the day.

He looked at his brother across the table. 'Totto, I'm sorry I got angry last night about my books. I realise that you couldn't risk them being found here.'

Totto's long face assumed its usual drear aspect. 'I'm sorry I had to do it. I know how much they meant to you. If I'd realised you were coming back I would have hidden them or taken them up to the farm.'

'It was very useful hearing about what Baccia and her cousin were planning. I really believe I may be able to find out the truth.'

That was the moment when the door opened to reveal a flustered Francesco.

The stout man staggered to the table and planted himself on a stool. 'Nicco, Totto,' he muttered as he regained his breath. 'Terrible news: Signora Mantini – Bianca Mantini, your cousin by marriage – has just been pulled out of the Arno. Early this morning she threw herself from a window of one of the shops on the Ponte Vecchio.'

XV

The impressive Mantini house in the Borgo Santi Apostoli was crowded with mourning family and friends. Several women kept up a wailing lamentation around the body of Bianca Mantini, which had been laid on a table in the main *salone*. Working his way through the throng, Niccolo gazed down upon the still young woman. All colour seemed to have been washed from her well-fleshed features by the water, which still dripped from her skirts where they trailed over the table's edge, to form a widening pool on the stone floor. Sudden anger grew within him at the sight of Baccia's best friend struck down by violent tragedy. Anger at the intrusion of death into a happy household. Anger at the vivid memory of his own wife lying thus, her life harshly extinguished. Anger because something about Bianca's sudden drowning was very wrong.

With Totto and Francesco he joined the queue of people waiting to offer their condolences to Bernardo Mantini, who stood in a corner of the room, his two small sons clinging to his legs. The widower was a tall, erect man, considerably older than Bianca, his long black hair already striated with grey.

He received Niccolo's words of sympathy with dignified gratitude. 'It's so good to see you again, Nicco,' he said. 'We heard of your return last night and Bianca was particularly excited by the news. She told me she had something to say to you but' – he shrugged – 'I don't know what it was. Her feelings about Baccia's death probably. She was very upset by that.'

Outside in the sunlit street Niccolo leaned against the wall, sunk in mournful thought.

'Poor Nicco.' Francesco clapped a hand to his shoulder. 'What a miserable home-coming.'

'Why, Francey, why?' Niccolo almost shouted the word. 'Was she melancholy of late? Had she any reason to take her own life?'

'She was deeply upset by Baccia's death,' Francesco replied. 'She would scarcely go out for weeks. But I thought she recovered herself eventually.'

Totto, who had joined them, suggested,

'Perhaps your return brought back the memory so forcefully that she couldn't bear it.'

Niccolo shook his head. 'Bernardo says she was looking forward to seeing me and had something to tell me.'

'Well,' Francesco said, 'whatever it was, it must have weighed on her mind. Perhaps she felt in some way guilty about poor Baccia.'

Niccolo looked at him in alarm. 'Francey, you're not suggesting that Bianca...'

'No, no, no, not that. But if she was the last person to see Baccia alive before the murderer and she left her alone in the house she might have felt that Baccia's death was somehow her fault.'

Totto agreed. 'If that's what she wanted to tell you, and if she lay awake all night thinking about it and eventually decided she couldn't face you...'

'But this is all guesswork,' Niccolo protested. 'For all we know she might have had something important to say about Baccia's death. She might even have seen the murderer.'

'Well, as you observe, Nicco, it's all guesswork. We shall never know what was so much weighing down poor Bianca.' Totto wore his most mournful expression.

'There's nothing more we can do here,' Francesco added. 'Let's go and have a drink.'

Niccolo shook his head. 'You go on. There's something I have to do here.'

After the others had reluctantly taken their leave, Niccolo went back into the house. He passed through the ground-floor rooms and reached the courtyard at the rear of the house before he found the people he was looking for – the Mantini servants. There were six of them, standing in a solemn group and saying little.

Niccolo questioned them closely about their late mistress. Servants, of course, always know more about their betters than their betters know about themselves and in the space of an hour Niccolo had learned a great deal about the life of the Mantini household. The signora had been utterly distraught at her cousin's death. She had been with her on the afternoon of her murder and had left her in high spirits. Bianca's maid was surprised when Niccolo asked her what her mistress was wearing that day but she described in detail a gown of red brocade with yellow sleeves. The same girl remembered the shock with which her mistress received the news of Signora Machiavelli's death. 'Poor Baccia,' she had muttered over and over again. 'I should have gone back. I should have warned her.' But to the question 'Warned her about what?' the maid had no answer.

All the servants confirmed that Signora Mantini had taken a very long time to recover from her cousin's death. She had been inconsolable. Was it true, Niccolo asked, that she had been too sorrowful to go out? Certainly the mistress had seldom left the house, the steward confirmed, but that was because she was afraid, not sad. 'Afraid of what or whom?' Niccolo demanded, but the man only shrugged in response.

When the conversation came round to the events of the last few hours Niccolo had to contend with the wails and tears of the female staff but eventually the story emerged. It was the maid who passed on to her mistress the news of Signore Machiavelli's return as she was preparing her for bed the night before. She was terribly excited. 'Oh, Maria,' she exclaimed, 'are you sure? Has he truly come back at last? I must go to him tomorrow. He will know what to do.'

'And that's all she said?' Niccolo demanded urgently. 'No details about what she wanted to tell me. Think, girl. Think!'

But at that Maria howled and fell into the arms of the cook who scowled at Signore Machiavelli for upsetting her so.

There was little more the servants could tell him. Their mistress had gone out early to the shops. It was her custom to do this twice a week to seek out the freshest produce in the markets – a habit which rankled with the steward since it seemed to cast doubt on his ability. Her route always took her to certain stalls on the nearby Ponte Vecchio, where tradesmen sometimes set aside their best comestibles for her, before heading for the large Mercato Vecchio. It was from the window of one of those bridge marketeers that someone had seen her leap or fall. The alarm had been raised immediately. Boatmen had pushed off from the bank but the current, swollen with spring rain, was running swiftly and, although air trapped in Signora Mantini's clothing had kept her partially afloat and she had been recovered from the water close by the Porte alla Carraia, she was already dead.

Niccolo thanked his informant and ran to the Ponte Vecchio. Several half-formed thoughts were stumbling around in his head like men in a darkened room but he had no time to bring them into the light for close scrutiny. It took him little time to discover the tradesman from whose premises Bianca had plunged into the Arno. He was a swarthy purveyor of spices and perfumes, a hefty brute of a man who, rather incongruously, was delicately arranging his little phials and pots and packets as Niccolo approached.

'And what's the signore's pleasure today?' the merchant enquired with a well-practised, subservient smile.

'My pleasure is to know about the lady who met her tragic end from your inner room this morning.'

The smile vanished. 'If a crazy woman chooses to throw herself in the water from my shop it's none of my business.' He turned his back ostentatiously.

'I believe Signora Mantini was a good customer of yours.'

The man did not turn round. 'She bought from me occasionally. All the ladies and gentlemen of discernment in Florence come to me for quality goods. They know I stock only the best.'

'How was it that Signora Mantini went

into your premises?'

The big man now faced Niccolo, hands on hips, his face reddening. 'What business is that of yours? I was out here when it happened. There's lots of folk around who will testify to that.'

'Calm yourself, man. I'm not accusing you of anything. I'm a friend of the family and the signora's distraught husband, not unnaturally, wants to know whatever there is to know about his wife's sudden death. Was she quite alone when it happened?'

'Quite alone.' The man nodded emphatically. 'I invited her to examine a newly arrived consignment of pepper. She went through to the back while I served another customer. When I went in minutes later there was no sign of her.'

'May I look?'

The shopkeeper waved Niccolo towards the doorway behind him. In the small chamber beyond, the air was heavy with the mingling scents of cloves, cinnamon, aromatic oils and several other pungent substances. Sacks and chests were neatly stacked around the walls and labelled. Two steps took Niccolo to the uncovered window. He noted that the sill was above waist height. It would not have been easy for

329

a woman in a heavy, wide-skirted dress to climb upon it.

'Satisfied?' The proprietor entered the room behind him.

'And you're absolutely certain there was no one else in here with her?' Niccolo watched closely for the man's reaction to the question.

'Absolutely,' he said firmly, but his eyelids flickered and he looked away as he spoke.

On the spur of the moment Niccolo decided on a wild gamble. 'So how do you explain the Dominican friar who was seen leaving this room after Signora Mantini entered?'

The merchant took a step back as though the question had become incarnate and punched his ample midriff. 'Who are you?' he demanded and swore vehemently.

'A member of the Ottanta which, as you know, has the power to close you down if you don't answer my question truthfully.'

The man crumpled almost visibly. He looked around nervously, as though hidden eavesdroppers might be concealed behind the sacks. 'Look, there's not much I can tell you, Consiglieri. He said he was from St Mark's and that he wanted a few words in private with Signora Mantini. How could I refuse one of Prior Savonarola's men? He could have made life very difficult for me.'

'Had you seen this friar before?'

'No, Consiglieri.'

'So, you let him use these premises for his assignation. You're in the habit of aiding affairs between holy men and married women? Prior Savonarola will certainly be interested to know about that.'

'Never, Consiglieri. Never!' The big man was very worried now. 'I've never had such a request before. You must believe me.'

'Well, perhaps I will – for the moment. So you let this renegade black friar in here and when Signora Mantini came along you found some pretence to lure her in?'

'I told you the truth about that. The lady wanted some pepper and I invited her in to examine my stock for herself.'

'Did you hear any sounds of a struggle? Did the signora cry out?'

'No, Consiglieri, not a sound, as God's my judge.'

'Yet you must have been alarmed when the friar emerged and the lady did not.'

'Alarmed? Of course I was alarmed. I came in here to see if she'd fainted or taken some injury. When I saw that she wasn't here... Well, Consiglieri, I went all weak at the knees. I didn't know what to do.'

'So you did nothing?'

'I was still wondering what action to take when people started shouting that a woman had thrown herself into the water. So, yes, I decided to keep quiet. I wasn't going to go upsetting any of Savonarola's brood.'

'Would you recognise this friar again?'

The man thought for a moment. 'Well, Consiglieri, he had his hood up but … yes, I'd know him again.'

'Then, if I bring him here you will identify him, or I'll have you before the Ottanta within hours.'

'Yes, Consiglieri, of course. Whatever you say.'

Niccolo began walking. He had no direction or destination in mind. He simply needed to think and the steady rhythm of his footfalls seemed to help. What had he discovered and was any of it of any use? Since it was not Bianca who had left her cousin's chamber masquerading as a Dominican it must have been the murderer who did so. Whoever killed Bianca used the same disguise. Obviously the two per-petrators were one and the same. Bianca had clearly been silenced because she knew something about the first crime, something which she was, apparently, intent on revealing to her cousin's widower. What she knew frightened her so much that she scarce dared leave her house. Who was it who walked the streets of Florence habited as a friar? One of Spini's men ordered to seek out his master's enemies? Or a madman who, having cast aside his robes, might be making his way along this very street?

Of all the questions that beat upon his consciousness seeking answers there was one which, though trifling in itself, worried him more than the rest. Without his volition that question directed his feet to where the answer lay. He found himself striding northwards past the quarter where the houses thinned out and the impressive bulk of St Mark's priory loomed before him.

At the gate he asked for Fra Roberto. He had to wait an hour before his friend was released from his duties to receive him in the cloister. After an exchange of pleasantries Niccolo explained why he had come.

Roberto gave a surprised laugh. 'Yes, I supposed I can check that for you but why ever should it interest you?'

'Just humour me,' was all the reply Niccolo offered.

Roberto went away and returned a few

minutes later with the answer to Niccolo's query. 'Was that what you wanted to know?' he asked as the two of them walked round the colonnaded perimeter.

Niccolo sighed deeply. 'It was what I didn't want to know. But perhaps I'm wrong.'

Roberto laid a sympathetic hand on Niccolo's shoulder. 'What's troubling you?'

'I need you to help me think, Brother. In Naples it was a great help to be able to talk things over with you. You enabled me to see through false appearances to the truth beneath.'

'I don't recall that I contributed much to solving the business of Prince Djem's death.'

'Oh, but you did; you really did. Just by listening and raising objections and asking questions you helped me to reconcile apparent impossibilities. Will you do the same for me now?'

Roberto smiled. 'If it's an ear you need, try me.'

Niccolo went over what he had learned about the circumstances surrounding Baccia's death and then went on to describe what had befallen Bianca. Where the ambulatory took another right-angled turn he stopped and faced his companion squarely. 'Roberto, I must ask you this and I beg you to answer as honestly as you can. Is there anyone sheltering here, in this cloister, who would be capable of such things? Some madman whose celibacy covers a hatred of women? Someone who genuinely believes that the daughters of Eve are the devil's whores set among men to seduce them from the path of holiness?'

The friar returned his gaze. 'Is that your way of pressing me for a confession? Because I once, in a moment of misplaced zeal, remonstrated with your wife and her cousin...'

'No, no!' Niccolo shook his head firmly. 'I've long since ruled you out, as you know. But if one of the brothers here' – he lowered his voice – 'can be guilty of "misplaced zeal", why not others? Your prior's holy enthusiasm is obviously highly infectious. Florence, as I hear, is in a state of pious frenzy. Men are capable of the most obscene devilries in the name of God. As a recent guest of the Inquisition, you know that better than most.'

Roberto raised a faint smile. 'Niccolo, you won't find your murderer here and I don't believe that you really came looking for him.

Back in Naples you were angry because someone was trying to make the details about the prince's death point towards you. Aren't you, now, attempting to do the same thing with these murders; make the facts fit some person you want to believe guilty?'

'Of course not. I'm only interested in the truth.'

'Are you? Then let's go over things again.' He drew Niccolo to the door of one of the empty guest chambers. 'We can talk in here without having to whisper.'

The following afternoon Niccolo entertained a small group of friends in the little garden behind the house on the Via del Proconsolo. For Paolo, Totto and Francesco it seemed like a return to familiar, happier days. Fra Roberto and Bianca's brother, Stephano Vernacci, were not *habitués* of the little Machiavellian 'academy' but they fitted in well and the conversation flowed freely.

Not that there was a spirit of gay camaraderie under the sparse canopy of fresh green vine leaves; the subject uppermost in everyone's mind did not permit levity.

Niccolo gave every appearance of being a

model, attentive host, ensuring that his guests' cups were kept filled but inside he was harrowed with an anxiety close to nausea. When he felt that the right moment had arrived he sat upon the wall around the well and delivered himself of a prepared speech. 'Friends, when the wise men of the Roman senate met to decide the fate of the state, in the days before tyrannical emperors reduced that ancient body to a cypher, each man who had a contribution to make expressed his mind freely and could not be prosecuted for anything said in the assembly. It was an effective way of arriving at the truth. Perhaps we could attempt something similar ourselves. Our beloved Baccia and Bianca can have no peace until we have discovered what happened to them. If we could bring together everything we know that might have a bearing on their deaths, however seemingly insignificant, we might be able to illuminate this dark and bloody sequence of events.'

He went on to rehearse the bare facts of both murders but said nothing of his conversation with the spice merchant. 'So,' he concluded, 'are we dealing with a madman or with a calculating murderer who has a grudge against the House of

Machiavelli?' Niccolo looked around expectantly at his friends.

Francesco was the first to make an offering. 'I think we can forget Doffo Spini. Apparently he was seen leaving Florence with bulging, gold-stuffed saddle-bags three days before the entry of the French.'

'What about his henchmen?' Stephano asked.

'The Compagnacci disbanded themselves, or so I understand. Many of them were marked men and some were sought out and "dealt with" in the days after the fall of the Medici.'

'Some sought sanctuary at St Mark's,' Roberto added. 'I can't imagine any of Spini's friends being so foolish as to draw attention to themselves by attacking your womenfolk.'

'Bianca was terrified of the black friars, that I know,' Stephano said. 'Saving your presence, Brother, I'm convinced it was one of your order who killed Cousin Baccia and drove my sister to her death.'

'Why are you so sure?' the friar asked.

'For weeks after Baccia's death we couldn't get Bianca to leave the house. Eventually, I persuaded her to come for walks and visits to friends but she would

338

only venture abroad with me at her side. I soon noticed that whenever a Dominican came in sight she would cross herself and cling close to me.'

'Didn't you ask her to explain her behaviour?' Totto enquired.

'Several times but she just shuddered and would say nothing. I suppose with Prior Savonarola being so powerful and so popular she was afraid to speak out. No one would believe her and she could find herself in very real trouble. In the end it preyed so much on her mind that...' He choked on the next words and had to compose himself before adding, 'And now, as a suicide, she cannot have a decent Christian burial.'

A respectful, sympathetic silence lasted for several seconds until Roberto suggested, 'May it not have been simply that the sight of a Dominican habit reminded her of her cousin's death? She and Baccia had rehearsed an irreverent masquerade, making fun of God's servants. As a direct result Baccia was struck down by an assassin. Is it not likely that your sister felt a degree of guilt for that? That, unable to confess it, she let it weigh on her mind – with fatal consequences?'

Before Stephano could riposte, Niccolo

said, 'Yes, I'm sure the women's good-natured little satire is important. Francesco, Totto, you helped them plan it, didn't you? Can you suggest anything that might be useful?'

His brother stared mournfully back. 'They didn't tell us exactly what they were doing. They just wanted us to help them set up their performance.'

'Totto, you told us you procured the habits for them.'

Sheepishly the elder Machiavelli nodded.

'Two habits, stolen from the washing line at St Marks?' Niccolo smiled an almost mischievous smile as he watched for his brother's reaction.

'That's right.'

'You're quite sure about that?'

Totto frowned angrily. 'Yes, of course!'

'Fra Roberto.' Niccolo turned to the friar. 'I imagine that caused some annoyance at the convent.'

Roberto laughed. 'Yes, Brother Simeon, our launderer, was incensed by it. He very nearly caught the urchins in the act as I told you yesterday. He discovered them raiding the line and gave chase. Unfortunately, he isn't the most agile of our number and the thieves managed to get back over the wall with one complete habit.'

'One? But I thought … Totto, didn't you say your young accomplices secured two habits for the ladies?'

'That's right,' Totto agreed. 'Obviously Brother Simeon made a mistake.'

'Impossible.' Roberto shook his head emphatically. 'Fra Simeon is a precisionist and immaculately conscientious. The joke at the convent is that he has an abacus for a brain. If he says one habit went missing, that's what happened.'

Niccolo shrugged. 'Oh well, I don't suppose it matters. I wonder what became of this habit or habits. Stephano, do you know if Bianca brought one home?'

'Knowing how she felt about Dominicans, it's very unlikely that she would keep something that reminded her of them,' the tall young man replied.

Niccolo continued, in musing vein, 'We were surmising the other evening that Bianca might have returned home in her disguise. In fact, she didn't. I was able to check that with her maid.'

'Is all this stuff about friars' uniforms important?' Paolo asked with an exasperated frown.

Niccolo wandered over to the doorway

341

leading into the house. From just inside he took a bundle wrapped in sacking. 'It's probably crucial,' he said heavily. 'You see, I found this hidden.' He unrolled a long, black, woollen garment.

One member of the company gasped and blurted out, 'You can't have...'

'What can't I have done, discovered where you hid it, Totto?' Niccolo stared through tear-misted eyes at his brother.

Totto jumped up, blustering. 'That's not what I was going to say.'

'Oh good; I'm so glad you didn't fall into my little trap. I didn't find this in a clever hiding place; I borrowed it from Fra Roberto. I'm sorry I let my suspicion embrace even you. Put it down to my grief. But will you do one more thing just to help me?'

Totto regarded him warily while the others looked on, bewildered. 'What?'

'Bianca was murdered; thrown from the Ponte Vecchio by a man disguised as a black friar.'

Astonished gasps broke from the company.

Stephano stared at Niccolo in mingled relief and astonishment. 'Are you sure? Bianca didn't take her own life?'

'Quite sure. Your sister's spirit is not doomed to endless purgatory. She died in innocence.'

'Nicco,' Francesco demanded, 'how do you know this?'

'I spoke yesterday to the spice merchant from whose premises she went to her death. Her assassin was waiting for her but – and this is the good news – the proprietor is sure he will be able to recognise the man. So, Totto, would you mind coming to the Ponte Vecchio and showing yourself to him – just to set my mind at rest?'

Totto glowered at his brother. 'Certainly not! Your grief must have driven you mad if you seriously think...'

There was a general murmur of support for the elder Machiavelli and Paolo said, 'Come now, Nicco, what is all this about?'

Niccolo sat down wearily and rubbed his eyes. 'It's all about little bits and pieces that seem to fit together into a pattern – a pattern that I hope to God I am wrong about. First of all there was the fact that someone was able to go into Baccia's room without alarming her. That someone can't have been a stranger. Almost certainly Bianca saw him, too, and was not surprised to observe him going into the house. Only later did she realise the implication of what she had seen. She couldn't bring herself to accuse whoever it was but as soon as she knew I was back in Florence she determined to unburden herself to me. Unfortunately, the murderer also realised this. He knew he only had a few hours to stop her.'

'But,' Francesco protested, 'several people knew of your return.'

'Yes, but only two people knew about the black habit. And, of course, there was only one. So why, Totto, did you insist that you acquired a costume for each of the women?'

Totto sneered. 'Oh, little brother, don't let me spoil your story.'

It was only at that moment, when he looked into his sibling's eyes and saw there deep hatred and pain that Niccolo knew that he was right.

In a subdued monotone he revealed the last steps of his reluctant reasoning. 'I knew nothing about the planned masquerade until Totto mentioned it the other evening but, of course, if he hadn't revealed it Francesco would have. So he had to think quickly. He said he had obtained two habits and the cousins had come here to try them on. He actually suggested that Bianca might have walked home in hers – a very odd idea

344

and one that I easily disposed of. So why lie about something so trivial? It could only be to conceal the truth. To account for someone else being in this house dressed as a black friar. What really happened, I believe, is that Totto arrived with one costume just as Bianca was leaving.' Niccolo gazed miserably round at the expressions of horror and disbelief on his friends' faces.

Stephano stared at the brother. 'Totto,' he implored, 'say this isn't true. Tell me you didn't murder my sister.'

Totto laughed. 'When Bianca died I was asleep in the same room as my dear brother.'

Niccolo shook his head. 'Your dear brother was slumbering so soundly that he would never have heard you slip out of the house and return within the hour.'

The elder Machiavelli looked around the circle with a long-suffering shrug. 'This ridiculous story grows wilder by the minute.'

'Prove that by coming with me to the Ponte Vecchio and I'll take back every word with the greatest happiness.'

'Oh, no, I'll not humour you any longer.' Totto strode towards the garden gate.

Stephano jumped up, dagger drawn, to block his path. 'I think I'd like you to prove your innocence too.'

Totto emitted a wild cry, drew his own blade and lunged at Vernacci. Stephano parried and grabbed Totto's wrist. The struggle was brief. The other men leaped forward and separated the combatants.

With tears sliding down his cheeks Niccolo faced his brother, who stood with his arms pinioned by Paolo and Francesco, breathing heavily, his face twisted in defiance and loathing. 'Why, Totto, why?'

'Why? You dare ask *me* that. The blame is yours – yours and these "friends" who fawn on you, just as our parents fawned on you. Always "pretty Nicco", "clever Nicco", "witty Nicco", "brave Nicco". I'm the eldest but all your life I've been pushed aside to make way for you. You've always had whatever you wanted. But it was *I* who had Baccia. Father arranged the marriage contract for *me*. I was to have the most beautiful woman in Florence *and* four hundred florins to set myself up in my own business. *Me! Me!* Poor old Totto. But, of course, you couldn't allow that, could you? Oh no, you had to step in and woo my betrothed and charm her father into favouring you for a son-in-law. And poor old Totto was expected to stand aside and watch you enjoy Baccia.'

346

Niccolo sank down on the wall, his face in his hands. 'Then why didn't you try to kill *me?* Why did you deliberately choke the life out of poor Baccia?'

The dishevelled captive glowered back, lips pursed, but said nothing.

It was Roberto who broke the silence. He sneered at Totto. 'Killing the object of your hatred is poor revenge, isn't it, you wretch? Much more satisfactory to see your victim suffer. You couldn't watch him burn in the fires of hell but you had the satisfaction of beholding him writhe in the flames of grief. How you must have relished Niccolo's anguish and hugged yourself with glee as he rushed off to Rome in pursuit of some hapless, innocent Dominican. And when the news came back that your brother had perished in a distant city, how did you feel then? Did you exult that your lifetime rival was gone at last? You had always believed that he would come to a bad end. Well, you were vindicated. And with Niccolo dead there was no chance that your crime would ever have been discovered. What a despicable...'

Niccolo held up his hand. 'Enough, Brother Roberto.' He stepped across the courtyard to stand in front of Totto, weeping now unrestrainedly. 'And yet, is there any truth in what the friar says?'

Totto looked away. 'I would have told you... Given time I would have confessed and faced my punishment... God knows I meant her no harm ... *I loved her.*' The last words rose as a wail from the depths of his being. What followed was little more than a whisper. 'I would have told you given time ... but you rushed off to Rome and...'

Niccolo lifted a hand to his brother's shoulder. 'Tell me now,' he said gently.

Slowly Totto raised his eyes to meet Niccolo's and for the next few moments no one else existed for either of them. 'I didn't plan it. You must believe that. I didn't ... I couldn't have planned ... I came here to bring Baccia her habit. The servants were out. Bianca was just leaving and she told me her cousin was upstairs. When I went into the room Baccia was changing. She was wearing only a shift and she looked ... lovely. I was mesmerised. I had to hold her, to feel her warmth and softness just once. Dear God, it wasn't too much to ask, was it? Just one embrace... But she pulled away. "Silly Totto," she said. "Silly Totto." Then she laughed. She *laughed* at me. And I had to stop her laughing. It was all over in a moment.' He sagged between his captors.

And everyone in the garden stood, as though frozen in the ice of time.

Such was young Niccolo's homecoming. The end of that sad episode is quickly told. For reasons of family pride it was decided not to hand Totto over to the authorities. Instead, he was taken to St Mark's and presented to the Dominican novitiate. In return for his life and the silence of those he had wronged he renounced his inheritance and gave himself to a regime of prayer and study. His penance was not destined to be of long duration. He died in his cell three years later. Bianca did have a Christian burial. Her brother, with the aid of the spice merchant, persuaded the authorities that she had been killed by person or persons unknown.

Meanwhile Niccolo, a little older and more than a little wiser, tried, not with much success, to find a new direction, a fresh purpose. He discovered that he could not write. Pithy apothegms and witty verses clogged up in his pen. When he went out seeking diversions, few were to be found in pious, po-faced Florence.

One morning, some three months after his return, he was aroused by Timeo with the news that a visitor awaited him downstairs. He washed and shaved, and descended to the living-room. Standing in the middle, a broad smile on his face, he discovered Alberto Reggio.

The brocaded courtier stepped forward to embrace him. 'My dear Niccolo, how delighted to see you again, and looking so well.'

Niccolo made a polite response. 'Are you staying long in Florence or just passing through?'

Alberto laughed. 'Nothing of the sort. I am here to see you. To bring you good news from his eminence the Cardinal of Valencia.'

Niccolo felt a sudden hollow in the pit of his stomach. 'What news?' he asked warily.

'His eminence has work for you and requires your immediate presence in Rome.'

Niccolo shook his head. 'Oh, no, my days as a servant of the Borgias are over.' He took Reggio by the elbow and steered him towards the street door. 'Please convey my gratitude to his eminence for the compliment he does me and explain that I am devoting myself to a quiet life of study.'

'I don't think you quite understand, my dear friend.' Reggio opened the door wide.

Outside stood a group of six armed horsemen in Borgia livery.

The publishers hope that this book has given you enjoyable reading. Large Print Books are especially designed to be as easy to see and hold as possible. If you wish a complete list of our books please ask at your local library or write directly to:

Magna Large Print Books
Magna House, Long Preston,
Skipton, North Yorkshire.
BD23 4ND

This Large Print Book for the partially sighted, who cannot read normal print, is published under the auspices of

THE ULVERSCROFT FOUNDATION